Someone To Care

by

Nelianne Taylor

Grosvenor House
Publishing Limited

This book is published by
Grosvenor House Publishing Ltd
28-30 High Street, Guildford, Surrey, GU1 3HY.
www.grosvenorhousepublishing.co.uk

A CIP record for this book
is available from the British Library

ISBN 978-1-906210-23-6

Acknowledgements

My grateful thanks to Alex, for his practical help, advice and for constantly keeping my computer in running order. To Steve, for his endless patience in answering queries and questions.

And to Doug, for his love, encouragement and unfailing belief in me, without which this book would never have been written.

Chapter One

"I publish the banns of marriage between Patricia Isobel Cameron, spinster...." John didn't wait to hear the rest. This was it, if he didn't move now, then he knew that he wouldn't do it at all. And maybe, somewhere in this church, someone was watching him, relying on his help, waiting to see if he cared. And of course he cared. Even in this odd situation in which they found themselves just now, Richard was still his brother. And whoever she was, she had cared enough about Richard too. He stood up and stepped from the pew into the aisle. "No," he said in a commanding voice he didn't quite recognise as his own. "No, this marriage can't take place." Was there a set formula for objecting to a marriage, could you just stand up and say No? He was walking towards the chancel steps from where the vicar had been making his announcements, and the older man watched him approach waiting, calm and unruffled, until John stood before him.

"Will you give us your reasons for this declaration?" he asked. This situation had never arisen during the years of his ministry, but the young man seemed serious and sensible enough.

John half turned to face the congregation, aware of all eyes upon him. Was she watching him, too, whoever she was? He took another deep, calming breath and said clearly and firmly, "This marriage cannot take place because the lady concerned is already married. To my brother." There was a collective gasp from the congregation, and from the corner of his eye he saw a man step from his seat behind a pillar into a side aisle and quietly leave the church. John turned back to face the vicar.

"I trust you have proof of what you are saying," the vicar said very quietly, and John nodded. "Can we speak together later? Could you call at the vicarage?" John nodded again. "Thank you," and with that the vicar resumed his morning service, drawing his congregation's attention back to him with the announcement, "The Mothers' Union meeting will be held..." as John, too, quietly left the church by the same side aisle and door. He had done it. He had spoken out. It was over.

"I should push your face in for that, made me feel a proper fool." The young man he had seen leaving earlier had been sitting on a tombstone, waiting for him. Now he stood up barring John's way. "I just hope you can prove all that you've just shouted to the world."

John stopped and regarded him steadily. The congregation of St. James, Hallinford was hardly the world, but he wasn't going to argue. He also saw that although the stranger's words had been belligerent, his look didn't give that impression at all. "Of course I can," he answered, almost scornfully. "Would you rather I had kept quiet and let you marry her? I'm guessing you are the intended bridegroom. Surely it's better to shout it to the world now than let everyone get hurt later. Yes, I can prove it all, but I'm not going to hang about here, they'll be out of there soon enough," and he nodded towards the church.

"Yeah, you're right. I'd rather have not been here at all just now, anyway. But you've got to explain. You can't just leave it at that." He had to make sure that Patricia's father couldn't find some legal jargon to get it all fixed again. "Where are you going now?"

"To get some breakfast if I can, I got up too late this morning. There used to be a little coffee shop down by the river. If it's still there, that's where I'm going."

"Right, then, I'm coming with you." He moved aside to let John pass, then fell into step beside him. He wore an expensive suit, beautifully cut, John observed, and his shirt was pale blue silk. Oh, yes, Patricia knew money when she saw it. Fancy shoes, too, probably Italian. But for all the man about town appearance, there was something immediately honest and likeable about him. "Breakfast's a great idea, I could do with it after all that. Explanations when we get there, but not while we're walking, OK? It's a bit too public."

"Suits me. I'm John Treherne, by the way. I didn't give the vicar time to tell me who you are."

His companion laughed. "No, you didn't, did you? I bet stepping out like that took some doing, though. It's Terry Kennedy."

The coffee shop John remembered was still there, and the two men settled themselves at a table in a far corner away from the door. A smiling woman came from behind the counter to take their order. "A big pot of coffee," Terry began, "and how about a couple of bacon sandwiches?" He looked across at John. "That OK?" When John nodded he turned back to the woman and smiled up at her. "Can you do that?" John envied his charm and easy manner with strangers. He may have stood up alone in the church amongst strangers this morning, but talking to them, face to face, was a fear that he'd never conquered.

"Just bacon, or bacon and egg," she asked.

"Bacon and egg?" He looked across at John, who nodded again. "You really know the way to a man's heart, don't you?" His smile was even wider now.

From behind the counter came a deep rumbling laugh. "She sure does, boy," and the big man standing by the coffee maker patted his stomach, which made the woman giggle. John smiled too, but felt a little awkward. He'd never been able to make people talk to him like that. Kids, yes, that was easy, but not strangers like this, and especially not women.

Their order arrived very quickly, and they settled to their late breakfast. "Go on," said Terry after a minute or two of eating and drinking. "Tell me what it's all about."

"It's just as I said there in church. Oh, you had left, hadn't you? Patricia Cameron is really Patricia Treherne – she is married to my brother Richard. That's it."

"So why isn't your brother Richard standing up and objecting? Why you?"

"He's in hospital. Has been for eighteen months. Paralysed from the waist down. Flying accident."

Terry Kennedy stopped eating, his sandwich held before him. "You mean it? Does he know what's going on? Did he ask you to speak for him? And why so dramatically in church?"

"No, he doesn't." John was silent for a moment, deciding just how much to say, but telling Terry couldn't hurt anyone. "Richard seems to have, well, I guess you could say he's sort of opted out of the world. There is nothing wrong with him mentally, he just isn't bothering with anything or anyone. His closest friend, right from the time we were all kids together, was killed in the same accident. Richard was the pilot. The shrinks think he feels guilty about being alive when Andy is dead, but as he won't talk to them, or us much either, we don't know. Patricia doesn't visit him at all now, hasn't for ages. But she hasn't divorced him either. I've checked it out. And I objected dramatically in church, as you put it, because there would be witnesses there. Her father can't find legal excuses and cover it all up."

Terry's face darkened with anger. "The cheating bitch. She ought to know no one cheats Terry Kennedy. She'll find that out tomorrow, anyway." John hid a smile. This good-looking, glossy man of the world sounded more like one of his thirteen year old pupils looking for a fight.

"Why tomorrow? She's probably regretting it right this minute."

"A couple of days ago," said Terry, pouring more coffee, "that London wedding shop sent me a bill. Me! It was for £650 for a wedding outfit or something. She'd told them to send the bill to me I suppose. Why me! She knows her father is paying for this affair. So I sent it back with a note redirecting the bill to her father. Do you know her father?" When John shook his head and explained that he only knew the man was a clever lawyer Terry continued, "He's Charles Cameron, the barrister. Pillar of the church and the local community. Chairman of the parish council. Secretary of the golf club. You name it, he runs it." He grinned across the table at his companion. "Thanks to you he now has a rather large bill for something that isn't going to happen."

John was puzzled and stared at him in bewilderment. "But this is the girl you were going to marry in a couple of weeks. You must still care about her, surely?"

"I don't know." This wasn't the moment to tell anyone, least of all a stranger, that he'd planned to back out of it all, waylay Patricia in the churchyard and tell her it was all off. When he had seen her arrive with her father, it seemed an even better opportunity. The old man wouldn't let her make a scene in front of his friends and neighbours. But he hadn't needed to do anything- this quiet guy across the table had done it all for him. Instead he said, "Maybe I'll find I still do when I've stopped being angry. Maybe. But I don't think so. Her cheating and conniving have changed the picture a bit. And now there's Richard, too. He changes the picture more than a bit." He was silent for a moment, deep in thought and then asked, "John, just now you said you thought you remembered this coffee shop. Don't you live in Hallinford?"

"No, not now. I used to teach at the primary school here for a while after I qualified, and lived in digs. That's when you know the eating places. Now I teach at Ashleigh boys school in Ledminster. Why?"

"If you don't live here, how did you know about the banns and which church and all that?"

It was a fair question. The letter was unsigned. Surely he wouldn't be betraying her confidence? Terry watched the other man's face and saw the frown crease his forehead as he tried to work out the right thing to do. Finally John reached into his pocket, drew out a letter and handed it across the table. "That's how I knew."

Terry slid the single sheet of paper from its envelope and read. "John," it began. "Patricia is planning to marry again. The wedding is in four weeks. The banns are being called in St. James's, Hallinford, from the 12th. I will go along with whatever you decide to do, but please, John, please speak for Richard. Don't let him be hurt and humiliated again." There was no signature, but at the very bottom of the page was added, "I loved him, once, too." He folded the letter, replacing it in its envelope. "Do you have any idea who sent it?"

John shook his head. "No." He picked up the letter and returned it to his pocket. "I have to go and explain to the vicar. I promised him I would. I guess he'll need to have someone officially cancel the wedding service. Why don't you come with me?"

"I may as well, I guess." Terry picked up the bill, and John reached into his pocket for money. "It's on me," Terry said. "I reckon I owe you that." He crossed to the counter, paid the bill and together they left the coffee shop.

When John had left the church that morning, the vicar calmly continued his announcements as though there had been no interruption, and then the congregation rose to its feet ready to sing the next hymn. Patricia picked up her bag and turned as if about to leave but her father laid a restraining hand on her arm. "Stay where you are." His voice was low, but she heard the command in it. "Where's your dignity, girl?" She had no choice but to stay and, full of resentment, wondered why he had chosen to accompany her today of all days when most other Sunday he attended the later service at All Saints. And where was Terry? He had promised to be here. Had he heard that wretched, interfering John Treherne? What business was it of his, anyway? The hymn dragged on and on, and her father stood erect and unbowed beside her, singing heartily and repeating the prayers in his usual, confident manner. What was he thinking? Then, for the first time in all these months, the realisation of what she had planned to do suddenly hit her. How was she going to talk her way out of this? But surely Daddy would understand. He always helped her with everything. He would know what to do. Anyway, if Richard was mentally ill, surely she didn't have to stay tied to him. There surely was some kind of law that made her free. And maybe Daddy could fix it so that she still got her allowance. And would she still be able to marry Terry afterwards? She couldn't even begin to guess. But he loved her. Wouldn't he forgive one little lie? When he knew just how useless Richard was now, he'd understand. She was so engrossed in her thoughts that the sermon and prayers continued around her, unheard and unseen.

When the service came to an end, Patricia and her father left the church together, her father's back straight and head held high as he smiled and nodded to neighbours and acquaintances. Outside she tried to speak, tried to make some kind of amends, but he said simply, "We'll discuss everything in private, at home please, Patricia. Your Mother deserves an explanation, too," and they walked to the car in silence. There was no sign of Terry among the people gathered in the churchyard, so perhaps he had overslept or something and hadn't come, hadn't heard John Treherne interfering anyway. Not that that solved the problem for her at this moment, but it just might be possible to sort it out before he heard. She didn't want to believe that this would be the end of their relationship. Terry was different - he might just laugh it off and wait for Daddy to fix things for her. He was like that. Yes, yes, that's what would happen. The car stopped outside the house, and father and daughter climbed out, still in silence, although she didn't think that he was angry with her. "We'll have coffee in the sitting-room," he told her. "I'll just go through to tell your Mother we are home, and then join you there." She nodded and went to hang up her jacket. He opened the kitchen door and then closed it quietly but firmly behind him. Perhaps he was angry, after all.

Isobel Cameron looked up in surprise as the kitchen door opened and closed. "You're back early, Charles. You didn't stay for coffee, then?" She saw from the look on his face that something was amiss. "I'll put the coffee on now," she said quickly. "It won't take a minute."

"Will you bring it through to the sitting-room, and then stay and listen? There is something we all have to discuss."

"Of course." When Charles spoke in that manner, "Will you" really meant "you will," but this had never bothered her in the least. She had been married for well over thirty years now, and knew almost every tone and inflexion and what it meant. It was a kind of private code, really. "Is there something wrong?"

"There is, but we'll all discuss it together."

Isobel made the coffee, put milk in a pan to heat and laid the tray. Placing the coffee pot and hot milk carefully on it, she carried everything through to the sitting-room. When she had poured their coffee, she took her own cup and sat in a chair by the window a little apart, from them and quietly waited to know just what was happening.

"This morning, in church," Charles told her, "a young man stood up and objected to the calling of the banns for Patricia's marriage." She gave a little gasp of astonishment, but Charles merely glanced her way and continued, "he objected on the grounds that Patricia was already married. I would not allow her to say a word until we were all here together." Now he turned to his daughter and asked directly, "Is it true?"

She looked down at her coffee cup, seeing the pattern, the silver rim, and tiny spoon with the little figure on the handle as though for the first time, studying them carefully. Then she said, "Yes. But it doesn't count now."

"Patricia!" Isobel Cameron was so startled by this answer that her coffee cup shook and rattled gently in her hand, and she put it down carefully. "Patricia! No!"

"I think you had better explain a little more," Charles was looking at his daughter in puzzlement. To Isobel he added, "The young man said she was married to his brother." Turning back to his daughter he asked, "Is that correct? If so, where is his brother? why didn't he object? Do you know?"

"Yes. Richard is in a nursing home. He's been there for eighteen months. He is paralysed. And mentally ill. He doesn't acknowledge me at all. I do not think such a marriage counts. Surely, Daddy, there is a law about it?"

Her parents stared at her in disbelief. "You do not think a marriage counts? You would have married Terry and not said a word?" Isobel's voice was strained, almost a croak.

"I told you. I don't think such a marriage counts. We have been apart now for two years. When I did go to visit him once he hardly spoke, didn't even open his eyes. He is sick in the head. Nobody has to be tied to someone who is sick in the head."

"You could have divorced him." Her father's tone was cold now. "It would have been perfectly straightforward and certainly kinder to Terry, not to mention your parents, too."

She made no attempt to answer this question, and her Mother asked suddenly, "Patricia. When and where did you marry this man? Why weren't we invited? And if you say such a marriage doesn't count, why marry a paralysed man in the first place? I just don't understand." Isobel tried to keep her voice under control, but it wavered a little, and she had to stop speaking for a moment.

"He wasn't paralysed then. He is, well, was, a captain in the army. We lived in a house just outside Oxford. Well, you knew the address where I was living, didn't you? He went away a lot with the army. He had learned to fly and bought himself a plane. Then he crashed it."

Her father suddenly became businesslike, breaking the tension for Isobel. "Tell me his full name, Patricia. And the name of the young man in church. I shall look into all this thoroughly, you can be sure. And if your husband is just as you say, then I think a divorce would be fairly simple. At this moment I just cannot express how I feel about you, and I cannot begin to think how Terry is feeling about it all. I suggest you take yourself off to your room or somewhere just now and leave Mother and I to talk together."

"His name is Richard Treherne. And it was his brother John in church this morning. Richard is in St. Lawrence's hospital and I can't tell you where John lives, but he teaches maths and history at Ashleigh Boys, in Ledminster. If that is all you want to know, Father, then I shall leave you to it. I will try to find Terry, I think." She stood up, smoothed her skirt and walked to the door. She wasn't going to tell them that while she stayed married to Richard she had a nice steady income. Perhaps her father would ferret that out, too, but she wasn't going to help. As she passed her mother Isobel turned her face away, not wanting to look at her. Patricia smiled faintly, left the room and closed the door softly behind her. Her parents sat where they were, neither speaking for a long while. Eventually Isobel sighed gently, and Charles said, "Don't upset yourself too much, my dear. I can probably sort something out," but he didn't really believe his words. He'd been very pleased at the thought of Terry marrying his daughter - a good, hard-working young man with ambition. But it didn't look very likely now.

"Terry was such a nice young man," Isobel said, as if reading his thoughts. "How could our own daughter treat anyone so shabbily?"

"I've just remembered something. This John Treherne told Oliver that he would call at the vicarage later and explain. I might be able to speak to him there." He crossed the room, picked up the telephone receiver and dialled a number. "Is your Daddy there, Hannah? Yes please." He waited a moment or two and then spoke again. "Oliver, I've just been hearing such a story from my daughter by way of explanation of this morning's event, and I wondered if John Treherne had called on you yet. Oh, good. Look, when he does, could you ask him to call and see me today? Yes, if you would. Thanks, Oliver," and he replaced the receiver on its cradle. "The boy hasn't been there yet," he told his wife, "so I left a message."

She nodded. She had heard the conversation too. "I'd better get back to the kitchen and prepare some lunch. Oh, Charles, how could she be so, so... callous? How did Terry react when he heard the objection? I gather he's not now coming to lunch."

"Terry wasn't in church today. Patricia was expecting

him to be there, but he didn't turn up. I can't imagine what he'll think if he hears the news from anyone else. Perhaps I'd better ring him." But he made no attempt to make the telephone call. Instead he poured himself a rather large whiskey. "Oh, I don't know, Isobel we'll have to try and put it right, somehow."

"Whatever you can arrange, Charles, the wedding will have to be cancelled, that's certain." Isobel became her usual practical self again, already mentally listing jobs she would have to do as she picked up the tray and went back to the kitchen.

Terry and John made their way through the quiet Sunday streets of Hallinford towards the vicarage. "So where do you live, Terry? Somewhere around here?" John asked, casually.

"No, I've got a converted barn, on the Ledminster road. I'll show it to you, if you like, when we've chatted to the vicar. It'd be on your way home and we might just find a couple of beers in the fridge." Terry always seized any opportunity to show off his unconventional home. "But maybe you have plans for this lovely, boring Sunday?"

John smiled. "I have to mark 9j's maths homework. And then sort out the accounts of someone who runs a local shop. Oh, yes, I know how to fill a boring Sunday."

Terry grinned. "So what do you do for fun?"

John kept a perfectly straight face as he answered, "Mark 9J's homework, and sort out accounts."

"No girlfriend, then?" He saw a shadow cross John's face and added quickly, "Sorry. That's me being nosey again. Tell me to mind my own business."

much to John's relief they had reached the vicarage.

The door was opened by a little girl wearing a much too long dress and a gold paper crown. Terry gave her a big smile and said, "Greetings, your highness. You must be Princess Pattikins?"

The child giggled, and the crown slipped over her eyes. "Bother!" she said and pushed it back into place. "No, I'm Princess Hannah. Did you want to speak to Daddy? He's having a glass of wine with Mummy in the kitchen," she added confidentially.

"Lucky man, I wish I was. Yes, please, Princess, we'd like to talk to Daddy. Tell Mummy we won't keep him more than five minutes."

Hannah picked up her skirts and ran off. Both men were aware of the security camera above their heads; the vicar would know who was calling, and a few moments later he appeared. "Would you like to come into the study?" he asked. They followed him across the hall and into a little room with a large desk and very little else in the way of furniture. He gave a wry smile; "No extra chairs here, I'm afraid," he said apologetically. "It's meant to discourage anyone from coming here to talk to me while I'm working."

Terry chuckled. "Does it work for you?" he asked. "I find they stand around and peer over my shoulder but still talk anyway."

The vicar smiled and nodded his agreement. "Now what can I do for you?" he asked. Of course he was aware of the situation, but he would keep it very formal.

John stepped forward. "John Treherne," he said, holding out his hand. You must already know Terry Kennedy, I imagine."

They exchanged greetings and then John began his

explanation of the morning's drama. "As I said in church, the lady in question, Patricia, is already married to my brother Richard." He reached into his pocket and drew out a folded paper. "This is a copy of the marriage certificate. Since I heard of the wedding plans I have done a great deal of research, but there is no trace of any divorce documents. The search took a great deal of time and is the reason why it was almost a last minute objection."

The vicar took the paper and read through it quickly. "But why are you objecting. I mean, why isn't your brother here? Is he ill or out of the country or something like that?" John related the story of Richard as he had told it to Terry earlier that morning. The vicar listened carefully and then said, "I see. Well, thank you for taking the time to explain it all to me, I appreciate that." He handed the copy certificate back to John and added, "Oh, by the way, Charles Cameron left a message here for you. He would like you to call and discuss the situation with him today." The look on his face was quite unreadable to the two men watching him.

John sighed. He had had enough of this drama for one day. Terry caught his look and said firmly, "I think you've done your bit for the Camerons already. Why don't you leave your phone number here, and let him contact you?" He turned to the vicar, "that would be the best thing, wouldn't it? Will you pass it on for John?" and when the vicar agreed it was all settled. "Don't leave your mobile number," Terry advised. "Give yourself a break." John shot him a look of gratitude and wrote his home number on the desk notepad. Terry officially cancelled the wedding and left a generous donation for any inconvenience the cancellation had caused, and in a few more minutes they were being ushered out of the house. The vicar stood a while watching them go, and then stepped back inside and closed the door.

—∿—

"Where have you left your car?" Terry asked as they reached the street.

"I haven't. It wouldn't start this morning. I came on the bus." He glanced at his watch and added, "There's not one for another hour and a half yet."

"Oh, to hell with buses," Terry grinned cheerfully, "I've got the car, Come on. We'll go to my place first and have a look around if you like. It's a great conversion job and I like showing it off. It's on your way home, anyway." Without waiting for an answer he set off towards the church, and John followed. The car, rather like its owner, was sleek and shining. "If you're in PR and advertising," Terry said by way of explanation as he saw John's admiring look, "you've got to sell yourself too. Otherwise no one believes in you."

They left the town and took the main road to Ledminster. After a while Terry turned the car into a quiet country road and very soon slowed, ready to turn into his driveway. As the car began the turn he cursed, pulled the wheel over again, and in seconds they were back on the road. "Change of plan," he said shortly.

"What's up?"

"Didn't you see the car? Patricia's. I don't know about you, but I'm not in the mood for any more histrionics." He drove on for a few minutes and then both their mobile phones began to ring. Terry pulled the car into a farm gate entrance as John struggled with his seatbelt, trying to reach into his pocket. The car stopped and John quickly released the belt and pulled out his phone. "John Treherne. Oh, hello Jane." He was aware that Terry had picked up his phone, swore and immediately switched it off.

"Are you visiting Richard today, John?" Jane's voice seemed very near in the confined space of the car.

"No, I can't, the car's playing up. Why? Is something wrong?"

"No," she said wistfully, "I just felt like some adult company. Thought if you were visiting you'd come for coffee or something."

"I'm sorry, Jane. I'd have come to you, anyway, if I'd been up there." He was suddenly aware that Terry had been listening and was now signalling frantically. Telling Jane to hold on a moment, he covered the mouthpiece and turned his head in enquiry. Terry immediately took the phone from him.

"Hi, Jane, I'm Terry. I was just giving John a lift home. We met up this morning in Hallinford. If you feel like inviting me for coffee, too, we could be with you as soon as he tells me where to go." He stopped speaking and then smiled. "We are on our way. Here's John," and he handed back the phone.

"John," said Jane, and her voice was full of laughter as she heard the car engine start. "Looks like I'll see you both soon. Bye," And she rang off.

John felt some resentment at having his day organised for him by someone else, someone he didn't even know properly. But he couldn't let Jane down now. She had sounded so lonely when she'd first called him. He looked across at his grinning companion. "You do know she lives outside Oxford, don't you?" He wasn't sure that he really wanted to go to Jane's with this guy in tow, but now he had no choice.

"No problem. It'll take about half an hour, not much more. I thought she sounded a bit forlorn, that's why I jumped in. Do you mind?"

"Not really," John lied. He didn't want to sound grouchy, and Jane would be glad of the company. "She gets a bit lonely sometimes. She's Andrew's widow. If Richard were OK, he'd probably see she was taken care of. But he isn't, so I try instead, but well, I don't know. I'm not much good with women. Oh, we'll have to stop off at a supermarket somewhere – with three young children she hasn't much money left over for entertaining."

"Again, no problem. There's plenty of places open on Sundays nowadays. Now, Tell me exactly where we're going."

They stopped at a supermarket in Ledminster and bought pizzas and salad for lunch. John added burgers and beans for the children and a big bottle of lemonade. "What about some wine?" Terry asked.

John shook his head. "Jane doesn't drink it, and you can't if you're driving. We won't bother." When they reached the checkout Terry drew his wallet from his pocket. "I'm not one of your bloody clients," John said irritably, "so you don't have to wave your wallet around at me. I'll pay for this lot."

Terry gave an apologetic look, but then grinned and said simply, "Sorry, mate. Sheer habit." And put the offending wallet back in his pocket.

The girl at the checkout smiled up at him. "I wouldn't object," she said brightly. "You could wave your wallet around with me anytime."

"Tell me about it another time, sweetheart," Terry laughed. "Right now I'm acting chauffeur," and he picked up one of the bags and followed John from the store.

Back in the car and clear of the traffic out of Ledminster, Terry asked, "So do you go to see Jane every week?"

John thought that this man reminded him of a puppy dog with a bone, never letting up on the questions. But you couldn't dislike him, he had such an easy manner and friendly smile. "No. I go to see Richard once a fortnight, and then call in on Jane for a cup of tea afterwards."

"But you said Richard didn't communicate."

"He doesn't. But I have to go. Something might change one day."

Terry was silent, trying to imagine himself going every other week to see someone who didn't talk to him. Why? Why bother? What good did it do? This guy sitting next to him must be some kind of a saint or something. And then spending more time comforting and helping someone's widow. He brooded on the situation until John broke into his thoughts with, "Take the next left turning, and then left again. Stephen's Lane is where we're heading. Number 27. OK?"

Terry turned the big car into a street of fair-sized houses in large gardens, but then left again took them into a narrower street where the houses were much smaller and a little old-fashioned. He slowed down and finally stopped outside number twenty seven. "Here we are then. I hope she was serious about the coffee, I could drink a potfull" and he reached over and took the bags from the back seat.

"She was," said John. "Come on and find out," and with that he climbed out of the car and slammed the door behind him.

CHAPTER TWO

Maria was sitting at the window as the car drew up outside the house. When John stepped on to the pavement she waved both arms in the air excitedly and disappeared from sight. As they approached the front door it swung open and a laughing, excited Maria ran to John, her hands held up to reach him. He lifted her up and swung her into his arms and said, "Hello dumpling. Will you say Hello to Terry," as the little girl hugged him tightly.

Maria turned her head to look at her uncle's companion. "Hello Terry," she said,. "Are you Uncle John's friend? Mummy said a friend was coming. I didn't know Uncle John had a friend."

"Yes, that's me." said Terry with a grin. "Hi, Maria." Jane was watching them from the front door and liked what she saw. She'd never known John have a friend before, either, and this particular friend was a total surprise to her. He was rather good-looking, tall and slim-built, but with a warm friendly smile that was almost boyish. A smart dresser, too, she noticed, and smiled as they came towards her, kissed John's cheek and then turned her head to the newcomer. "Hi, Terry, I'm Jane. Come on in, the coffee's already bubbling." She led the way into the house, the two men followed and John set Maria down and closed the front door.

The sitting room was small but bright and cheerful. They handed over their purchases to a delighted Jane, who disappeared into the kitchen to fetch the promised coffee. Maria fetched a thick sketchbook and put it in John's lap as he settled himself into an armchair. "Can't I have my coffee first?" he teased her. "We've been busy all morning and I'm thirsty." The child giggled, but left the book where it was and ran off to tell her Mother.

Terry had remained standing, looking around with interest. After a moment or two his gaze had travelled to a silver-framed photograph on the mantelpiece. "Andrew!" he exclaimed in surprise. He crossed the room in a couple of strides to stand beside the mantelpiece. "Hey, John," he said in a low urgent voice "what is Jane's other name?"

John looked startled at the question and the odd note in Terry's voice. "Lawson," he said. "Why?"

"So it was Andy Lawson in the plane crash? You didn't tell me the guy's other name."

John stared at him for a moment, uncomprehending. "Yes, it was. Didn't I say that. No, I suppose I didn't. Did you know him, then?"

"We were at Durham together. A real nice guy, Andy. Great cricketer, too."

"You should tell Jane about it – she loves to talk about him."

"Tell Jane about what?" She had come from the kitchen, carrying a tray and was setting it down on to the table.

"Andy and I were at Durham together. Same year, too, but different studies." Terry explained. "We were both in the cricket team. I was only good as a batsman but he was a great all rounder. I have photos at home of that cricket team." He picked up the photograph and looked down at the smiling face pictured there, remembering.

"We were part of the same crowd. Everyone liked Andy. He was a great guy altogether," he added softly, as he returned the picture to it's place.

"He was," Jane said slowly, and added, "And if you remember him well, wait until Jamie comes home from his Sunday school outing. He's Andrew in miniature." Then she became brisk "How do you like your coffee, Terry?" With that, the mood had changed. "Come on, tell me all about this morning and how you two met up. Judging by your gear, it was important. John is wearing his Speech Day suit." John pulled a face at her and she laughed. "Come on, tell. Why were you in Hallinford this morning all dressed up, John?"

Between them they related the morning's events. Jane looked from one to the other as they spoke, comparing the rather flamboyant Terry with quiet, steady John whom she had known for most of her life. They were quite unalike, almost opposites, but didn't they say opposites often became the best of friends? She hoped this would be so, John was a loner, or at least she thought he was. And Terry had known Andrew. She hoped she would see him again after today - it would be a sort of comfort to talk about him to someone who had known him well. When the tale was told she asked incredulously, "Did you really stand up and interrupt the service, John? It was so out of character for him. Then she stopped smiling and asked, "Does Richard know?"

"No. there didn't seem any point in telling him, he wouldn't answer, anyway."

"I bet it took some doing, all the same." John nodded, he was growing bored of the whole business and picked up Maria's sketchpad from his lap. Maria climbed on to the arm of his chair.

"Will you draw Terry for me, Uncle John?" she asked, turning to a clean page. John began to draw, leaving Jane and Terry to talk together. Just for a while he was tired of talking, he seemed to have been doing it all day. But Jane was happy, and Richard had been saved the possible embarrassment of a bigamy case, and even Terry seemed to be OK so perhaps he'd got it right today. He worked quietly and finished the drawing, wrote "Terry" underneath it in neat, clear letters and handed the book back to Maria. She looked at it, looked at Terry, and then gave her uncle a huge smile before sliding from the arm of the chair in order to show the picture to her Mother. "Look, that's Terry."

Jane took the pad and studied it. "It's good, John," she said, and handed the book to Terry. He stared for a long while at his image and then began to turn the pages. A girl rather like Jane, "Debbie", a small boy, "Jamie", a teddy bear with "Pongo" written beneath it, a doll, pictures of all Maria's favourite toys with their names. And two pictures of Jane, one smiling and one serious.

"These are really great, John," he said enthusiastically. "Do you paint, too?"

Jane pulled a face at John. "No, he doesn't now," she said reproachfully, "and he only draws for Maria and the other children. He used to paint a lot when we were young. It's sheer wasted talent." Then she began to giggle. "Tell Terry about the time you drew people in Bournemouth." John shook his head but didn't answer so she went on, "He went one day to Bournemouth. He drew a girl sitting on a bench and when she saw the picture she was so delighted, that she fetched a friend who also sat on the bench to be drawn. He charged them fifty pence for the pictures. By the end of the day he had fifteen pounds." She turned to John, "You were about sixteen, weren't you?"

"Fifteen," John said flatly, "And my Father nearly had a heart attack when he found out." "Very bad form, you know," he mimicked. But his voice had a bitter edge, and Jane quickly changed the subject.

"You know, John, Patricia's father is going to want to know Freddie's details, for it's a good bet he'll want to talk divorce. And money, too," she added shrewdly. "It might be wise to let Freddie know before the morning, so he can stall if he feels it's necessary."

John sighed inwardly. She was right, of course, but he was tired of the whole sorry business. "I'll give him a ring when I get home."

The other children arrived a little later, and the two men spent a happy afternoon playing games and laughing with this little family. Eventually Terry said, "I think we had better be making tracks, John, don't you? I've got a few things to do before the morning."

"Yes, I suppose we'd better move, I still have 9J's homework to mark before the morning." He stood and stretched, almost reluctantly. Although he was tired he found he didn't really want to go home. Somehow, this particular trip to Jane's had been much more comfortable than usual. Everyone went with them to the front door. "Will you come and see us again, Terry?" Maria asked. "You could come with Uncle John, couldn't you? He wouldn't mind." Terry raised an enquiring eyebrow to Jane who nodded.

"Sure, we'll do that. And soon, too, as long as you're good." They all stood in the porch and watched as the two men climbed into the car and Terry started the engine. John waved from the window, and Jane blew him a kiss. "Soon," she called. He nodded and they drove away. John sat quietly for a while, as Terry concentrated on negotiating the narrow streets. Finally they turned on to the main road, and Terry broke the silence.

"They're lovely kids, aren't they?" he said, and there was a wistful, almost yearning, note in his voice. "Jamie is the image of Andrew, too. He must have been about six when Andrew died, but he has the little mannerisms I remember, the way he holds his head, the way he walks. It's uncanny." John agreed and Terry went on, "I'd love to have a family like that one day."

John looked at him in surprise. "You would? I saw you as the up and coming businessman." He was silent for a moment and then added, "I can't see Patricia settling for that and missing out on all the glamorous social life that seems to go with your type of business. It's just not her style."

Terry shook his head. "No. It wouldn't suit her at all. Being with those kids today has been a revelation and taught me something. Well, a lot of things. Patricia would have made a real business asset, socially. She has the style and flair to attract the clients, you have to admit that. She's stunning to look at, charming and sociable. But marrying to improve the business was a crazy idea I was really stupid to even think about it. I know now that just wouldn't have worked for me, or even for her for that matter. We were fine together as a couple, but when she came to stay for weekends, well, things were a bit different. That's when the doubt began. After those weekends, nothing could put those doubts right. I'll be honest, John, I was going to confront her today and call the whole thing off. I guessed her father would make difficulties for me, maybe even block business from coming my way. He could make a bad enemy if he chose to, I think. but I'd decided it was best. And then you did the thing for me, without my having to pay any penalties to him. I could hardly believe my luck."

"So why the threats and demands for explanation, then?"

"Like I said, I couldn't believe it. I thought you might be one of those TV shows that set people up to look stupid. Only while we were having breakfast did it really seem true." Right now, the thought of John being a TV sleuth made him smile, but at the time it did seem possible.

They drove on in silence for a while as John turned all this new approach over in his mind. Terry would make a great family man, he'd seen that this afternoon. The kids had adored him, right from the first moment. He had the same easy manner with children as he did with adults. And then his thoughts were startled back to the present as Terry said quietly, "John, I'm minding someone else's business again, so shut me up if you want, but have you ever asked Jane to visit Richard with you? Don't you think it might ease his guilt or despair or whatever it is he's brooding on if he saw her well and reasonably happy?"

Despair? That described it exactly, didn't it? "Yes," John answered. "I've asked her a couple of times but she refused. I thought perhaps she felt it would upset her, you know, Richard living and Andy dead, and so I didn't push the idea again. Why?"

"That's what I thought you'd say. I guessed you didn't know the truth. It was Patricia. Again." Terry's voice held a hint of bitterness and he frowned deeply. "She told Jane that the psychiatrists thought a visit from Jane would make him even more depressed and guilty. I didn't say anything at all in case it was true, but I had my doubts."

John felt suddenly angry now, but mostly with himself. "Oh, why didn't Jane tell me that? How would Patricia know what anyone said about Richard, she hasn't been near him for months. He doesn't have a psychiatrist, anyway. No, it's not true, and I was damned stupid not to find out Jane's reasons before now. Oh, hell, I could kick myself for this."

Terry felt sorry for this quiet, unassuming man who seemed to have taken on all his brother's problems without any kind of recognition for his efforts. "Oh, don't give yourself a hard time," he said cheerfully. "This at least can soon be put right." He turned into the gate of John's little cottage. "Home, sweet home," he grinned. "Now for all that homework marking."

John pulled a face and sighed as he unbuckled his seat belt. "I suppose you're going home to put on your glad rags and go out on the town now."

"Actually, no," Terry said seriously. "Believe it or not, I have a stack of paperwork on my desk which has to be done tonight. I'm lecturing at a seminar tomorrow morning, and must tidy up my notes, too. Shake off the playboy image for tonight, anyway." He smiled at John's surprised look. "Even the ringmaster has to do his books, you know." And as John opened the car door he added, "I'll be in touch."

"You do that," John agreed, "Goodnight Terry. Thanks for the ride." He watched as the car backed out into the road and was gone. Then he let himself into his cottage, closing the door thankfully behind him. It was good to be on his own again. He laid his jacket carefully over the back of a chair, switched on the gas fire and went through to the kitchen and made tea and toast. Now he could really relax for a while. The pile of workbooks was still waiting where he had left it that morning, stacked neatly on his desk, and after a while he sat down to begin his task. But first, he must ring Freddie.

Freddie's wife answered the phone. "Good evening, Mrs. Greenwood, may I speak to Freddie? It's John Treherne. No, I promise, only a minute." Then, after a short pause, "Hello Freddie, John Treherne. Have I interrupted something big?"

"Not at all," said the jovial voice at the other end. "I was being thoroughly trounced at backgammon. What can I do for you, John?"

Quickly John explained the morning's events and added, "I think her Father will want to arrange a divorce, and as quickly as possible. I wanted you to know first. He's a barrister, I gather. Charles Cameron."

"Oh, yes, I know of him. What does Richard say about a divorce? Does he want me to agree?"

John's heart sank. He supposed Richard had to be told, even though he probably wouldn't bother acknowledging it. Another trip, and still with no car. Life seemed to be quite perverse, just at this moment. "I suppose I'll have to visit and ask him," he said, with the faint hope that Freddie might go instead. No such luck – Freddie simply agreed that that would be best. "Can you stall, if Mr. Cameron approaches you, until I've seen Richard?"

At the other end of the line there was a rich fruity chuckle. "Moira could refuse the Queen herself if I asked her to. Yes, John, no problem. Let me know as soon as you can though, won't you? Even Moira can't stall forever."

There wasn't time even to pick up his pen after speaking to Freddie, for the phone rang as soon as he replaced the receiver. "John Treherne?" a crisp voice demanded. When John agreed the caller continued, "Charles Cameron here. I've been trying to reach you all afternoon. I left a message for you with the vicar, you know." John made no comment, and the barrister's voice became a little sharper. "I'd like to know more about this business in church this morning, if you please."

John took his time answering. Then he said carefully, as if explaining something to his year nine boys, "It's exactly as I told the vicar. Patricia is married to my brother Richard, so the banns had to be stopped. That's all there is to say."

"Of course that's not all there is to say. My daughter tells me that your brother is mentally ill. That he went into a mental hospital and so she was left alone and came back home to live with us. I take it you are managing his affairs for him."

John's voice was controlled but razor sharp. "Patricia is wrong, and speaking of matters of which she knows nothing. Richard is in a perfectly normal nursing home. He is there because his wife couldn't or wouldn't take care of his needs. And when she let the house they once shared, he had no option but to go but a nursing home where he could be looked after. It is unlikely that Patricia would have any knowledge of my brother's progress or medical condition. She has not been in touch with him for eighteen months at the very least. His affairs are managed by his solicitor, Frederick. Greenwood of Hamilton & Greenwood in Oxford. Now, if you will excuse me I have a pile of homework to correct before morning school," and he replaced the receiver carefully back on its cradle. Charles Cameron could throw his weight about in court, perhaps, but not here. He was about halfway through the correcting when the phone rang again, and he muttered under his breath as he lifted the receiver. "John Treherne," he said with a sigh.

"Oh, John, I'm sorry, have I disturbed you?" Jane's voice was full of concern.

John relaxed. "No, 9J's homework is always good for an interruption. Is there something wrong?"

"No, no, nothing like that. I just wanted to say thank you for coming this afternoon. I'd been feeling a bit low and it was just an impulse to ring you. And it's always great to see you again anyway. The kids enjoyed it all, didn't they?"

"You can thank Terry, for that. My car really is off the road but he was listening as I took your call. We were in his car. He's not a bloke to hang around waiting for decisions, is he?" He gave a laugh and added, "Or invitations. Did you like him?"

"Yes, very much. He's great fun to have around and the kids adore him. If you have his number, I'd like to ring and thank him too. But I guess he's out on the town somewhere by now."

John laughed again. "I said that, too, and he told me that even the ringmaster has to do his paperwork. No, he's at home all evening. And yes, I do have his number, he gave me his business card. Hang on it's in my jacket." He fetched the card, read the number aloud to her. After some further conversation, Jane prepared to finish the call. "Hold on a minute," he said quickly, "There's something I want to ask you."

"Ask away then."

"Terry told me that you wouldn't visit Richard because Patricia had warned you off with phoney doctor's reports. Is that true?"

"Yes. But I didn't know about phoney, She said she'd spoken to Richard's psychiatrist and that he felt any visit from me would remind Richard that Andy was dead and that he, was still alive. That it would upset him and make him even more depressed. It seemed logical, so I accepted it. Why?"

"Because there's not a scrap of truth in it. Oh, Jane. How could you believe her? Why didn't you tell me all that? Richard doesn't have a psychiatrist, anyway, he's not a mental case. I'm convinced that he wouldn't be in such a state of despair if he saw you and felt that you were reasonably happy and didn't blame him." He realised he was quoting Terry, but went on, "Jane, please, will you come to visit him with me next time? Please, Jane? Now I think it is important."

"If you're sure it won't do more harm than good of course I'll come. I've always wanted to see him and tell him it's OK and I'm not mad at him, or anything like that." After a minute or two more John said his good-byes, replaced the receiver. Then he bent down and pulled the telephone plug from its socket, fetched himself a glass of whiskey from the kitchen and settled down to work. Blessed silence reigned in the tiny sitting room except for the occasional turning of pages and the plop as another book joined the corrected pile. It had been quite a day, one way and another.

Terry scanned the front of his house as he turned the car into the drive. There were no light shining and no car at the front door. Usually he felt a great sense of satis-faction, returning to the barn conversion, but tonight he felt more anxiety than pride. Then he sighed with relief at the realisation that Patricia's car wasn't there, she had given up waiting for him. He had avoided another confrontation. Letting himself into the house, switching on lights as he went, he headed for the kitchen and made a pot of coffee, then set about the task he had planned during the journey home. Fetching a suitcase from the bedroom and working systematically room by room, he removed every item which belonged to Patricia, whether it cost pennies or hundreds of pounds. Each was carefully packed in the suitcase. Upstairs he searched wardrobes and drawers, checking carefully that not one item was left behind. Then he closed and locked the suitcase and stood it in the hall.

In his office he set the coffee on the corner of the big desk and surveyed the papers waiting for his attention. No, these two letters must be done first. Taking a sheet of company headed paper he began to write. "Dear Mr. Cameron, I am writing to you to make my intentions clear. After the events of this morning, I think you will understand that I no longer feel able or wish to marry your daughter. It would be wiser for her to be told this now, rather than believe that a divorce from Richard Treherne would solve the problem for her and all would be as it was before. I believe this is how Patricia will view the current situation. It can never be so. I write to you as her father and as a lawyer, in order that there may be no misunderstanding. Patricia, I have found, has a rather cavalier attitude to truth. I am returning, with this letter, all your daughter's personal possessions which have been left here during the last few weeks. These are contained in a suitcase for which I enclose the key herewith." Terry read the letter through and signed it. Then he folded it into an envelope, added the suitcase key and then sealed and addressed it, and laid it to one side. After a moment's thought he drew a fresh sheet towards him and began to write, "Dear Patricia, This is to confirm that I consider that I am no longer engaged to you, as you are not free to be so. You may keep the ring. I have explained this to your father, and he has the key to the suitcase in which I have packed all your possessions from this house." This too he signed, folded into an envelope and addressed. Then he reached for the telephone, and dialled a number.

"Jimmy Hancock." The gravely voice at the other end made Terry move the receiver a little further away from his ear.

"Jimmy, it's Terry Kennedy. Sorry to ring you on a Sunday, but I wanted a job done first thing tomorrow. What do you reckon?"

"Hi, Terry. Sunday, Thursday, what's the difference? What's up, then?"

"Can you do a job first thing tomorrow, say eight o'clock? I want something delivered before the old man goes to the office. Could you do it that early?"

"Where?"

"Oh, it's OK, it's only Hallinford. But I don't want to go myself."

"'Course I can. I'll be with you about ten to tomorrow then, OK? Anyway, Terry, I was just doing my accounts, so I'll bring yours along with me. Save me a stamp."

Terry was puzzled. "My account, Jimmy? What account's this? You and I always settle things in cash."

"Yeah, usually we do. But your girlfriend had Dave do two runs up to Oxford, and he had to wait about a bit up there. Time's money, Terry, you know that." After a pause he asked, "Didn't you know about it?"

Terry wondered what more he would find out as time passed. "No, but don't worry about it, we'll settle it when you get here. Oh, and Jimmy, do you know of a local locksmith?"

"Sure. Jerry Cunningham, top of East Street."

"The shoe mender?"

"Yeah, and he's a good locksmith, too. He's an agent for a dry cleaning firm as well. Knows how to make a bob or two, does Jerry. But don't try him on a Sunday evening, he'll be in the Six Bells by now."

"Thanks, Jimmy, see you tomorrow." and they both rang off. For a moment or two Terry sat looking thoughtfully at the desk in front of him. Now, what did she have to send someone to Oxford for? Twice? He shook his head, oh well, that was Patricia. He poured himself more coffee, pulled the pile of papers towards him and picked up a pen. And then the telephone rang. "Terry Kennedy," he said a little sharply, still with Patricia on his mind.

"Terry," Jane's voice was apologetic. "I am sorry, have I interrupted you? John did say you were working at home tonight. I can always ring again….."

Terry interrupted her quickly. "Jane, it's marvellous to hear from you. No, I was afraid you were someone else, that's why I was abrupt. I haven't really got stuck in yet, anyway. And thanks for a lovely afternoon - you have the most amazing kids, do you know that? They're great."

Jane laughed. "Thanks Terry, they feel the same about you, especially Debbie. You really made a hit there. Maria will always be Uncle John's girl. And truly, I rang to thank you. Everyone had a great time and already they're asking when you're coming again. You'll have to,

Terry, or I shall be the ogre of the month and I shan't get a minute's peace."

"Thanks, Jane, I'd like that," Terry said quietly." "I'll talk to John. His car's off the road so he may be glad of a ride."

"I've just been talking to him. He wants me to go and see Richard. I guess you told him my reasons for not going, didn't you? I think he was a bit put out because I hadn't explained them before. I've told him of course I'll go with him if he thinks it will help. But I'll have to find someone to mind the kids for a couple of hours."

"No problem," Terry laughed. "We'll come up together, he can take you in and, if Richard acknowledges you and decides to talk, he can leave you with him. Then we'll mind the kids together. They'll feel safer if John's with us, I guess. That'll be no hardship for either of us, I reckon. And if Richard doesn't want to talk to you, well, you'll know you tried. We'll all go off somewhere for a treat, or something."

She was silent for a moment, wondering how John would react to being organised in this way. He was quiet and easy going normally, but might not like having his day arranged for him like this, especially by a comparative stranger. "Talk to John, see what he says," she said diplomatically, and then added, "but I wouldn't ring tonight, he seemed a bit, well, tired and edgy I suppose. Not his usual calm self."

"No, I'll leave it tonight. And don't worry, I won't let him feel he's being organised again. I'd hate the thought myself. And I really do have a pile of papers to deal with as well as some notes for a lecture. But one, or perhaps both of us will be in touch before next weekend, that's a promise."

"I'll look forward to that," she said, "and thanks for the offer. Now you to your papers and me to mending Jamie's school trousers. Again. Bye Terry."

Terry replaced the receiver and sat quite still for a moment or two, deep in thought. In this one day he had been saved from a disastrous marriage without having to face either Patricia's tantrums or the wrath of her father. He'd met a woman he found attractive, but in a new and relaxed kind of way. A woman who seemed to be from a different world, a world of children, and shortage of money and yet was on his own wavelength, at least he thought so. And he'd met John the loner, who had been the catalyst in a way, for all this change in his outlook. John the loner, who took on his brother's problems without recognition or thanks. And judging by Jane and the children's regard for him, had seen them through the problems of losing Andy. Life could be very strange sometimes. He shook his head as if to rouse himself from all these deep reflections, and reached for the first of his papers. Enough of daydreaming, he still had a living to earn. Judging by the size of this work pile it was going to be a very late night, or more probably, an early morning, too. He drained the last of his coffee, reached for his pen and began to write.

CHAPTER THREE

On Monday morning John tapped on the headmaster's half-open door. Putting his head around it he asked, "Can I have a quick word, Brian?"

The older man looked up from the pile of letters on his desk. "John! Yes of course. Come in and close the door. Is there a problem?"

John did as the headmaster had asked, and stood in front of the desk. "Well, yes. I know it's short notice, but do you think we could find someone to cover for me this afternoon? Something has cropped up and I really ought to go to Oxford and sort it out."

The headmaster looked at him thoughtfully. In the two years that he had been in this job he had never once known John Treherne ask for help or time off. Indeed he was always the one who was willing to step into any breach. "What do you have on this afternoon?"

"A double period with 9J for history. The other is paperwork time, and I can catch up with that this evening."

The headmaster smiled. "Oh, 9J for history? Well now, that shouldn't be too bad. Yes, I'll cover for you there myself John. But you're not on playground duty, are you?"

It was John's turn to smile. Everyone knew how the Head disliked having to do any playground duty. "No," he said. "That's tomorrow."

"That's settled then. You can leave as soon as morning school finishes. I take it this is your brother's business again?" he added quietly. He felt, somehow, that this young man had taken on too many family worries.

"It is," John answered resignedly. "Right, I'll get off to class then, before they start rioting. Thanks, Brian," and he turned and left the office.

He bought a sandwich at lunchtime and ate it on the bus. The damned car really had to be fixed somehow, and soon. Probably he was wasting his time again this afternoon as well, but still felt he ought to keep Richard aware of what was happening. More so this time as this problem would involve Richard himself and his financial advisers. He wouldn't care, of course, but Freddie couldn't go ahead without some kind of authority.

On reaching the hospital he made his way to Richard's room in the private wing. The door opened as he approached and Karen stepped into the corridor.

"Hello, John," she said with a smile. "We don't usually see you in the week. Nothing wrong, is there?"

"Not really. I just wanted to make sure he knew something before someone else told him. But I don't suppose he'll care much."

The young nurse looked at him sympathetically. Every two weeks he came here, told his brother the news, and got only the odd grunt or monosyllabic answer. Why did he go on doing it? But then, why did she go on caring so much. The same reason, she supposed, they both wanted to help Richard. That Richard didn't want their help made no difference to them both. Now she said simply, "See you later then, perhaps," and stepped aside in order to let him pass into the room. As usual Richard was dressed and lying on his bed, staring out of the window.

He made no effort to turn his head or speak as his brother approached the bed.

"Hello Richard," John said as he pulled a chair to the bedside. "I really must get the car fixed; travelling by bus is a real pain. How's things?"

Richard said nothing, and continued to gaze out of the window. Did he actually see anything out there, John wondered.

"I came up to tell you that Patricia's father called me last night. He wanted to know who managed your affairs. It seems that Patricia is looking for a divorce. She wants to marry again." He thought it best not to go into too much detail just now. What would be the point?

Still Richard did not turn, but this time he actually made a reply. "OK, Tell Freddie," was all he said.

"I already have. He is holding Mr. Cameron off until I'd told you what we think is in the wind. He needed to be sure that he knew what you wanted him to do. Well, Moira is stalling for him," John added with a forced smile. "I'll tell him to go ahead then, shall I?"

Richard said nothing. After a couple more attempts at conversation which drew no reply John had had enough. "Right," he said, standing up and pushing back the chair, "I've told you, and I'm assuming you agree. You will have to talk to Freddie at some stage you know. You'll probably also have to talk to your accountant. I'll see you again soon," and as Richard made no answer, he left the room, fighting the urge to slam the door, and walked quickly along the corridor and out into the sunshine and fresh air. He needed to get away from the hospital as quickly as he could. It was all so depressing. Now he wasn't even sure why he'd bothered to come, anyway. But Freddie needed someone to say yes or no.

As the door closed behind his brother Richard gave a muffled groan. Why did he take out his resentment on poor old John? Or anyone else, come to that. Because they were free? Because they could walk away from him and live their lives as they pleased? He didn't know, he just knew that it was too much to ask him to talk about things he had no part in any more. And now Patricia wanted to marry someone else. Well, that was no real surprise. He almost smiled as the thought came to him - had she told the poor guy that she was pregnant, as she'd tricked him into marriage? But whoever he was, he'd be rich, that was for sure. Probably good-looking, too. She had always despised ordinary people, like his brother John.

Sitting on a bench in the bus station John watched the people milling around him. He thought about getting another bus and going to see Jane, but it was all too much of an effort just now. Visiting Richard was no picnic. He'd seen Jane on Sunday, anyway, and she'd been OK. He had some work to catch up on this evening, too. Finally the Ledminster bus crawled into its parking bay ten minutes late, and he climbed aboard thankfully. 9J's history antics would have been more interesting than this afternoon's fiasco. The bus had almost reached its destination when he remembered something else he had to do today. He'd promised to call at David Brownlow's office after school. Was there still time, he felt as though he'd been away for weeks. After checking his watch he decided to go straight to the builders' yard from the bus station. Another walk, perhaps someone at the yard would look at his car for him. He'd ask, anyway.

During their journey home together yesterday evening John had told Terry about David Brownlow's call. The builder had wanted to ask John if he could sort his bills and invoices into some kind of order before he presented them to his accountant. He had heard that John sometimes did this kind of job for small businesses like his own. Terry had been greatly amused. "He has a wonderful accounting system," he laughed. "There are two boxes on his desk, one for things paid out and one for things paid in. At the end of the year he takes them to the accountant. That's it! It must cost him a small fortune to have the bloke sort it all out."

"Sounds like a challenge," John grinned. "He wants me to keep his accounts up to date on a regular basis, once they are sorted. Seems like his accountant has had enough. Or maybe it's getting too costly."

With this conversation still in his mind John made his way to Brownlow's builder's yard. There was a small wooden cabin in one corner with "Office" painted on the door. He knocked, waited a moment and then went in. The cabin had been partitioned into two small rooms and in this one a young woman was bending over the desk, clipping papers together. She straightened up at John's approach. "Can I help you?" she asked. She was small and slender and her long dark hair had been swept into a knot at the back of her head, but here and there strands had escaped. This, together with her slight figure gave the impression of a little girl playing grownups. She tucked the loose strands behind her ears impatiently, giving a little, exasperated sigh.

John smiled nervously. "John Treherne," he said. "Mr. Brownlow has asked me to look at his accounts for him."

"Oh, hello, John." She had a warm, friendly smile which made her dark eyes sparkle. "I'm Kitty Brownlow, David's sister, secretary and general help. He has had to go out, but he says to take you through to his office. He asked can you work there, he'd rather the papers stayed here. Can you manage that." She gave a soft little laugh and added, "someone ought to work in there - David never does." She opened the door to the second room and led the way in., "I cleaned it all this morning ready for you, and tidied the desk. I even watered the geranium, poor thing. No one else ever comes in here, except to drop papers in a box." There was laughter in her voice, and John couldn't resist a smile, too. This smile stayed with him as he saw the desk. Highly polished and perfectly clear save for two large boxes. Terry hadn't been joking – how did that guy know so much about so many people? "If I lay papers in separate piles on the desk will anyone disturb them?"

"No," she answered, "I told you. No one uses the office.

He glanced at his watch. "What time do you go home?"

"I leave at five fifteen, so I'll have to lock it all up then. Would you like some coffee? It won't take a minute."

"Oh, yes please!" It was just what he needed after this afternoon's hassle. He sat at the desk a little bemused. Kitty brought a large mug of coffee and then left him to his work. Picking up one of the boxes he put it in an empty drawer beside him, then started work on the other. This was the paid out box, just as Terry had described, and he was soon engrossed in sorting the papers into monthly order. He was surprised when Kitty reappeared, ready to lock up and go home. He looked at the piles of papers dubiously and wondered aloud if it was safe to leave them there or should they be put away somewhere. It could be risky, leaving them piled up like this. She thought for a moment and then fetched a sheaf of large envelopes. Together they put the various piles into separate envelopes, marking them with the month, put everything away in the drawers and left the inner office with Kitty solemnly locking the door behind them.

"Excuse me, Kitty," said John a little nervously "but does your brother or any of his men know much about cars?"

"Cars? Probably. Why?" She was rinsing mugs at the sink in the corner

"It's just that my car won't start," John began rather sheepishly. "I have to find someone who might fix it for me fairly quickly. I need to go up to Oxford regularly and the bus takes forever."

"Oh, mending cars you mean. My Dad is an expert. He'll look at it for you. I'll ask him tonight." She was tidying the outer office and switching off wall sockets and lights. "Listen," she said impulsively, "Why don't you come with me now and we'll talk to him about it? It's only a couple of streets away. Are you in a hurry?"

Was he being organised again? But he really did need the car. They walked companionably together for about ten minutes as Kitty explained about her father. "He's been off work for a while. He wanted to go back today but the doctor said another week. He's a bit bored, so he might be glad to do your car for you. Here," she said, and John followed her through a gate and along the path. As she opened the front door she called, "Dad. I'm back," and then to John, "Come on in. Dad'll be in the kitchen."

Ray Brownlow turned away from the stove as they entered the kitchen. "Hello, Cats," he said. "Do you want tea?" He was already filling the kettle and now switched it on without waiting for an answer.

"Dad, this is John Treherne. He's trying to sort out David's accounts. His car's out of action. Do you think you could look at it for him? Maybe fix it, too?"

John held out his hand, and Ray shook it with a grip that almost made John wince. "Hello, John, what's wrong with the car, then?"

John flushed; he felt a bit foolish having to admit his ignorance. "I don't know, it just won't start and I'm no mechanic, I'm afraid."

Ray was not surprised. He had noted the thin hands with the long tapering fingers. Here was a man for fine work, not motor car engines. "I'll have a look, anyway. Where do you live? Is the car there or somewhere else? I could look at it tomorrow, if you're free."

"I have to be in school by eight forty five and don't finish till well after four, but my cottage is in Archers Lane, number 3, it's only ten minutes walk. The car is parked in my drive,. Do you think you can help?"

"You're a teacher? God, you must have some patience." That explained the hands. He smiled and added, "It wouldn't be the job for me, though. I'd want to shake the little blighters. Ok. Suppose I get to you by eight fifteen? I could have a quick look, and then maybe work on it during the day. Maybe, if it's nothing too serious, I can have it running by the time you finish work. Would eight fifteen be OK?"

"That's fine for me, thanks." John watched as, without asking, Ray put three mugs on the table and began to pour tea. "Not for me, thanks," he said quickly, as Ray held the sugar basin up inquiringly.

"I thought you were an accountant," said Kitty. "What subjects do you teach? Which school is it?"

"Maths and history," John answered. "Ashleigh Boys. I only tidy up figures ready for the accountant."

Ray laughed aloud. "You must like a challenge if you've taken on David's books. Cats thought she might be able to help but she didn't know where to start. He's a damn good builder, but not much shakes in the office. That's why Cats took the job there."

"Oh, Dad, I wish you wouldn't keep calling me that," said Kitty ruefully. "It makes me sound nasty and spiteful." Ray grinned at her, and as he opened the oven door she asked, "What's for supper?"

John, feeling that this was his cue to leave, finished his tea and stood up. "I'll see you in the morning, then, Mr. Brownlow. Thanks for the tea."

Kitty went to the front door with him and watched as he walked quickly away down the street. Then she returned to the kitchen.

"Not very talkative, your friend," her father said conversationally, but she could tell, that he wasn't being critical.

"No, he isn't, is he? Do you think he's shy?"

Ray looked at his daughter thoughtfully. Obviously John Treherne had made an impression. "No," he said after a pause, "I think he's just a quiet man by nature, that's all. Does it matter to you, Cats?" But she made no answer, she had already turned away and busied herself laying the table for supper, and Ray held his peace.

That same morning, just as Charles and Isobel Cameron had finished breakfast they heard the postman's step in the porch and the rattle of letters falling into the wire basket. Charles laid his napkin neatly beside his plate and stood up. "I'll pick up the mail and take it through to the study," he said.

Isobel nodded, and began to stack the breakfast dishes. "I have to go out for a short time later, Charles, but I'll let you know when I'm leaving." She put all the dishes and the coffee pot on the trolley ready to wheel it through to the kitchen. She crossed the room to open the window and saw a small silver-blue van approaching the house. When it drew up she was able to read the neat inscription "J.H.Couriers" painted on the side; Probably some more work for Charles. The driver climbed out and reached for a dark blue suitcase, some letters and a small clipboard. Charles was already in the hall and would deal with it himself, so she could head for the kitchen. As she stacked crockery into the dishwasher, Charles appeared in the kitchen doorway. "Oh, some mail for me?" she asked, seeing the letters in his hand.

"Well, not exactly, but I think you should read it," he said grimly. "The courier just brought it." He handed Terry's letter to her, and she read through it quickly.

"Well," she said, handing the letter back, "I think that's pretty final, don't you? I'm not surprised though. She has treated him very shabbily."

"Yes, she has," her husband agreed. "And perhaps you'd better look at this, too," and he handed her the second envelope he was carrying. Again Isobel scanned it quickly, and looked up in surprise.

"Charles," she said slowly, looking at the frown on his face, "You look a bit, well, put out. didn't you know about this? Didn't she agree it with you first?"

"She did not. I knew nothing until this bill arrived. As there isn't going to be a wedding now, what do we do with a bill for a going-away outfit, whatever that might be? What exactly is a going-away outfit, Izzy? He looked at his wife, appealing for her help in a situation he didn't want to deal with.

"Leave it with me," she answered. "I have already planned to cancel the dress, that's why I was going out today. There is a branch of this store in Ledminster. I'll call in there this morning and explain it all. I think we may have to pay a certain percentage of the cost for inconvenience, you know what some of these quality stores are like, but I'll see what I can do."

Charles Cameron smiled at her with relief. "Thanks, Izzy," he said gruffly, and went back to his study. Isobel put away the napkins and other small items and was just leaving the kitchen when Patricia appeared.

"Hello, mother," she said as though nothing unusual had ever occurred between them, and she sank gracefully on to a chair at the table. "Is there any coffee? Are you just about to make breakfast?"

"We've had breakfast, Patricia," Isobel told her in a dangerously calm voice. "Your father is already at work in his study, and I have work to do upstairs. As for coffee, there's the kettle, there's the coffee pot. There's the toaster. It's all yours." She walked towards the kitchen door.

Patricia looked at her mother in surprise. "I don't think Daddy would be pleased if he heard you talking to me like that," she said carefully.

"Then I suggest you ask him to make your breakfast and your coffee," Isobel snapped, and left the room. Ten minutes later she put her head around the study door. "I'm just off, Charles," she said. "I have that bill with me. I'll be back long before lunch."

Her husband looked up, pen poised over his papers. "Drive carefully, Izzy," he said softly. She wondered why the old familiar name had suddenly crept back into his conversation. Then he asked suddenly, "Is Patricia up yet?" When his wife agreed he added, "Will you ask her to make me some coffee and bring it through here, Izzy? No," he said, as she opened her mouth to speak, "Patricia can do it." She nodded, said goodbye and went to the kitchen. Patricia was still elegantly slumped on the chair, but had switched on the kettle.

"Patricia," Isobel said from the doorway, "Will you make some coffee for your father and take it through to the study?"

"Couldn't you make it for him, mother, now you're here? You know just how Father likes his coffee."

"Patricia." Her mother's voice was patient. "You will see that I have my coat and gloves on, and my car keys in my hand. That means I am going out. Your father asked me to ask you for coffee. That's all," and she turned and walked away.

Fifteen minutes later Patricia opened the study door and walked in, carrying a tray on which stood two cups of coffee. "Mother said you wanted coffee," she said, not waiting for him to stop his writing. Putting the tray on the corner of the desk, she added, "She's gone out."

Charles laid down his pen. "Sit down, Patricia," he said. When she did so he handed her a letter. "That came by the courier this morning. I think you should read it now," he added, as she made to tuck the letter in her pocket.

She opened the envelope, took out a single sheet and slowly began to read. When she had read it all through she said, "Oh, Terry must have been in a bad temper after that silly business in church. I'm sure he doesn't really mean it. I'll go round there this morning and make him understand."

Her father looked at her in silent disbelief. That "silly business" had made her parents feel humiliated in front of their neighbours. And what was there for Terry to understand? The letter said he understood perfectly. Then he reached into his pocket and drew out a key. "That is the key to the suitcase in the hall. Terry has returned all your possessions. I think he means it quite definitely."

"Oh, Daddy, you don't know him as I do. He's always quick to react. It will be all right, you'll see, once I've talked to him. We'll probably laugh about it together. Mother was in a funny mood today. She seems to be rather cross about something. Has something happened to upset her?"

"Take your letter and take your key and take your coffee, Patricia, and go. You are trying my patience beyond all limits and I have work to do." He picked up his pen and then added, "And I think it's high time that you found some work to do too. Terry won't want you hanging around his office now. Go and find yourself something to do."

She looked at him in astonishment. "Daddy!" she exclaimed, but Charles was writing again, intent on his papers and did not look up or answer. After a few moments of stunned silence she picked up her coffee and walked out. Whatever was wrong with everyone this morning? She would get dressed and go round to see Terry. It was only a question of delaying the wedding until Daddy had sorted out the divorce, surely? And Daddy would make sure that Richard paid what she deserved. It would all blow over.

An hour later she turned the car into the driveway of the barn conversion. This was not Mrs. Paget's day for working, so Patricia went to the front door rather than the office. She tried to slide her key into the lock, but it would not go in. She looked at the keys, had she used the office key? She tried again, without success. She rang the doorbell several times. Nothing happened. Terry must be out. She tried the key once more, and then, very slowly, it dawned on her; this was a new lock. She walked around the building to the office door. This had a new lock, too. She went back to the car, climbed in and took her mobile phone from the passenger seat. There was no answer from the house phone or Terry's mobile. There was nothing else to do but turn the car and drive home. Terry was more angry than she had thought.

Much later that afternoon Isobel quietly opened the study door and put her head inside the room. "Charles?" she said questioningly. He looked up and smiled and she continued, "I'm just going out to the pillar box with these. Have you anything that needs posting?"

He looked at the sheaf of letters in her hand. "My word, Izzy, what have you been doing," he asked. "What are all those?"

"Cancelling the wedding invitations. I bought plain cards and did the rest on the computer. Have you anything to go?" When he shook his head she added, "I'll only be ten minutes, then I think you might break for a cup of tea with me don't you? She didn't wait for an answer, but withdrew her head from the study and closed the door. Truly, Charles Cameron reflected, Izzy is a remarkable woman. So many things she did without question or complaint. And now, after the events in church yesterday and his daughter's behaviour since he had to admit that Izzy had been right all along. Patricia might have learned to be an elegant and sociable woman at that expensive school, but she was not, and now he accepted it, never would be truly adult. Perhaps this was what they called arrested development, or something. He had tried to hide it from himself all these years. He'd tried to believe that the daughter of a well-known barrister had to be perfectly normal.

Ray Brownlow was as good as his word, early the following morning John heard a car in the drive then an unhurried step on the gravel path. "Morning Mr. Brownlow," he said as he opened the front door and stepped out.

"Ray," said the older man. "Nice morning, too. If you've got the keys, I'll take a quick look and then you can get off to school. Lord," he added, taking the keys from John's hand, "you must have the patience of Job to teach those little hooligans."

"It's not that bad. Most of them are OK," John laughed. "I like teaching. Not so mad about all the paperwork they've introduced, these days, though."

"Tell me about it," said Ray with a grin. "I reckon I spend as much time filling in forms and dockets and what have you as I do mending cars. That's the way it goes, though." He unlocked John's car and took a look at the dashboard, the came around to the front and lifted the bonnet. John went back inside the house, reappearing some minutes later with a small satchel of books and papers.

"Can I leave you to it, Mr. Er Ray?" he asked. "I'd better get into school now."

"Course," said Ray. "I reckon I might have this little lady running for you by this afternoon. OK if I take it away to work at home where the tools are?" John agreed, at once, but wondered as he hurried along the street how you took a car home when it wouldn't go. Still, it would be good to have it working again. Then he could go to Oxford and take Jane to see Richard. He was quite convinced now that this would snap him out of his misery, convince him that Jane didn't blame him and was managing on her own. If it didn't work, well, then they'd all know, wouldn't they, that there was nothing they could do for Richard? With his mind still working along those lines, he turned into the school gates and moved swiftly across the playground, ready to tackle that day's classes.

That afternoon there was a staff meeting, which seemed to go on forever. When John finally reached home he was a bit disappointed to see that the driveway was quite empty – obviously Ray was still working on the car. Well, at least he hoped that was the reason. He entered the cottage, picking up the mail and as he went straight to the kitchen to fill the kettle. Staff meetings were thirsty work. He was just making his tea when the phone rang. He picked up the receiver of the kitchen extension at once. "John Treherne."

"Ray here, John. Thought I'd better let you know that the car is safely locked in David's yard. I've fixed it, but I've put the battery on charge. OK?"

"Thanks a lot, Ray. I was going to the yard tomorrow anyway to do the books, so I could pick it up myself, if that suits you. How much do I owe you?"

"Oh, Cats has a couple of invoices. She'll tell you all about it. But I'll bring it back myself tomorrow, anyway. Like to see that it's running nice and smooth. I'll be with you about half eight, OK?"

When he had replaced the receiver John felt a sense of elation. He had a genuine reason to speak to Kitty tomorrow, something to say that wasn't trite or forced. Even 9J's history workbooks didn't seem quite so bad tonight. He prepared and ate his meal and then settled down to work.

—⁂—

Kitty was working at a rather elderly typewriter when John walked into the yard office next day. She looked up and smiled. "Hi, John. Want some coffee? I'll give this old thing a rest," and she stood up and came around the desk to unlock the inner office door. "Dad's fixed the car, then?"

"Yes, he brought it back this morning." Stupid thing to say, of course she'd know that. He felt his face begin to redden as it always did when he talked to women. He says you have the bill." He had to smile as she pulled a face at him. "Yes, I'd love a coffee, please." He walked into the inner office, sat at the desk and was soon engrossed again in David Brownlow's accounts. Kitty brought coffee and biscuits and sat on the corner of the desk watching him. "I think I might try a bookkeeping course later," she said. "Do you think it might help me with these?" indicating the papers on the desk. "I'd like to be able to keep David's books in order myself. Do you think I'd be any good at it?" She wanted to make him talk to her.

He looked up and reached for his coffee cup. "I can't see why not," he said. "Yes, it would be a good plan. Any qualification is useful in the job market. Now he was sounding pompous. " You'd take away my pocket money though," he added with a faint smile.

She laughed aloud. "No, I shall only take over when you've sorted out this lot. But really, David needs some organising. It's funny," she went on, "Dad is so methodical. All his tools and stuff are always in order. David is always in a mess." The phone rang in her office and she left him to his work, and only returned when she was about to close the office for the night. They tidied the papers away and left the building together.

"Oh, lord," said John suddenly remembering, "I still haven't paid for the car repairs. How much did it cost? Do you know offhand?"

"Dad's got the invoices," she said innocently. "Why not walk home with me now and sort it out with Dad, if it's bothering you. It isn't bothering him any." And so without realising he was being manipulated, John found himself once again walking home with Kitty. He felt just a little more relaxed with her now, and they talked easily, not the awkward, stilted conversation he usually had with women. It was true, she did most of the talking, and she was certainly different. She opened the front door and called, "Dad, I'm back," before turning again to John. "Come on in. He'll be in the kitchen, as usual."

Ray looked up from the newspaper he had spread across the kitchen table. "Hello Cats. Hello again, John. Tea?" He got up and switched on the kettle without waiting for an answer.

"Kitty says you have the invoices for the car parts, so I'd like to settle up with you for the repairs," John said. Ray looked surprised, caught Kitty's eye, thought for a moment and then answered, "Oh, sorry, I thought I'd given them to Cats." He turned to his daughter, "See if they're in my jacket pocket, will you love?"

She gave him a huge, delighted smile. "No rush, Dad, let's have some tea first," she said, and sat down at the table. Both men quickly followed suit. "You're not in a hurry, John, are you?"

John smiled at them both. "No," he said, "for once, I don't even have homework to mark.

Ray watched his daughter over the rim of his mug. The boy was either disinterested, or shy or reserved. It was a mystery to him that both his daughters, pretty, outgoing and vivacious, chose men who were quiet and unassuming, thoughtful and reserved. He did not remember now Ray Brownlow the quiet, unassuming engineer apprentice their mother Alissandra had loved and married all those years ago. But Cats wasn't making much headway here just now. He could sense that it was important to her, too. "Well, in that case," he said, "Why don't you stay and have a bit of supper with us? It's only chicken casserole, but there's plenty." From where he sat, he could see Cats' hands under the table – she had her fingers crossed on both of them and it was as much as he could do not to laugh.

"Well, if you're sure, I'd like that." John was also watching Kitty, who turned and smiled back at him, uncrossed her fingers under the table and then picked up her mug to finish her tea.

As they ate, Ray asked, "John, the sill on your front window is badly rotting. Did you know?"

"Yes. I keep meaning to do something about it, but haven't got around to it yet. There's lots of other jobs, too. But I'm no handyman and need to find someone, and I keep put it off."

The boy looked quite shamefaced and Ray grinned at him. "Until it all falls down around your ears, you mean?" Then he became more serious. "Why don't you ask David to do some of these jobs you have instead of paying you for the bookkeeping?"

John looked up quickly. "Would he do that?"

"He'd jump at it," Ray laughed. "The taxman can't touch barter, you know. Cats can ask him in the morning, can't you, love?" She agreed enthusiastically, giving her father a radiant smile for his understanding. "Well, that's settled then. Anyone want any more chicken?"

CHAPTER FOUR

On Thursday evening Terry rang. "John, are you planning to go up to Oxford this weekend?" he asked.

"Yes. I've had the car fixed. I told Jane I'd take her to see Richard when I could. I was just about to ring her."

"Listen. I promised I'd mind the kids for her while she visited. You won't need to stay with her while she chats to him, will you? I think the kids might be happier if you were with me. So I was thinking we might go up together, taking my car as it's bigger. I've picked up some bits that might amuse them for a while. What do you think?"

Here we go again, John thought I'm being organised once again, but he supposed it made a lot of sense. Someone must mind the children while she was with Richard. Jane had been quite adamant that no way were the children going into the hospital. Well not this time anyway. "Ok, that's fine," he said. "You'll pick me up Saturday morning, then?" When Terry agreed, they fixed a time and rang off. John supposed that it wouldn't be such a bad thing this time, but he wasn't going to trundle back and forth to Oxford with Terry in tow from now on. Or was it he who was in tow? He felt rather resentful, and then smiled at his own childishness. He was getting to think like some of his pupils. Then he picked up the telephone receiver and dialled Jane's number. She was delighted with the arrangements,. She was looking forward to it all she said, even visiting

Richard. Perhaps Jane needed to make this visit as much as they hoped Richard needed to see her. It was impossible to guess.

When Terry's car drew to a halt outside his cottage on Saturday morning, John still felt a niggle of resentment. Terry didn't get out but simply sounded the horn, which didn't improve matters. Finally, Terry got out of the car and came to the front door, just as John opened it. "Everything OK?" he asked.

"Sure. I just wasn't ready, that's all." Terry said nothing, and they climbed into the car, but before they started out, Terry slipped a cd into the player on the dashboard. John sighed inwardly, Terry was sure to go for some modern pop stuff. But slowly he began to unwind and relax as Rachmaninov's piano concerto softly filled the air. This man was really full of surprises. He couldn't stay offhand with him for long. The music, the fine day they had chosen, and not having to concentrate on the driving all fused together to fill him with a sense of peace and well-being. "It's going to be a great day to take the kids out," he said. "There's a little park near the hospital, we can take them there."

"Great. That's what I was hoping. I've got some bits and pieces in the boot for them. They'll keep them happy for a while. Me and you too I should think."

Jane was in the kitchen when they arrived. "Scrambled eggs on toast for lunch," she announced. "Is that OK for everyone?" They all agreed and as she worked, John made coffee for the adults. "Do you really think this will work," Jane asked tentatively. "Seeing Richard, I mean?"

"I honestly don't know Jane, but it's worth a try, isn't it? Sorry, Janey, am I pushing you into something you don't want to do?"

She shook her head. "No, not a bit, but if he won't talk to anyone else, is he likely to want to talk to me?"

"Who knows where Richard is concerned?" John's voice was matter of fact and level. He noticed that for once Jane was wearing a neatly fitting sweater; usually she wore one of Andy's old ones. He supposed it gave her some sense of comfort, or continuity, or something. Today she looked so neat and pretty – just like the old Jane Lawson, the pretty but practical business management student. He smiled at her; "You look nice, Jane."

Coming from the quiet, reserved John Treherne this was quite a compliment, Jane thought. But she said simply, "Thanks, John," and went on stirring the pan of eggs.

Just before two o'clock they all piled into Terry's car and set off for the clinic. When they arrived Jane and John got out and walked towards the main door, leaving Terry in the car with the three children. John had told neither Richard or Karen, his nurse, of Jane's visit so that his brother would have no chance to cancel it. when they entered Richard's room Karen turned from the sink to greet the newcomers. Jane put a finger to her lips, and Karen understood, nodded and said simply, "Oh, hello, John." Richard made no move at all. He was dressed and lying on the made up bed as usual. Jane pulled a chair forward and sat down, putting her hand over his as it lay on the counterpane. There was no reaction. After a moment or two Jane signalled to the other two with her finger to her lips again. Then she moved sharply as if to snatched her hand away and stand up, pushing her chair back, making it scrape loudly.

"Right then, Dickybird," she said crossly, looking down at the inert figure on the bed. "If you're just going to lie there like the proverbial beached whale, I'm off. No one ever ignores Jane Lawson, you should know that by now." But as she spoke the hand on the bed gripped her fingers tightly. John and Karen watched as Richard's face changed, cleared, losing at once the look of apathy and his head turned very slowly towards his visitor.

"Jane?" Richard's voice was hoarse, almost a croak, through lack of use. "Jane! Oh, it is you." His mouth moved as if to say more, but no words came. John took Karen's arm and they left the room together, closing the door gently behind them. In the tiny adjoining office Karen turned her face away, but not before John had caught the glimmer of imminent tears. "Oh," she said in a choked voice, "Oh, John, it's not fair, is it? All these months you and I have talked to him, cared for him watched over him without ever getting an answer, or a smile, and she walks in and now he's smiling, talking, and oh," she broke off for now the tears really began to fall.

John felt uncomfortable and embarrassed, but said gently, "Karen, listen. Don't you know who she is?" When she shook her head he went on, "Richard's friend Andy died in the crash, you know that? Jane is Andy's widow. I brought her here hoping that if he saw her happy and well he might feel better about himself. Now I'm supposed to be helping my mate mind the kids for her, so I've got to go. Make them some tea and put a cup on the tray for yourself. Jane might be finding it hard and be glad of someone else in the conversation. OK?" It was the longest speech Karen had ever heard John utter but she simply nodded, and he made for the door with a sense of relief. Comforting tearful women was not his strong point.

Terry was telling the children a story as John got back into the car. He sat quietly until it finished and the children fell about laughing. Terry raised an enquiring eyebrow; "Everything OK?"

"I think so. He's talking, anyway. I've left them to it. Let's go get some fresh air now." When they reached the park Terry opened the boot to reveal a box of bats and balls, skipping ropes and other energetic toys, and a highly coloured inflated beach ball for Maria, who squealed with delight and hugged it like a new doll. For the next hour all five of them were happily absorbed in various and novel games, so that when at last it was suggested they all go to fetch Mummy, three happy but rather rosy and dusty children climbed back into the car.

Karen took the tea into Richard's room as John had suggested. "Oh, lovely, tea," said Jane, looking up and smiling. "Are you going to have a cup with us? I've been catching Richard up to date with the family news, and I could just murder a cup of tea right now." Karen smiled and nodded as she set the tray down and began to pour. She handed a cup to Jane and set Richard's on the table beside his bed and propped him up on his pillows.

"Thanks, Karen," he said gruffly but with a rather crooked smile. She nodded again for she found she couldn't speak – this was already one big step forward for her patient. Then he turned back to Jane. "And the baby?"

Jane laughed. "She wouldn't thank you for calling her a baby now, she's almost four." She felt that Richard was leaving Karen standing and she turned to the young nurse and explained, "John is looking after my three children for me at the moment, but Maria, the youngest, will always be his favourite. He's really good with them."

"Yes, he would be," and the nurse smiled back at her. "He's always so calm and patient."

"Will you bring them to see me one day?" Richard asked quietly. "If Jamie is so like Andy I'd so like to see him. And the girls too, of course."

Jane hesitated, and a slight shadow crossed her face. "Look," she said at last. "I'd love you to meet them again Richard, see how they've grown and all that. But I don't want to bring them here, to see you in bed, to stand about not knowing what to say or what to do. Isn't it possible for you to get up into a wheelchair, and meet us in the garden, or the dayroom or the coffee shop, or somewhere? Somewhere where the kids will feel comfortable."

Karen held her breath. Was he going to snarl and refuse again? She had tried several times to persuade him into a wheelchair. Richard looked first at Jane, and then at her. "Yes," he said slowly, "I understand. And yes, I think I can manage that in a little while."

"Oh, Richard, you know you can," Karen's voice was soft but compelling. "It's something we've always wanted you to try, you know it is."

He didn't answer or look at her for a long moment, but still gripped Jane's hand. Then he said slowly, "OK, Jane. We'll see how it goes."

They talked on for a little while longer, but Jane could see the new effort he was making was tiring him and she prepared to leave. "I really have to go now," she said. "Terry and John will be exhausted minding those three." She bent and kissed Richard's cheek. "No more gloom now," she said softly. "Now everything can get better, you'll see."

He still held her hand, but she withdrew it gently.

"Jane," he said urgently, "You will come again, won't you? Soon?"

"I'll try, but I don't have transport and there's always the kids. But I'll tell you what," and she looked around the little room. "Oh, don't you have a phone?"

"He could," Karen said quickly. "He just thought it wasn't necessary."

"If you had a phone you could ring and talk to me," Jane said. "Once the children have gone to bed, it's more than quiet all evening. It'd be nice to chat then." She moved to the door. "Bye, Richard. Bye Karen."

"Jane," Karen called urgently. "Your number? Give Richard your number."

Jane came back, took a pen from her bag and wrote the number on a scrap of paper Karen produced from her pocket. "Thanks," said Karen, "I'll organise a phone as quickly as I can if Richard agrees."

"Bye, Janey," Richard said, and lay back on his pillows. But when his visitor had left he turned to Karen again. "She doesn't hate me," he said in a tone of wonder.

"Of course she doesn't." There was the shine of tears in Karen's eyes again. "You've known her so long, did you really think she would?"

Whatever they might say, Richard thought, it was partly his fault that Jane was alone now. But if he made the effort, if he became a bit more mobile, couldn't he be a bit more use to her? "Karen," he said suddenly, and now there was an urgent note in his tired voice. "That physiotherapist woman that came once, is she still around?"

"Chloe? No, she left to have a baby. There's a nice young man, Steve, who has taken her place now. Why?"

Richard looked a little sheepish. He knew now that those long months of self-imposed inertia would have weakened all the working muscles he still had left. Even talking had been an effort. "Do you think this new man could give me some treatment? I know I refused before but I really do want to see those kids again."

Karen offered up a silent thank you for Jane Lawson and her unknown children. "I'll fix it on Monday," she said. For patients in the private wing, anything could be fixed, just as long as they pay for it, she thought sadly. "And I'll see about the phone as soon as I can. You know, I think perhaps Jane gets a bit lonely in the evenings. You will ring her, won't you?" She wanted to keep up this new interest, keep him motivated, keep him talking, too.

He nodded, but said no more, and she picked up the tray and left him to his thoughts.

When John came out of the school gates the following Wednesday he found Patricia waiting for him, leaning elegantly against her gleaming car. A group of his year nine pupils stood a little way away, watching curiously. She stepped forward just as he saw her. "Hi, John, I've been waiting for you." There were whistles and comments and a cheer from Monty in the crowd.

John looked surprised and embarrassed. Usually Patricia barely acknowledged his existence. "Hello," he said shortly. "Is there something wrong?"

"I just wanted to talk to you. Ask your advice."

Well, he wasn't going to discuss anything with all of year nine's ears wagging, and he certainly wasn't going to get into her car, either. She drove like a maniac. Such a move would make his life somewhat difficult in the morning to say the least. "Let's go across for a cup of tea," and he indicated a café across the road.

She wrinkled her nose in distaste, but as he was already moving in that direction, followed him anyway. She sat carefully on the edge of a chair, arranging the folds of her dress across her lap, while John went to fetch two mugs of tea from the counter. "Right," he said, setting one in front of her, "so what's the problem?"

"Have you seen Terry?" she asked. "He won't answer his phone and he's changed the locks on his house as well so my key doesn't fit. Mrs. Paget always says he's busy."

"Then he's busy," said John unhelpfully. "he does have a business to run. Maybe he doesn't want to talk to you."

"If he doesn't it's all your fault, anyway." She looked at him disbelievingly, but then changed the subject. "Richard is divorcing me?" John nodded and she continued, "He's going to sell the house when the lease to that company is finished. Did you know that?"

John avoided the question. He hadn't known but he wasn't going to give Patricia any kind of satisfaction. "Well, he can't live there, can he? Not in a wheelchair."

"No one asked me if I wanted to live there." Patricia's voice was petulant.

"And do you? There are thirteen rooms in that house Patricia, could you really clean and cook and look after the garden and everything on your own?" He was being blunt, he knew that, but how else could he get the message across?

"Oh, we had a lovely couple who did all that. He did the garden and she cleaned and made an evening meal. They really worked hard and were neat and quiet."

"And could you pay their wages? Nobody works for nothing, Patricia. It could be quite costly. Could you manage that?"

65

"You really don't like me John, do you?" For a moment he thought she was going to cry. Then she changed tack again. "Daddy says I have to get a job."

Now that did surprise him, but all he said was "Good idea." He was watching the clock, he didn't want to be stuck here half the evening.

"I don't know what I want to do. I expect Daddy will sort it out. He says I should work in an office. I'd like to work in Terry's office, but I couldn't do all that stuff Mrs. Paget does, so I don't suppose he'll let me."

"Why don't you choose something you are good at?" He was feeling a bit sorry for her now, she was just like a Dresden figurine, really. Every strand of hair, every eyelash in place, every fold of her dress draped artistically, but like the Dresden figurine she was of no practical use whatsoever. When she raised her eyebrows questioningly he went on, "Look, you could use your skill teaching other women how to look as beautiful as you do. A beautician maybe. It's something you know about, isn't it?"

"Yes," she said blankly. "I'll ask Daddy about it tonight."

John lost his patience with her and stood up. "Sorry, Patricia, but I really must go. I have a lot of work to do this evening." She followed him as he left the café and crossed the road again. He paused as they reached her car, then said his goodbyes and walked away down the street as quickly as he could. He just hoped that he'd been rough enough to make her avoid him in future. If he had turned to look back, he might have caught the cat-like smile of satisfaction on Patricia's face as she watched him go, and then climbed into her car.

Later that evening Terry turned his car off the road into his driveway and braked suddenly. The garage entrance was blocked by Patricia's car, and she was sitting in the driver's seat, waiting for him. Now she climbed out and came across to the car as he switched off the engine. She was as beautiful and elegant as always, but now it didn't matter to him any more. His thoughts, when he had time to think about anything except the contract he was chasing, were always of Jane, wearing Andrew's sweater for comfort, and surrounded by her little family. He opened the door and stepped out but waited for Patricia to speak first.

"Terry, I've been waiting for ages. Where have you been?"

"Patricia," he said roughly, "some of us have to work, you know, earn our own living? What do you want?"

"I thought we might talk a little, spend the evening together and sort things out."

He looked at her incredulously. "Sort things out," he repeated. "What things? There is nothing to sort out, and I have a mass of work to do before the morning. No way, whatever it is you want to say, say it now and then go away."

She looked at him in utter disbelief. "Surely we are only putting off the wedding until Richard divorces me," she asked. "Surely we must think about another date."

"Patricia." Terry spoke loudly, as if she were deaf. "There is not going to be a wedding. Not ever. Your Mother has cancelled all the invitations and sent the presents back. I've checked. You have got to start believing in reality. Your Father knows there is no wedding. Your Mother knows, too. So you should know. Now, will you move your car so that I can put mine away? I have to work this evening." She made no move, but simply stood where she was, staring wide-eyed at him. After waiting a moment he added "If you don't move it, Patricia, I shall have to call a tow truck and have it taken to your home. Then you'll have to walk. So, will you move it now, please?" To make his point, he was already pulling his mobile phone from a pocket.

"John Trehern was horrible to me this afternoon. Now you are being horrible to me too. All right, I'll move the car and go home. I'll talk to you when you are not in a bad mood." She walked slowly to her car, climbed in and started the engine. Terry watched her drive away with a sigh of relief, but also quite sure that he hadn't seen the last of her yet.

Walking the school corridor the next morning John met Paul Fellows the head of English studies leaving the headmaster's office. As they exchanged greetings the headmaster followed Paul into the corridor.

"Ah, John," he said,. "Can I have a quick word?" Involuntarily John glanced at his watch, but followed the older man back into his study and closed the door. Then he stood where he was and waited.

"John, it's about Keiran Montgomery. Do you find him disruptive?"

John half-smiled. How the boy hated his named. "Monty?" he said. "No, I don't, but I can see that he could be. He has to be sat on a bit sometimes or he'd get out of hand."

"Good, that's just what Paul said." Seeing John's enquiring look he added, "Mr. Hapgood has complained that he's disruptive and wants him removed from science lessons."

John said nothing. It was the Head's problem. Old Basil was a great scientist, but not much good at keeping young boys interested and in order. Brian would sort something out. "Is that all you wanted?" he asked at length.

"Well, no," the headmaster said slowly. "It's a bit more serious than that. A young woman came to see me yesterday, to tell me she thought you were unfit to teach young boys as you were a homosexual."

The young schoolmaster stared at him. "What?" John was so taken aback he could hardly get the words out. "Was she a parent?" The headmaster noted how the shock was genuine in the young man's voice.

"No. She was much too young for that. Stunning to look at, mind," and the Head grinned at the thought. Then his smile faded as John let out a gasp of disbelief.

"Patricia! She was waiting for me outside the gates when I left yesterday. Said she wanted to talk to me. Brian, the woman is a little mentally retarded. What did you say?"

"I gathered that she wasn't too bright. She suddenly changed the subject twice and got herself quite lost. I suggested that she put her complaint in writing, with her name and address and proof of her claim, and bring it to me. She said her father was a barrister. I think that was supposed to make me jump to attention."

"And to think she sat there in the café across the road asking my advice about what job she should do. And I was a bit hard with her, which won't help. If her old man chooses to make a complaint, I've had it."

"Well, we shall have to wait and see what happens. And of course there is still the question of proof, isn't there? I think this should stay strictly between you and I for the moment. If nothing further is said, it would be best forgotten quickly. But," he went on carefully, "if he does advise her to make a complaint, then it's out of my hands. You do realise that, don't you?"

"Of course. But do you believe her? Do you trust me?"

Brian smiled back at him. "Without question. Mrs. Lawson wouldn't trust you with her precious children, especially young James, if she thought you were, well, different."

John looked at him in amazement. "You know Jane?" he asked.

"Well, not personally. But my parents live in French Street, and I've seen you pass with the little ones when I've been up there. My Mother was once a teacher, and can't quite give up on it. She teaches the older two in Sunday school. She is full of admiration for the way Mrs. Lawson copes. She's doing a grand job single-handed, according to Mother."

"She's a wonderful person. I've known her since I was six." He glanced at his watch, "I'd better get a move on. I'm in for a lot of comments this morning as half the year nine boys watched Patricia waiting for me. Especially Monty," and he grinned at Brian across the desk.

The headmaster chuckled. "Good luck to you," he said and picked up his pen, ready to start the day's work.

Charles Cameron was working in his study early in the evening when Patricia opened the door and walked in. "Daddy," she said at once without waiting for him to speak, "I had a talk with John Trehern and he said I might train to be a beautician. I said I'd ask you. What do you think?"

Charles laid down his pen and put his arms on the desk. "Patricia," he said slowly, "I think you should talk to your Mother about it. I know nothing of beauticians and that sort of thing."

Patricia tossed her head impatiently. "Oh, it's no use talking to Mother, she never agrees with anything. She wouldn't know anything about beauticians, anyway."

"Listen to me, Patricia. I have made a great apology to your Mother today. I now realise she was right; I was wrong to spoil you and pretend that everything about you was fine. So now, if you want help, go to your Mother. She is a very wise person and will know just what to do. She always has, but I didn't listen. Now I shall and so should you."

Patricia scowled at him. "But I want you to write a letter for me."

"Ask your Mother, she'll help you write a letter too. Now please, leave me to finish my work for we are going to Cornwall for the weekend."

"Cornwall, Daddy! Oh, Cornwall is so boring. Couldn't we go to London?" Patricia looked at her father appealingly.

"Your mother and I are going to Cornwall to find a holiday cottage. I expect she will have made some arrangements for you. Just go and ask her. Now leave me to work, please." Charles picked up his pen and bent his head over his papers.

"A letter would be no use coming from Mother," said Patricia sulkily. "It needs someone important like you."

Charles sighed and, against his better judgement asked, "what letter is this?"

His daughter's smile was brilliant. "Oh, I knew you'd do it. I went to see John Treherne's headmaster today. I told him that John shouldn't be allowed to teach young boys as he was a homosexual. But the headmaster didn't believe me, and said I had to write a letter with my name and address and say why I knew this. So I thought you might write it and then no one would doubt the word of a barrister."

By the time she had finished speaking Charles Cameron's face had darkened and was flushed with anger. "If you are making such an accusation, then it must be you who writes the letter with your signature on it, and giving your reasons for accusing him. It's nothing to do with me. Have you reasons for saying such a thing?"

Now she was a little nervous. Daddy had never been angry with her before, well, not really angry like now. "Well, he must be," she said at last,. "He's twenty nine and has never had a girl friend so he must be gay."

Charles stood up and walked around the desk to stand in front of her. He took her shoulders and pulled her to her feet. His face was only inches from her own and she was frightened. "Patricia," he said, slowly and clearly pronouncing each word, "if you make such wild accusations ever again, I shall disown you. I shall put you out on the streets and lock the doors against you. Do you understand me?" She didn't answer and he shook her shoulders a little, but never hurting her. "Do you understand me?" he repeated.

"Yes, Daddy. I'm sorry."

"Now, go and talk to your Mother about being a beautician or whatever, and leave me in peace. Go on," and he pushed her gently but firmly towards the door. When she left he returned to his desk and sat for a long while with his head in his hands. If he had ever doubted her, he knew now for certain that Isobel had been right all along. Patricia was, well, retarded, he supposed. And all these years he had refused to admit it, not wanted the daughter of a well-known barrister to be anything but normal. But Izzy was strong, she would know how to go on from here. Thank God for Izzy. After a while he drew a sheet of notepaper towards him and began to write. "To The Headmaster and Whoever It May Concern. I understand that my daughter Patricia Cameron, called on you recently with a complaint against one of your teaching staff, John Treherne. This complaint was quite unfounded, and I wish no attention be paid to it. My daughter, although adult, has the mind of a fourteen year old, and thus is not in any position to judge anyone. In this instance her word is not to be trusted and there is no grounds for this accusation. I suggest you keep this letter as proof of the young man's innocence. Should any problem arise regarding this accusation you will be in a position to justify any lack of action with your superiors. With my apologies to the young man concerned, and for any inconvenience this action may have caused you." He read it through carefully, looking for any possible repercussions and then, satisfied, signed and addressed the letter. Leaving his study he went to find his wife in the kitchen.

"Izzy, has Patricia been to chat to you?" She looked up in surprise and he continued, "remembering our conversation this morning, when Patricia came to see me just now I told her that from now on she discuss everything with you. She has some idea about being a beautician. I said you would know more about it and the best course of action to take."

His wife smiled back at him, but shook her head. "It won't happen overnight, Charles. But sooner or later she will need some sort of advice and have to ask. Till then, well, we'll just wait and see. Supper will be ready in about fifteen minutes." She looked at the letter in his hand. "Do you want me to post that tomorrow?"

"If we have fifteen minutes before supper, then I'll walk to the corner and post it myself. Begin as I mean to go on, you know." They had talked for a long time that morning, about Patricia and his attitude to her, about his health problems and the possibility of retirement just a little earlier than they had planned. Izzy was so practical, so full of common sense. He was not quite ready to retire yet, of that he was sure, but it was a good idea to plan for it now. He picked up his hat from the hall table and, calling goodbye, left the house.

CHAPTER FIVE

During the days that followed Jane's visit, Karen arranged for the telephone to be installed in Richard's room, and organised an appointment with the physiotherapist. As he waited for the young man to arrive Richard was feeling a little apprehensive about this. Karen had explained that Steve was blind, and Richard was sure it was all a mistake on her part. It surely meant that he would be clumsy, or slow moving or need help finding things. But Steve came striding into the room, greeting his patient with a broad smile. "Steve Miller," he said cheerfully. He set down his bag and took a small hand-held computer and earpiece from it. Tapped at the keys, he listened to Richard's notes and then began work, running expert hands over the muscles that were now so flabby and useless. "I'll work on these now," he told his sceptical patient, "and I'll teach you a series of exercises. If you do them regularly, you'll get all the use back - they must have been pretty well toned up before. It might make you ache a bit, but it will wear off as time goes on. OK?"

For some time he worked in silent concentration, and then Karen came in with coffee. "Do you want a drink, Steve?"

"Can a duck swim?" he grinned at her. "The wards are so hot, I could murder a pint right now, but I'll settle for coffee. But I'll have it in a minute, OK?" He turned back to his patient. "How does that feel?" Richard groaned, but then smiled back at him, quite forgetting it wouldn't be seen. "We'll have a coffee break and then I'll teach you the exercises while Karen's here so she'll know what you're up to."

They talked easily together for a few minutes. Karen wanted to know if Steve was still riding. Richard looked enquiringly from one to the other, but didn't ask any questions.

"Twice a week I ride out my aunt's horses," the young man explained. "Not on my own, mind, that might be a bit tricky to say the least. No, Sim and I ride out together. Sim's my twin sister, Simone. She lives in the flat above mine. She works here too as a speech therapist."

Richard was impressed with this so confident young man. "Do you live with your parents, then?"

Steve chuckled. "No way. That would really cramp my style, wouldn't it? No, there's just me and Sam."

"The riding must keep you fit, though," Richard observed. Later he asked Karen about Sam – was it a man or a woman? She laughed and told him it was Steve's guide dog.

"That and a morning swim in the pool here. One of the perks of the job. But I need to be fit, or I can't lecture the patients who aren't, can I?" and he grinned broadly. "Now, what about these exercises. Will you do them regularly? Those muscles won't respond with just a bit of a rub from me."

A bit of a rub, thought Richard ruefully. They were already aching a little, but he followed Steve's instructions and repeated the exercises once to show he understood. He was thoroughly tired, but felt good. "Sure. I'll do them as often as you say," he said at last. "I've got a plan for a wheelchair outing to see a small boy called Jamie."

Steve was already putting his equipment into his bag, and then made a couple of brief notes on his computer before stowing that away too. "Right," he said, "I'll see you tomorrow, about the same time. Is that OK?"

"Fine," said Richard. "I'm not going anywhere. See you tomorrow, then." After Steve had gone he lay back on his pillows for a while. The long-idle muscles must be made to work again. Now that he had started, he didn't want just to be put into a chair and moved about and then lifted out again; he wanted to choose what he did, when he did it and to do it all himself. Was that possible? He'd ask Steve tomorrow. The young physiotherapist was so capable and independent, he'd understand. Just now some form of independence, however small was important to him, and he'd already wasted so much time. He could have done all this a year ago. Oh, God, how stupid he had been. But he'd do these exercises till his arms dropped off, if necessary. For a little while he slept, and later that evening he telephoned Jane. Karen might be right, although Jane had always been an army wife, and accustomed to long absences and evenings on her own.

Through the next ten days, whenever she came into the room, Karen found Richard working away at his exercises. Sometimes he looked quite tired, but kept up the pace, determined to win this battle. Steve had taught him some tips to make it easier for him to get off the bed and into his chair a little more independently, although he would still need some help. "It will be a lot easier when you go home," the young man had said. "Hospital beds are higher than at home. You'll be able to have an overhead hoist fitted above the bed now that those arm muscles work, too, and be a bit more independent. Are you planning to go home now that your body is a bit more flexible?" Richard frowned. Home? He hadn't got one. Fallowfields was no longer available, let to a big insurance company. "It's not going to be quite so comfortable here, I reckon, when all the changes take place." He turned to Karen and asked, "How does it go for you, Karen?"

She pulled a face, then remembered Steve wouldn't see the reaction, and said, "I don't think any of us are going to like it much, do you?"

"I'm only a day-boy, I don't think they can change my job much."

"Come on you two. What's it all about, then?" Richard asked. "What are all these changes?"

Steve was already tidying away his equipment into his bag,. "Staff deployment, top priority," he said, assuming a mock-military tone. "Jump to it, all you nurses! At the double!."

Karen laughed and said, "Steve, remember your patient is a military officer here." Richard winced at the memory, but said nothing.

"Sorry, sir!" and Steve gave a mocking salute. Then he became serious again.

"You know, Richard, I don't think you need me any more. I'll call in next week, just in case there are queries, but you can do the rest yourself now, can't you? It's only keeping those muscles exercised and toned up. OK?"

"Yes. I reckon I can cope on my own now, Steve. And thanks. You've been great."

Steve grinned at him; "all part of the service. See you." And he opened the door and strode off down the corridor.

"Karen, what are all these changes? How do they affect you, or maybe me? What's going on? And where does the military fit in?"

"The new staff manager calls it staff redeployment. He is ex-army, by the way, and likes to be addressed as major. And it will certainly affect both of us. You see, I am over-qualified just to be nursing you and the other patients in the private wing; none of whom have specialist needs just now. So the thinking is that I should be sent wherever those qualifications are needed. Then any nurse available, and not necessarily the same one each time, will come and do what I do here. I suppose it does make sense really, but I hate the thought of being moved here and there and not knowing which job I'll do next." She sighed and looked a little disconsolate.

"Oh, God," said Richard, "and I get a stream of different nurses all the time." Karen nodded, and Richard suddenly became thoughtful and silent. What had the boy said just now? "When you go home..." What home? Life here had just drifted on until Jane came and changed it for him. He had never given a thought of going home. He didn't want to go back to that great house again, though. He couldn't move in with John, even if he wanted to. Or Jane. But he was going to have to live somewhere, and by the sound of it, fairly soon, or be uncomfortable and dissatisfied here.

Karen watched him as his thoughts chased each other across his face. Then she said quietly, "You could leave here, you know, now that Steve has got you a bit more mobile. It would have to be well organised of course, but it could work. What you pay for this room could go a long way towards the rent of another place of your own. Social Services could help, too. Why not talk to Jane about it tonight? She might have some ideas." If Jane had convinced him that life was worth the bother, she might well work on him on this one, too. She sighed inwardly; why was she encouraging this man, the man she had grown to love over the last few months, to go out of her life now? But she wanted Richard to be happy, and with all the new arrangements, she was sure that the hospital room was not the place for him any longer.

As always, Jane's advice that evening was practical and down to earth. "I think it's a great idea, Richard. And it's a shame it's taken you so long to get there." He winced at her bluntness and pulled a face at the telephone receiver; Jane had always been forthright and outspoken, it was why his own father had discouraged him from inviting her to call at their house as youngsters. "Not good in a woman," he would say. "They should know their place." Now he supposed that bluntness was sometimes necessary. "The first thing you need to do," she went on, "is to talk to Freddy. Find out if you can buy or rent a place and still afford a live-in help. Work out the money side first between you, and we'll sort the details out when we know how your finances stand." He didn't think for one moment that there would be any problems with finance, although he supposed the divorce would take quite a chunk from his income. But of course she was right; he had spent far too long letting any decision roll over him. "How's the mobility going?" she asked.

"Really well. The physio lad doesn't need to come again, as long as I work at it myself. And I am," he added quickly before she could ask. "How about getting someone to bring you and the children on Saturday, so that I can prove it? What do you say?"

"Terry might be here at the weekend. I'm not sure if John is coming, but I'll ring and ask. One of them could bring us. The kids will be glad to see you again."

He doubted very much if they would even remember him, they were so small when he'd been a regular visitor at the house in Stephens Lane. After his disastrous marriage he'd tried to be out of the country as often as possible, but he didn't say so, and they talked for a little while of other things before they said their goodbyes. He would ring Freddy first thing in the morning, see if he could fix an appointment that day. It was great to feel that he was in charge of his life again. Jane's words re-echoed in his head, "why did it take so long?" A question he wouldn't like to have to answer honestly.

That evening John's telephone rang unexpectedly. "John," Kitty said rather breathlessly, "David has tickets for the show at the Community Centre on Friday. Our neighbour is in it so we are all supporting it. Will you come with us or will you be busy then?"

She sounded so nervous he tried to make her smile. "Yes and no in that order he said, "I'd like to join you all."

She giggled. "John, do you know what the show is, then?" He didn't, but it didn't matter. "It's 'Oklahoma!" she said. "Is it still OK?"

"Fine." He would sit through the telephone directory set to music if it meant spending the evening with Kitty. "Do you want me to pick you up?"

"No, Dad's coming too. He's taking Polly's daughters. Polly is our neighbour, so she'll already be there. I'm going with Dad and the girls so we'll pick you up on the way past. Is that OK with you?" He was rather disappointed, but couldn't find the words to say so. "David and Laura will meet us there," she continued. "You haven't met Laura yet, have you?" She talked on for a moment or two and then she said goodbye. John replaced the receiver with a smile; perhaps things would be easier in a group. Perhaps he'd be able to talk to her and not get so tongue-tied and embarrassed. It was all so ridiculous at his age. How he wished he had Terry's flair with women. But he hadn't, and wishing wouldn't get him there, either. He must make the most of this opportunity, though.

Just as he was checking the doors and switching off lights on Friday evening Ray's car turned into the drive-way. John left the house, closed the front door firmly behind him and went to greet the occupants. Kitty sat in the back seat with two smiling teenage girls, and John thought how pretty she looked – more like a teenager herself than her twenty five years. Her long dark hair fell about her shoulders, and her dark eyes smiled happily back at him. Ray leaned across and opened the passenger door. "Glad of some male company at last," he laughed. "This bunch of beauties have been chattering away like monkeys." John smiled, settled himself into his seat, and they were on their way again in a couple of minutes.

The big hall of the community centre was filling up rapidly when they arrived. They took their seats and settled down to wait, with Kitty and Laura scanning the crowds for people they knew, Ray and David talking business while John began to read the information about their local operatic society on the back of the programme. Kitty slipped her hand through John's arm; "There's a nice-looking blonde boy keeps looking at you," she whispered. "Every time I catch his eye, he winks at me." She giggled, and added, "third row from the front, left side, on the end."

John looked to where she had indicated and gave a mock groan; "Monty!" he said. "What on earth is Monty doing at a show like this?"

"Who's Monty?" Kitty wanted to know.

"One of my year nine boys. The class character, you might say, or the class comedian." Now he realised the name he had just read on that back page of the programme was Sarah Montgomery. Monty's sister. The boy turned, caught John's eye, grinned, and gave him a thumbs up signal. Then he winked at Kitty and turned away again. Luckily, John was saved from any further explanations for the music started, - the show was about to begin.

At the interval they headed for the coffee shop. As they were crossing the wide entrance hall Patricia stepped into John's path. "John, how nice to see you here. Are you going for coffee?"

John took Kitty's arm, guiding her to the right and moving her on as he said, "Good evening, Patricia," and passed her without another word or a backward glance.

"Oh, John!" Kitty exclaimed. "Why did you snub her like that? Don't you like her? Who is she, anyway?" She glanced back over her shoulder, but Patricia had turned to speak to someone else. "She didn't seem to notice, though," she added thoughtfully. "How odd."

"She is odd. Her name is Patricia Cameron. She loves to make trouble. Make sure you avoid her if you want a quiet life." She heard the bitterness in his voice and looked back at him rather puzzled and slightly worried, but as they moved on another figure stood in their way.

"Hi, Mr. T.," Monty said with a grin. "Having fun?"

Monty's parents were seated at a table beside him. Mrs. Montgomery was a comfortable, easy-going woman with a cheerful smile. Now she said, "Good evening, Mr. Treherne."

John smiled back at her, he really liked Monty's parents. "Hello, Mrs. Montgomery, Mr. Montgomery. Have you met Kitty Brownlow," and he drew Kitty towards the table.

Mrs. Montgomery smiled up at Kitty. "Hell, Kitty. It's nice to meet you. Will you both join us for coffee?"

"We'd love to, but my father and brother David are waiting for us with coffee over there," and Kitty waved her hand in their direction.

"Ah, you are David Brownlow's sister," Mary Montgomery's smile was even more wide and cheerful. "He has done some really good work on our house, hasn't he Keiran?" Mr. Montgomery, also named Keiran, smiled and nodded. He left all the chatter to his wife.

Kitty was pleased. "He'll be delighted to hear you say that." The two women talked for a few minutes and Kitty and John moved on to join Ray and David who had already set coffee on a table. As they left Monty's table, Patricia paused to speak to the family. "I think that man is a bad influence on young boys," she began. "If I were a parent, I wouldn't let him teach my child."

Mrs. Montgomery's face lost it's smile. She'd met Mr. Trehern at PTA meetings and parents evenings. She liked him a lot and so did Keiran, although he would never admit it. She stared frostily at Patricia and snapped, "Then it's just as well you're not a parent, isn't it? Your child would certainly be the loser. John Treherne's a really fine teacher. Obviously you know nothing about children. Good evening, Madam," and she turned away and began to speak to her husband. Patricia moved on, apparently unruffled. Monty stared after her with suspicion. What game was this woman playing? What had old T. done to upset her?

On the way back to the hall he met Darren. "You going home, Daz? Thought you had to help backstage."

"Yeah, so did I. "Come and help backstage," she says, and I trail around moving' things. Now she says "get off home, Darren, you're in the way." So I'm off."

"Aren't you going to see the rest of the show then?"

"Nah, not my scene, man, I'm off."

"Listen, Daz. Do you remember that bird who waited for old Treherne after school on Wednesday? Had a brilliant car, dark blue and real clean and shining?"

"Yeah, I remember the car mostly. Saw it parked under the trees as I came in. Why?" Daz was looking interested now.

"She's making trouble for old Treherne. Hinting he's homo. My Mum gave her the big freeze." He grinned at his friend. "Don't think she liked her much."

Darren's face crinkled in a frown. He had a lot to thank old T. for. "I might just wander past that car," he said, patting something in his pocket. "Just to see how pretty it is, like."

"Thought you might. Look, I'd better go or Ma will be yelling the place down. Don't do anything stupid, will you? You're already in trouble with your Dad remember."

Darren grinned. "Stupid? Me? See you, Monty," and he sauntered out of the door, grinning broadly.

When the show was over many of the audience lingered, some for coffee and some just to chat. Kitty and John stood together, listening to an elderly man praising the show, and waiting for Ray. When he came to them, the other man wandered off, and Ray began to apologise. "Look, I've got to go and look at Laura's car, she needs it for tomorrow. I'll have to take mine so that I can get back later. Will you get a taxi home, Cats?" He slipped a five pound note into her hand and she froze. John had seen it, even though Dad had tried to be careful. She could see John's expression change and his face redden as the anger flared up in him, and she wanted to cry. Oh, Dad, she thought, you've blown it now! Just when John was beginning to relax. She was knew her father was trying so hard to help her, and now John was angry. Ray hadn't noticed, and simply said, "See you in the morning, I expect. Don't know how long I'll be. OK?" She nodded, and he turned and hurried away.

"I'll get that taxi," John said grimly. What did the man take him for? Did he think he was too mean to pay for a taxi? Perhaps he thought schoolteachers couldn't afford such luxuries. He found that everyone, or so it seemed wanted taxis and they had to wait quite a while. Kitty tried to ease the situation with chatter about this and that, but John was too preoccupied to join in. Perhaps her father though I'd just walk off and leave her to find her own way home or something. What kind of a bloke does he think I am? He knew he was making Kitty miserable and a bit uncomfortable with him, but he was too angry to be kind to her. She watched him, miserably aware of his anger, but she didn't know him well enough to smooth it over. Now, perhaps, she never would.

When their taxi finally arrived they sat in silence for some minutes as they drove through the darkening streets. And then John felt rather sorry for her, she looked so small and forlorn, and it wasn't really her fault. "Look," he said on impulse, "I'm driving up to Oxford tomorrow. Would you like to come with me for the ride? You could visit your sister, she lives there, does-n't she?"

"Oh, John, I'm sorry, I can't." Now she looked even more forlorn. "I've promised to look after my friend's two little girls while she goes to her cousin's posh wedding. Truly," she added, as though he might think she was making excuses not to see him again.

"Doesn't matter," he said gloomily. "It was just an idea." He had told the driver to take her home first, and now they had arrived. "Will you come in for a drink," she asked, picking up her bag.

"No, not tonight. I'll get off home now. Goodnight, Kitty," and he stood watching her as she opened the front door of her house. She waved to him, stepped inside and closed the door. He climbed back into the taxi, gave the driver his instructions and slumped miserably in his seat. That was the end of that. Why had he been so mean and angry with her, it wasn't her mistake. He just wasn't any good about talking with women. But suppos-ing she had made up all that excuse for tomorrow. No, he didn't want to think about that, either. When he let himself into the house the phone was ringing. He glanced at the screen – Jane. No, he didn't feel like talking to Jane just now. He made coffee and sat staring at the empty fireplace. The phone rang again, and again it was Jane. He'd better answer, he supposed, it might be important. "John Treherne," he said abruptly.

"John?" Jane's voice was full of concern. "Is some-thing wrong?"

"No, not really," he lied, "I've just got the blues, that's all." She may have known him for years and years, but he wasn't going to tell her how he just blown it with Kitty. "How are things with you?"

"Oh, we're all fine. John, Richard has been working like a slave over his muscles and exercises, and wants us to go to visit tomorrow with the children, in the hospital garden or the coffee shop, depending on the weather. But he's moving around, John, that's the important thing."

"Great!" said John, trying to feel some enthusiasm. "It's taken him long enough. Do you want me to take you all there?"

She hesitated for just a moment, but long enough to put him on his guard. "No, Terry's here for the weekend, and he's offered to take us. But will you come too, just to make it an occasion? The children will love to see you, you know that."

So Richard was moving around, Terry was staying the weekend and Jane no longer needed him. Wonderful. That just made his evening complete. "No," he said flatly, "I don't think I'll bother. You don't need me if Terry's driving, and I'll catch up with Richard later."

There was a silence at the other end, and he thought she had gone. Then she said quietly, "John, the children and I love you for who you are, as well as for what you do for us, you know. They will be disappointed if you don't come this week. Please, John, won't you come? Won't you see how well Richard is doing now? Please."

"Perhaps," he answered, relenting a little at the pleading in her voice. "I'll see how it goes tomorrow. How are the kids, anyway?"

She chatted about the children and her day, and then brought the call to a close. "See you tomorrow then, maybe? Bye for now." she said.

Ray and David Brownlow were among the last to leave the community centre. As they crossed the car park they were stopped by a stunningly pretty and elegant woman coming towards them. "Can you help me," she asked, although her tone was more of a command. "My car, look," and she pointed to where a sleek, dark blue car was parked under the trees.

"What's wrong?" Ray asked. "Won't it start?"

"Look at it," she said crossly. "Someone has scribbled over it. And I know who it was, too," she added, her voice growing louder with her indignation. "That awful John Treherne. He did that, I know he did."

Ray and David stared at her. "No," said Ray, "it wasn't John. He's been with my daughter here at the show all evening."

"Well, perhaps she came with him." Patricia's voice was sulky now. "I know it was him. I told his headmaster he shouldn't be teaching young boys, it wasn't right, and now he's getting his own back. I think he's homosexual."

Ray and David exchanged glances. They had moved towards the car, and on they could see on the windscreen, in big red letters the word "Liar". David spoke sharply. "Even if we cleaned it off you couldn't drive it. You've got a flat tyre, look," and he pointed at one of the front wheels. "Have you got a spare?"

"Spare?" she echoed. "Spare what?"

"Wheel," said Ray patiently. "In the boot, probably."

"Oh, that. No it made things smell all rubbery, so I took it out. Aren't you going to scrub that writing off for me?"

Ray looked at David, but his son shook his head. "No, we're not," he answered. "You'll have to call a taxi and get the garage to pick the car up in the morning. They'll change the wheel and clean it up for you."

"My Father's a well-known barrister," said Patricia.

"Good for him," said David, already turning to walk away, "but it's a garage you need, not a barrister. Come on, Dad, Laura's waiting for us." Ray looked back as they walked towards their own cars. The woman had stopped someone else now. Ray hoped she had a mobile phone, for the Centre was now in complete darkness, closed for the night. He hoped, for John's sake, that she wasn't telling too many people of her theories. "What do you make of all that, Dave?"

"No idea, I've only just met the guy,. Might explain things, but I don't think I believe her. Kitty is quite a good judge of people, wouldn't you say? I don't think the woman's quite all there. We'll talk about it indoors. Will you follow us?"

Ray nodded, left them and minutes later the two cars pulled out of the car park. But Ray was troubled; whatever David said, he thought he ought to warn Kats about what was going on. He didn't want her getting hurt.

Saturday dawned bright and sunny. John did some shopping, a bit of desultory cleaning, made some lunch and then wondered what to do with the afternoon. He had kept it free to drive to Oxford but now, well, it wasn't worth the petrol. But it was a lovely day, and he was at a loose end and just a bit ashamed of his, well, sulks he suppose you could call it. Eventually, a little later than usual, he set off for Oxford. He'd drive straight to the hospital and maybe spend an hour there with them all. He thought of Kitty and wondered how she was coping with her friend's children. But perhaps she had made it all up as an excuse. No, that was unkind, he was sure she hadn't. He didn't think Kitty could do a thing like that – she was too honest. He had behaved stupidly, so now he must try and get things back on a level course again. And then he remembered something, smiled and almost shouted aloud "Of Course!" He was still working through David Brownlow's accounts. He could see her again on Monday. He felt better, and began to hum tunelessly as the car purred its way to Oxford. First he'd put things right with Jane, and then try to work out what to say to Kitty on Monday. She was too nice a person to hold a grudge, just so long as he could say the right words. That was all he had to do – find the right words.

CHAPTER SIX

Richard and Karen were sitting at a table in the hospital garden when Terry and Jane arrived with the family. The children seemed a little subdued by the event, but Jane hoped it was simply the strange surroundings. This time Karen was off duty, and dressed in a soft turquoise sweater and dark trousers. Her dark hair swung loosely about her shoulders. Jane introduced Terry, then the children. The adults settled themselves at the table while the children ran around the garden, exploring. "Where's John?" Karen asked.

Jane looked across at her and answered, "he said he might come, but didn't. I rang last night and he seemed a bit fed up, or disappointed, or something. Not his usual self."

"Oh, never mind John," Richard said with a touch of malice in his voice. "I'm sure we can all manage without John."

For a moment there was silence and then Karen got to her feet abruptly. She stood over Richard's chair, something she knew he hated anyone to do. "I'm not going to sit here and listen to you sniping at John," she exclaimed angrily. "You of all people to say we can manage without him. He's really someone special, and you particularly ought to know it. Who do you suppose fetched and carried for you all these months? Who brought your summer shirts and your winter sweaters, and your shaving things? Who has been keeping your solicitor up to date with what's going on? Not you, Richard Treherne, but John. I'll go and get coffee for us all while you think that over," and with that she turned and walked away from them. "Come on, kids, let's go and buy ice creams."

The children ran after her, and Richard watched her go. "I've never heard her speak like that," he said. "I've never even heard her raise her voice before. Do you suppose she's in love with John?"

"Richard! Are you blind as well as everything else? Can't you see what's right under your nose?" Jane was incredulous. Then she continued more quietly, "but she's right about John being special, you know. I don't think I could have coped with that first Christmas without Andy if John hadn't been there to help. He remembered all the things Andy would have done, like lots of batteries and things like that. bought half their presents as well, because my money wasn't sorted out. And even now he keeps Jamie in school uniform, and pretends it came from the OBNO shop. Honestly, Richard, both you and I owe him a lot more than either of us can pay back, and that's the truth." Then she laughed and added, "and before you ask another stupid question, no, I'm not in love with him, either."

Terry sighed dramatically. "Oh, I'm so glad to hear it. There's hope yet. But what's an OBNO shop?"

"Outgrown but not outworn. Most schools have them." She gave him a look which he couldn't interpret and added, "Oh, yes, there's always hope." They laughed together, but Richard was silent. All those silent months, all that guilt, and he hadn't even thought of Jane having to struggle and manage without Andy's money. He looked across at Terry and was going to speak, say something about families, but Terry got in first. "If it hadn't been for John," he said, "I'd have been married to your wife." He saw Richard's look of genuine surprise and went on, "Hasn't anyone told you about that?"

"You were going to marry Patricia? Oh, I see, that's why she wants me to divorce her. No, I've heard nothing. What's it all about. But were you really going to marry her? Didn't you know about me?"

Between them, Jane and Terry told the story of the interrupted banns, and all that had followed. When they had finished Richard asked, "and John actually stood up in church and objected? I thought that only happened in books. How did he know, anyway, he doesn't live in Hallinford?"

"Someone wrote him a note, anonymously. Someone who said she'd loved you once." Then he grinned at Richard, "I'm sure it was a she."

"Oh, yes, I reckon a woman wrote it, don't you, Richard? It's quite a broad field, someone who loved you once." Jane was laughing at him now. "every girl in the sixth was in love with Richard at one time or another," she told Terry.

"Except you." Richard's voice was rather abrupt.

"Ah, well, I knew all that boyish charm too well." There had never, ever been anyone else for Jane but Andrew.

As John passed the coffee shop on the way to the garden he caught sight of Karen with the children. Suddenly Maria saw him and her little face lit up. "Uncle John. Oh, oh, Uncle John," and she ran towards him, both arms raised, and the other two children were close behind her. John hugged them all in turn and Maria went on, "Terry slept on our sofa last night, and me and Debs jumped on him this morning. He says he's going to sleep in the shed."

John bent down and in a pretend whisper that the others could hear he said, "then the mice will jump on him in the morning instead." Her eyes widened and her hands flew to her mouth. "Ooooh, I'm going to tell him. Come on Debs," and the two little girls ran off.

"I'm glad you came," Karen said softly as John took the tray from her hands. "Jane thought you were a bit down in the dumps."

"Oh, you know how it is, sometimes. Come on or those will melt, for Karen was carrying the ice creams. "He's got a good day for his first outing hasn't he?" and together they walked out into the garden.

Richard was looking really well, John thought. The greyness and the lines had gone from his face. They had all settled down again and Karen had poured their coffee. Richard turned to his brother. "John, they've just been telling me about the interrupted wedding banns. Terry says you had a letter about it. Did you keep it?" he asked.

Of course, thought John, no one had told Richard; Karen didn't know, and Jane had avoided mentioning Patricia. But did he want to show it to Richard? Was it just Richard's vanity, needing to know who wrote it? Oh, well, he supposed it didn't matter now, anyway. "I think so," he said. "I haven't cleared my pockets for ages." He pulled all the papers from his inside pocket and riffled through them. "Yes, it's still here," and he handed the letter across the table.

His brother slipped it from the envelope but didn't need to read it. His face creased into a wide smile "Frankie Brownlow," he told them all, and his voice had softened now. "She used to write to me when I first joined the army. I'd know that writing anywhere."

Frankie Brownlow?" John queried. "Is she related to David?"

"Yes, she's his older sister. They have a little sister, too, but I forget her name." He turned to Jane; "You must have known Frankie Brownlow."

"I did, well, until the family moved. Their Mother died and their Father sold up and moved to Ledminster. Isn't Fran's husband French?"

"Not really," came the reply. "he just had a French name. Works at the university here, I think. Admin of some sort."

The conversation went on around him, but John wasn't listening. Had Kitty known about the letter? She and her sister were very close. How glad he was that he had acted on it, and not let them down. Not that Richard seemed to care one way or the other. But still, if Kitty had known, then she would know now that he had done the right thing. It made him feel better.

He came out of his reverie to find that Maria had climbed or been lifted on to Richard's lap and was taking centre stage, as usual. She looked down at her small legs in their scarlet trousers and said, "You know, Uncle Richard, if my legs didn't work I'd make Mummy push me to the sweet shop every day."

"She wouldn't get you up the steps," said Debbie practically. "Then you'd have to have whatever she chose for you. You wouldn't like that. You couldn't choose your own."

"You could build one of those slidey things," Jamie said. "What's it called Uncle John?" and when John told him he went on, "That's it, a ramp. You could have a ramp up the steps."

Debbie began to giggle. "If there was a ramp up the steps, we could all whizz into the shop on our skateboards. Wouldn't that give Mrs. Thompson a surprise?" Privately Jane thought it would probably give her a heart attack, but Debbie began to mimic the old lady's Welsh accent, "Now you get those nasty noisy things out of my shop, you children, or there's no sweets for you today." With this Debbie and Maria went into fits of giggles which only ended when Maria slid off Richard's lap in a heap.

But Jamie had another idea. "If you fixed a motorbike engine under that chair, you could go anywhere by yourself," he said. He squatted down beside Richard's wheelchair, and his uncle felt a sharp stab of real pain; how many times had he seen Jamie's father squat like that beside a broken down truck, or a motorbike that wouldn't start? "Don't you think so, Terry?" and Jamie turned to Terry for confirmation.

"Not a petrol engine," said Terry with a grin. "You wouldn't want your uncle queuing at the pumps, amongst all the trucks and things would you? No, a car battery engine."

Jamie gave him a huge smile. That was the great thing about Terry, he never laughed at you. "Brilliant," he said. "There you are, Uncle Richard. That's the answer." But the conversation ended there for the girls had run off and now Debbie was calling him.

"Jay," she said. "Come and look what we've found," and he turned and left the adults to their talking.

Late the following morning Patricia's dark blue car drew up in the quiet street where Jane lived. She climbed out and crossed the small garden to the front door. As she waited, after ringing the doorbell, she looked up and down the street. If she had been married to a man like Andrew Lawson she wouldn't have been living in a place like this, with its old fashioned houses and narrow pavements. Jane must have chosen this house, not Andrew. She remembered a conversation with Richard once, long ago, when he had been packing to return to camp. She had asked him to stay, not to go, because there was building work to be done in the house. He had only answered, "You are an Army wife now. Army wives have to learn to cope with whatever comes up when their man is away." Then he had flung his luggage in the car and driven off, leaving her alone. Yes, definitely, Jane Lawson had chosen this house. Suddenly she was aware of Jane standing, silently in the open doorway.

"Oh, hello, Jane," she said in what she thought was a truly friendly manner, "I've brought a few sweets for the children." She handed Jane a carrier bag with a box inside.

"Oh, thanks," Jane said abruptly. "I'll tell them, but I don't suppose they will remember you, they didn't get a lot of chance to know you, did they?"

Patricia ignored this remark. "I came to tell you that I may be getting married in September. It all depends how long the divorce takes. Did you know Richard is divorcing me? Daddy is fixing it for me."

"Do you mean the divorce, or the marriage?" Jane asked.

"Oh, the divorce of course. He is a barrister, after all." She was making sure to wave her left hand about a great deal, where Terry's ring still sparkled on the fourth finger there. "I'm going to marry a man called Terry Kennedy.

He runs his own business you know, and I should be able to work for him afterwards as his secretary." She was delighted to see that she had caught Jane Lawson's attention at last.

"Really?" Jane said, trying to sound interested. "Oh, why don't you come in and tell me all about it?" and she stood aside to let Patricia pass. The younger woman swept by in a cloud of expensive perfume. And Jane closed the door and followed her. Patricia settled herself elegantly into an armchair, and Jane perched on the arm of another. "When did you say the wedding is?" she asked.

"Probably September. We're not sure yet. But it should be sometime this year, anyway." She paused for a moment and then asked, "Jane, what's that noise?"

"Just a friend cutting the grass for me. It's almost done now." As she spoke she heard the back door open and close, then the sound of running water and then footsteps. Terry appeared in the doorway, slightly flushed and a little disheveled from his exertions. "Oh, Terry," Jane said as she moved towards the door, "Patricia has just been telling me about your wedding plans. I'll leave you two together, then. You both know where the front door is," and she closed the door firmly behind her as she left the room. They heard the kitchen door bang and then the door to the garden.

For a moment Terry looked startled, and then he turned and hurried to the kitchen. Jane had locked the garden door from the outside, and he could see her out there, digging furiously in a flower bed. Now Patricia came to stand beside him, watching her too. "What does she imagine she looks like?" she asked. "That's a man's sweater and those awful faded jeans. No-one will ever look twice at her, dressed like that. Why does she have to wear a man's sweater, for heaven's sake?"

"Because it was Andy's and it gives her some kind of comfort."

Patricia was scornful. "She wouldn't be comforted if she knew what I know about Andrew Lawson." She saw Terry's raised eyebrows and smiled triumphantly. "I had an affair with Andrew. Would she go on being comforted by his old clothes if she knew that?"

"Oh, she knows about that. Even I know about that." Terry was dismissive.

"How could you know? You never even met Andrew. Who told you that, or are you making it up?"

"Jane told me. And you're wrong again. I knew Andy at university."

"Jane told you! She couldn't have done. How would she know? You are making it up, Terry, aren't you? You're just being spiteful."

"She knew because Andy told her all about it. He told Richard too, and apologised." And now Terry turned angrily on this she-cat who stood beside him. "What the hell have you been saying to Jane? What wedding plans? What lies are you spreading now?"

"Daddy is working on the divorce, you know that. We could be married before the end of the year."

He wanted to shake the stupid smile off her face. "Patricia," he said forcefully, "we are not going to be married. Never. Not ever! I told you that in a letter, and I told your father that too. We are not engaged and if you want to find a new man, you should take that ring off that finger. Now just go away and leave us alone. Do you understand now? Have you got the message this time? Just leave us alone."

"We were going to be married. You can't suddenly change like that and say you don't care about me any more. You should be angry with John Treherne, not me. He was the one who spoiled everything for us, didn't he? And why do you keep saying "us" like that? Do you mean you and her," and she jerked her head towards the window. "Just look at her, Terry. You can't mean that, surely?"

Terry suddenly realised that anger would get him nowhere with this simpleton. "Well," he said at last, "Jane doesn't want to talk to either of us, so we may as well leave her where she is. Come on," and he turned her towards the front door. She smiled back at him, she could always get her own way with Terry. He opened the front door for her, and ushered her out. He was such a gentleman, with lovely manners she thought. He walked across the garden to her car at the kerb edge. "Goodbye, Patricia," he said. "Drive carefully, now."

"Will you come with me?"

"No, I must get my car from Jane's garage and go and see someone before I go home." He closed the car door for her and stepped back. "Bye, Patricia," and he went back into Jane's little house and through to the kitchen. She was still digging out there and the back door was still locked. He pulled a stool near the sink, opened the kitchen window and climbed out. Maria spotted him at once.

"Oooh, Terry's climbed out the window," she laughed and ran towards him, her arms raised to be picked up. He lifted her up and swung her round. Jane stopped digging and came striding towards him.

"Terry, put my daughter down and go away," she said crossly. "Just go away and leave us alone." She turned as if to go back to her digging. Terry set Maria down and grinned at Jane's retreating back.

"Shall I climb back through the window, then?" he asked innocently. He set off towards the open kitchen window and after a moment Jane stomped past him and, putting the key in the lock, flung the back door open. She turned away, but he had seen her shoulders shaking, he hoped with laughter, not anger. He walked through the house, picking up his jacket as he went, and opened the front door. As he crossed the little garden a window flew open in the sitting-room and a red-faced Jane flung a carrier bag onto the flower bed.

"And take her present with you. We don't want them," and the window was banged shut again. Terry grinned, blew her a kiss and sauntered off up the street, leaving the offending parcel where it lay in the flower bed.

About an hour later the two older children returned from Sunday school and Maria regaled them with her version of the morning's incident. "Shall I climb back through the window, then?" she said several times, accompanied by fits of giggles, and "Take her present with you" and Mummy threw the sweeties into the garden." Maria and Debbie almost rolled about on the floor with laughter, and Jane, listening to Maria's version of the story, felt the same sense of the ridiculous. She couldn't help but join in with them. She'd ring Terry later and apologise; now it all seemed a bit, well, childish.

That same evening David Brownlow rang John. "I've got a chippie with no work to do on Tuesday afternoon," he said. "If it's OK with you, he could come and fix that windowsill for you."

"Yes, that's fine by me. Shall I leave the key somewhere for him to find?"

"I'd rather you dropped it into the office, if you could," David answered. "That way we'll know it's safe. Kitty will go with Paul to tidy up after him and bring the key back here. Is that OK?"

"Sure. I'll leave it with her after school. I could do a bit of work on those books while I'm there. Kitty is doing pretty well now, keeping all the new work up to date. I just have a bit more sorting the backlog. And thanks, David."

"No problem. Not like those blasted accounts. Bye then," and the line went dead. John replaced the receiver and went to find the spare door key, dropping it into his jacket pocket ready for the morning. Had it really only been a couple of days since he and Kitty had driven home in utter depressing silence? What could he say to make it easy for her now?

When he opened the office door the next day she was sitting at her desk, typing. She looked up and smiled. "Hi, John. Coffee?" she asked, pushing her chair back.

"Thanks. I'll do an hour on the books. You'll be able to take over soon, won't you?"

"Maybe." She unlocked the door of the inner office and he went through and sat down at the desk. After a few minutes she brought coffee and sat with him for a moment, looking thoughtful. "Did you enjoy the show on Friday? We got rather interrupted and I didn't ask."

He flushed at the memory. "Yes, very much."

"The Montgomery's are a nice couple," she said idly. "David likes working for them. The boy is very attractive, isn't he?"

Suddenly John stiffened and stared at her. Was this some kind of a trap? Had they heard Patricia's spiteful rumour? "I wouldn't know," he said coldly. "I'm just paid to teach him maths and keep him in order. His work is all I know about Monty," and he began furiously to sort the papers on the desk.

Kitty was appalled. Oh, no, you stupid bitch, she cursed herself. Dad had told her about the woman in the car park, and the malicious rumour she was spreading. She'd been hurt and angry with him but he'd said he didn't believe it, just thought she ought to know what was being said. And now she had said just the wrong thing altogether and put him on his guard with her. This stupid rumour was obviously getting to him already. Aloud she said, "OK, I'll leave you to work," and left the office, closing the door quietly behind her.

He had not been working long before he heard the telephone ringing in the outer office. Some minutes later Kitty came back to stand in front of the desk. "John," she said, "I have to go over to help Laura. Will you stay here and lock up afterwards, or leave now, whichever suits you best. It's OK, Laura has checked with David...."

He looked up sharply. "Checked with David?" and his face set in a frown. "About what, exactly?" he asked coldly. Did they think he wasn't to be trusted with the office, either?

"John," she said quietly but firmly enough to make him aware of her strength of character, "David and Laura are both business people. I work for David, so of course she checked that it's OK for me to go." She smiled down at him and added, "don't jump to so many conclusions. Now, will you stay, or will you leave with me?"

He felt a little ashamed. He had jumped to conclusions, and the wrong ones, too. This silly rumour was clouding his whole judgement. "I'll stay for a while, I've just got this particular bundle in order, so I'll enter them up. What shall I do with the key? Oh, and the key to my cottage, David said to leave it with you."

"Could you take it to Dad? It isn't really out of your way, is it? You can leave your key with him, ready for Paul tomorrow, too. Will you do that?" When he agreed she turned away saying "Goodnight then, John," and left the room. He heard the sound of closing drawers and then the outer door closed and the sound of her footsteps on the gravel path died away. He worked on quietly until all the paperwork he had set out was completed, then took his empty cup to the little corner sink and rinsed it out. In his usual methodical fashion he checked the lights and other switches and then he left the office, locking the door carefully behind him.

It was only a few minutes' walk to the Brownlow's house, and very soon he stopped at their door, rang the bell and waited. Ray opened the door almost immediately saying "Oh, John, good to see you again. Come on in, the kettle's on," and without waiting for an answer began to walk back along the passage to the kitchen. John hadn't meant to stay, but he could hardly shout "No thanks" at Ray's retreating back, so stepped inside and closed the door.

"Grab a chair," said Ray, busy at the sink. Seconds later he turned with the teapot in his hand and began to pour tea into two mugs. "Cats said Laura was in a panic,. That's not a bit like Laura. She's always so organised."

John drank some of the scalding tea and said, "Kitty asked me to bring you the key to the office. And the key to my house. David's men are working there tomorrow." He laid the two keys, one with its bright yellow label, on the table.

"Not before time, either," Ray laughed. "I bet Cats has been giving him reminders. She's made a tremendous difference to his business, you know. And she keeps him in order as well, I shouldn't wonder. But I'm glad you came, I wanted to talk to you." He watched the young man stiffen and his face close up. "Don't worry, John, we're all friends around here. But you ought to know that some woman is putting rumours about?"

"Yes," John said heavily, "Patricia Cameron. She called on my headmaster with her complaints about my suitability. She says its because I spoiled her wedding." He hoped Ray would tell Kitty of this explanation.

"And did you?"

"Well, I stopped it. So I spoiled it. But she was already married to my brother." When Ray enquired he told the whole story as briefly as possible. If Kitty had known about that letter, then she would know his part in it all. Now he looked thoroughly miserable; "Does Kitty know about this?" he asked.

"Yes, I told her, but she simply said it's a load of spiteful rubbish. Did you know this Patricia also complaining that you vandalised her car?" John's look of total surprise gave the older man his answer. "It was the night of the show," he explained. "David and I came out late and found this woman looking for help. The word "Liar" was daubed across the windscreen, and she had a flat tyre. She told us you'd done it. When I said you'd been with Cats all evening, she suggested that you'd both done it." For the first time that evening John began to smile. The thought of dainty little Kitty vandalising cars was just too much. Ray grinned at the thought, too. "David asked if she had a spare wheel and she said no, it made her clothes and things smell rubbery when she put them in the boot, so she had taken it out."

"That's Patricia!" John said grimly. "So what did you do?"

"Nothing. David was so angry with her for making wild malicious accusations that he just told her to phone a garage and get a taxi home. I felt a bit mean leaving her there, but David wasn't having anything more to do with it. Without a spare wheel, we couldn't have helped her anyway." They drank their tea in silence for a minute or two, and then Ray asked, "Do you have any idea who might have done it?"

John shook his head. "None at all, except it wasn't me or Kitty." They both laughed, and after a few minutes of speculation, John finished his tea, said his goodbyes and left.

That same evening Jane called Richard. "So how did the meeting with Freddie go?" she asked.

Richard had decided to consult his lawyer and had been a bit apprehensive about it. Freddie Greenwood had been crisp and businesslike over this appointment, not his usual easygoing self. After all, Richard had refused to see him for eighteen months, and left all the consultations to John. The old solicitor rather liked the quiet, unassuming young teacher, and still felt that he'd had a raw deal under the terms of his father's will. He would have preferred to do business with John.

"Oh, fine really." Freddie suggests I sell Fallowfields. I don't want to live there again, I couldn't anyway for it's too big. It's a family house, isn't it? It's let to an insurance company at the moment, and Freddie thinks they'll jump at the chance to buy. There's still a couple of months to go on the lease, but by the time everything is sorted over the divorce, that will be up. I think it's a good idea so I agreed that's what we'll do. He's arranging for the accountant to come and talk to me on Wednesday. Alan Holgate knows everything about my finances, he was my Father's accountant, too."

"Richard," Jane said slowly, choosing her words carefully. "Wouldn't it be a nice idea to ask John if it was OK with him? He wouldn't want it anyway, and couldn't afford it if he did, but it was the family home after all, and it might make him feel, sort of, involved. Perhaps there might be something there he would like to have, you know, as a sort of memento. I imagine you'll be selling the whole lot, furniture and all?" She thought of John, and his bullying father, and doubted it, but Richard ought to be told. He had always taken everything for granted.

For a brief moment there was silence at the other end, and she expected him to ask what business it was of John's. Their father had left the business and the house to Richard, with only a small token legacy to John. She held her breath, and then let it out in a long sigh as he said quietly, "Yes, you're right. It would be a nice gesture. I owe him that." He owed John a great deal more than a nice gesture, thought Jane, but she would be content with that little concession for the time being, and so didn't press the matter. Instead she asked, "So will you be look-ing for somewhere to live soon?"

"Yes, but there's something else I need to sort out first. Do you know if Terry has a computer?"

"He does, well, he has two really. A state of the art job

that sits on his desk, Very proud of it he is too. And a laptop that travels around with him in the car. Why?"

But Richard was evasive. "Oh, just something I'd like him to search the internet for. Do you think he has the time to do it? Business is business and I know he's chasing a contract just now."

For the last two years Richard had ignored his business and left it all to Freddie and John to sort out. But she kept her opinions to herself once again. "He lost that one," she said, "but already he's off after a couple more. But I think he'll be happy to help. Do you want his number?" When he agreed she dictated it to him over the telephone. "He's probably spent the day working at home so might be glad of a diversion." She hadn't called Terry, nor had he called her, but she didn't think he was angry. She smiled again at Maria's telling of yesterday's incident. It wouldn't amuse Richard, though. "So are you going back to work, taking over the reins again, now that you're with us again?"

"Probably later when I'm settled somewhere. There's several things to sort out first. If I move out of here I have to find a live-in helper. I have to sort out the finances of that too with Alan but they seem to be looking good and Freddie is optimistic."

"Have you thought of asking Karen? About the live in help, I mean."

"I've thought of it. But would such a, well, menial job be of interest to her, do you suppose? She's so highly qualified."

"Then why not talk to her about the problem but without any kind of commitment. Ask her advice," said Jane, practical as ever. "She'll tell you what she expects out of life. And it just might be you. Have you thought of that?"

"I don't think I dare, Jane, and that's the truth. What have I to offer now?" For once in his thirty two years Richard Treherne sounded almost humble. Did he really care, or was it fear of being refused? She didn't know. But it was only a job they were discussing here.

"Well, just talk to her." She stopped speaking abruptly and then said, "Look, Richard, I must go. Maria seems to be having one of her nightmares. Ring me again tomorrow if you want to. Bye" and she replaced the receiver and hurried upstairs.

Terry answered the telephone almost as soon as he heard the sound. "Terry Kennedy. Oh, hi, Richard. Everything OK with you?" He listened to the other man's explanation and then grinned. "No problem. I can download all the information tonight and get it in the post to you tomorrow. No, it's no bother. I reckon when you get out of there the first thing you should buy is a computer. Do your own shopping without moving far. Brilliant." He had made it sound, Richard thought, as though he was a prisoner. Well, in a way, so he was, but voluntarily. But it was almost impossible for Terry to imagine wasting two years of life! Just now he couldn't imagine wasting two hours.

Richard replaced the receiver for the second time that evening, and sat back to think over all the conversations. Karen would be here in a little while to help him get to bed. Maybe he'd talk casually to her about it all then. But very casually. He sat on for a while, and then the door opened and a middle aged nurse came bustling in.

"Hello, dear, I'm Brenda and I've come to put you to bed." Richard winced at the silly expression and the jolly tone. "Now, do we have a shower before bed? No? Right then, let's get you organised."

"Is Karen off duty, then?"

"No, she's been sent to Maternity to help a difficult delivery. The maternity ward is short staffed at the moment." The nurse bustled around him, and Richard felt small and uncomfortable as he submitted himself to her care. But at last the ordeal of Brenda was over, and he could settle down to think. If this was the new regime, then he must get out of here as quickly as possible. But he couldn't manage on his own, he had to be honest about that, and what if he could only find helps like Brenda? It didn't bear thinking about.

The discomfort of the new arrangements continued the next day. He woke to find Brenda drawing the curtains and bustling about again with his morning tea, heaving him up on his pillows like a sack of potatoes. "Now," she said, "you drink your tea, and later on Jenny will be here with your breakfast. She'll help you get up. I'm off duty in a little while, but I expect I'll see you again this evening. Bye-bye dear," and she bustled out again. This was awful, where was Karen? Suddenly he realised that it wasn't just her nursing routine and quiet ways he was missing. He was missing her. But would she really consider giving up her job here and moving with him? It seemed a lot to ask. Could he bring himself to ask? Although the accountant wasn't coming until tomorrow, Richard suddenly needed to make everything happen – and fast! Throughout his military career he had been able to snap out orders and make things happen. Now the frustration of relying on other people's help was really getting to him. He closed his eyes, trying to work out what he, Richard, could do for himself to ease his situation, but instead, drifted off to sleep.

CHAPTER SEVEN

Jenny proved to be a pretty talkative blonde nurse, who hoped to use the time here with the three private patients to study for her last exam. And once breakfast was over and he was dressed and into his chair, she disappeared, but assured him that she would come immediately if he needed her. She tapped her pocket to show him she was wearing her pager. He settled down to read the paper, but after a few minutes laid it aside and tried to work out what it was he wanted to do. After a while Jenny reappeared in the doorway.

"You have a visitor, Mr. Treherne," she announced and stood aside to let someone pass. It was Patricia. Now what did Patricia want with him? Jenny was just about to close the door when Richard called

"Jenny, could you stay here, please? This lady and I are going through divorce proceedings. She has only a nodding acquaintance with truth, so I really need a witness to anything I might have to say to her. Can you stay? If not, we shall have to ask this lady to leave and make another appointment."

"I can stay, Mr. Treherne, unless someone pages me" Jenny said. Patricia had taken the only other chair, so Jenny sat on the end of the bed opposite Richard, smoothed her apron and crossed her legs.

There was a time, Richard thought, when I might have just rolled her backwards and…. Well, better not remember it now. Those days were past, and best forgotten. "So what is it you came to see me about, Patricia?" he asked.

"Do we really have to discuss our private affairs in front of her?" his wife asked petulantly.

"Yes," he answered firmly. He was going to say as little as possible.

"Well, I came to see how you were." She stopped and looked at him, but he made no answer. "I'm glad you're better." Again she stopped, and Richard saw Jenny looking at him, waiting for his reply. Let them wait. "Daddy says you are probably going to sell Fallowfields. Surely that's my home too. Don't I have to agree?"

"No. You made it clear that you did not wish to live there with me. Fallowfields is my family's home, left to me by my father. So I can sell it. I shall ask John first, of course, it was his home too. But I know he won't want it. He couldn't afford to buy it, anyway. I can't live there on my own it's too big."

"But I could. You didn't ask me if I wanted to live there, did you?"

"No. You know you couldn't in any case, it's too big for you, too. I don't remember you being any good at housework and cooking and gardening."

"But the Trimbles did the work."

"Oh, Patricia," Richard said in exasperation, "the Trimbles have retired. And I have to sell Fallowfields. No arguments."

She stared at him. "When you sell it, do I get half the money?"

So this was what it was all about. "Patricia, your Father and my solicitor are probably working out a settlement with that in mind. I have no doubt your Father will make sure you get what you deserve." He wished he could give her what she deserved for her lying, cheating and extravagant ways. "Now, if you don't mind, I'm rather tired. Jenny will show you the way out. Goodbye, Patricia," and he sat back, closed his eyes and waited. For a moment or two she hesitated, uncertain of what to do. Then she said angrily, "Do you know your brother vandalised my car?"

For once, Richard forgot his position and made to rise, then fell sideways. Jenny slipped from the bed to help him, but he recovered quickly and said gruffly "It's OK." Then to Patricia he demanded, "Why should John vandalise your car? Another of your lies, I suppose?"

"I know it was him. He was trying to get back at me because I told his headmaster he was a homosexual."

Richard was incredulous. "You did WHAT? God, Patricia, he teaches young boys, he'll lose his job. What in hell's name did you do a thing like that for? What's poor old John ever done to you?"

"He spoiled my wedding."

"No he didn't. He saved me and his mate from total embarrassment. God, Patricia, you really are a spiteful, malicious interfering little bitch. Get out of here right now, and don't you ever come near me again. Go on, go!" For a moment she hesitated, began to speak but Richard turned away and would not listen. Finally she stood up, swept past Jenny and left the room, closing the door with a bang. Richard sighed heavily. "Thanks, Jenny. Any chance of coffee before you get back to your books. I need reviving after that." Jenny looked at her handsome patient for a long moment, her face full of concern. Then she nodded and went to make the coffee, leaving him to brood on this latest problem.

Just before lunchtime the door opened quietly, and Richard looked up from his book. "Karen! Oh, Karen, you're back. That's wonderful," and quite involuntarily he held out his hands to her.

"Sorry, Richard, only for a few minutes. I just thought I'd pop in and see how you were before I go back on duty in Maternity." She pulled up the chair beside him. "How's it been?"

He groaned. "Karen, it seems I'm being pushed into moving out. The new system is already driving me mad. When will you be back?"

"I've no idea. The new system is pushing me around too. Are you really serious about moving out on your own?"

"I am now," he said firmly. "But it will all take time and I want to talk to you about it, ask your advice. But not like this, not in a couple of minutes between shifts. And Patricia has been here making trouble, too. I wanted to ask you about that as well. Do you know, she has told John's headmaster that John is gay?"

Karen was horrified. "Oh, no! John, gay? It's ridiculous. Will he lose his job? What has she against John, for goodness sake? He's so quiet and caring and well, gentle. And he loves his job."

"I know. I'll see if Jane or Terry know any more about it all later. Oh, God, Karen, I do miss you."

She went quite pink, smiled and touched his hand lightly. Then she stood up to leave. "I have to go, Richard, I'm sorry. I'll try to come back after this shift if I can, but in Maternity you often have to work on until the delivery is finished. I'll do what I can. Can I ring you, if I'm late home? Say, before eleven?"

"Any time at all." He tried to keep his voice light as he

added, "I have no job to go to tomorrow so don't need to worry about sleep." But he was afraid he sounded bitter. She had already moved across the room, now she blew him a kiss, opened the door and quickly stepped out, closing it quietly behind her.

"Hi, Karen," Jenny called from the office doorway. "How's the baby farm?"

"Don't ask. The whole thing really puts me off having children."

"Just as well, really, with him the way he is," and Jenny kept her voice low and nodded to the closed door of Richard's room.

"Oh, Jenny, it's not like that." But Karen's voice held no sound of conviction as she added, "He's just a patient."

Jenny laughed back at her. "Yeah, and I'm the Queen of Sheba. I caught the look on his face when you opened the door. When I go in it's that 'Oh, it's you' sort of look. But you'd better get moving, Kar, or you'll have the sergeant major after you. Does he check up on you?"

Karen pulled a face. "He does. All the time. He has the idea that I should be made up to Sister. No way."

"I reckon he fancies you, Karen." In her teasing mood, Jenny's voice had grown louder now.

"Oh, do me a favour! I've got enough problems and he's definitely not my type. Hey, I must fly."

"And don't worry, I'll take care of things here."

Karen was already hurry along the corridor, but turned and smiled back at the younger nurse. "Perhaps that's what bothers me," she murmured, and walked quickly away.

Sitting quietly in his room, Richard slowly became aware of the two nurses talking outside his door. He was slightly annoyed that Karen had left to go to work, but had stopped to talk to Jenny anyway. Jenny was laughing, Karen answering softly, words he couldn't hear. And then, higher pitched with excitement Jenny said "I reckon he fancies you." Richard held his breath for the answer, but when it came he wished he hadn't listened. "Oh, do me a favour I've got enough problems." He didn't want to hear any more. It served him right for eavesdropping anyway. But that certainly changed things, didn't it? And that evening, when he had been helped into bed he switched off the telephone, switched off the light, and lay awake for what seemed like hours with the words chasing themselves through his mind. "Oh, do me a favour! I've got enough problems."

John got home from school a little later than usual that day. There had been a visit from an irate parent and although he wasn't the teacher involved, he had been asked to stay. These days no teacher stayed alone for long with irate parents. The first thing he noticed as he walked the short driveway was the new windowsill, its new timber stark in its coat of primer. So David's men had been busy. He opened the front door and immediately was aware of the smell of cooking coming from the kitchen. Puzzled, he dropped his case on the hall table and went to investigate. As he opened the door Kitty came toward him wearing an apron, her hair tumbling about her shoulders. "Hello, John, I came with Paul to make sure everything cleaned up. He doesn't always bother. So I stayed and made some dinner, for us both, is that OK?"

"It's great," said John enthusiastically, "and the place is really clean, too. I expected sawdust everywhere. Thanks, Kitty."

She switched on the electric kettle and John pulled out a chair at the kitchen table. He couldn't think what else there was to talk about. After a minute or two she set a mug of tea in front of him. "Had a bad day? You were later than I thought. I always imagined schoolmasters ran for the door when the bell rang." She was laughing at him.

"Nice thought," said John. "We had to deal with a very cross parent. What are you cooking?" He knew there wasn't anything in the fridge that morning. He'd been going to get a takeaway.

"I'm not really much of a cook," she confided. "Dad rather spoils me and does most of it at home. So I bought some pies. We're having mash and peas with them, is that OK?" She looked a little worried about it all, and he tried to reassure her.

"Fine. I'd have probably had beans on toast. So I'm more than happy with pie and mash. Thanks Kitty."

"I got Paul to re-hang a couple of cupboard doors here in the kitchen units. Is that OK, too? They didn't shut properly."

John felt a little uncomfortable. "Thanks. I knew they didn't but, well, I just mean to do something one weekend, and never do."

She smiled at him. "Let's eat now," was all she said.

After their meal they washed the dishes together. John remembered that the sink had been partly blocked that morning. "Paul fixed the sink, then too?" he asked, as the water drained away quickly.

She laughed. "No, I did." When she saw his look of surprise she added, "don't you know the old-fashioned remedy for blocked sinks?" He shook his head, mystified. "Bicarbonate of soda, vinegar, and later, boiling water. Works like a charm. Ask your science master," she teased. The thought of Basil Hapgood clearing clocked sinks made him want to laugh out loud.

"Thanks for the tip, I'll remember that one." They finished the dishes and tidying the kitchen and then John went through to the sitting room to light the gas fire while Kitty made coffee. She sat beside him and looked across at the pile of books on the desk. "Do you have to mark all those tonight?" she asked.

"Not necessarily. They have to be done by Friday." He was about to ask why she had asked, but the telephone rang. He sighed and reached for the receiver. "John Treherne," and then after a moment, "Oh, hello Richard. How are things with you?" Covering the mouthpiece he told Kitty, "It's my brother."

She nodded. Fran had told her about the handsome Richard Treherne. How she'd had a real crush on him once, until Alan had made all other men look nothing. She listened to John's end of the conversation, wondering what this Richard was like, now that he was an invalid.

"Well, yes, of course I understand. Really, it was too big for us as children, wasn't it?" and then after a pause. "Yes, if it's still there. Do you remember Father bought a picture? He hung it in his study, but whether it is there still I couldn't say. I only collected up all your personal gear, so I didn't go in there. If it's still around, yes, I'd love to have that. Or would that be raiding your assets?" He listened again. "Right then. We'll talk more about it when the time comes. Clearing the old place will be quite a job. Yes, of course you will. Right then, Richard, thanks for ringing, and thanks for thinking of it. Bye, then," and he slowly replaced the receiver. Turning to

Kitty he said, "Richard is going to sell the house. My Father left it to him in his will, along with the company. Richard asked if there was anything there I'd like as a memento."

Kitty nodded. "And was there?"

"Only a picture and heaven knows if it is there still. When my Father bought it I admired it a lot. Too much for his liking, so he took it down from the hall and put it in his study. I never saw it again. Sorry about the interruption," he went on, and looked at his watch. "Let me know when you want to go home, and I'll drive you there."

"Do you want me to go? Have you work to do?"

He flushed a little. There he was again, putting his foot in it and giving the wrong impression. "No, there's no work. I just wasn't sure what time you wanted to be home."

She took a deep breath. She was going to put herself in the firing line. "I don't have to go home at all. could stay if you wanted me to. If you'd like that."

Thoughts chased themselves through his mind; he hadn't changed the sheets on his bed this week. She was so neat and dainty, he couldn't ask her to sleep in grubby sheets. And his laundry was piled in the corner, and all the stuff from this windowsill here was piled on the floor. Would she understand? But he had hesitated just that little bit too long and ruined his chances, as usual, for she stood up and collected the coffee cups. "I'll just take these to the kitchen," she said softly. "And don't worry about it, John. I'm sorry," and she left him, headed for the kitchen, closing doors behind her.

He sat staring at nothing. He'd messed it up again. She wouldn't bother with him after this. He must go after her, try to explain. Terry would know how to smile it all away, but he wasn't Terry, was he? She was so lovely, he didn't want to lose her. But as he opened the sitting room door she was pulling on her jacket in the hall. Her face was flushed and her eyes brighter than usual. "I've just called a taxi," she said. "It'll be here in a minute. I'll go down to the gate and wait for it. Goodnight John," and she opened the front door and was gone. Now she'd really believe this bloody rumour that Patricia was circulating. And who could blame her? He wrenched open the front door. "Kitty?"

She was hurrying down the drive to the gate. "Leave it, John," she called over her shoulder. "Goodnight."

He went back inside and slumped into a chair. Now he truly had blown it. She had taken a big step, and he had humiliated her. Of course he hadn't meant to, but she didn't know that. He groaned aloud, like an animal in pain. He'd lost her. No chance of getting back now.

David Brownlow was just going into the supermarket when he met Mrs. Montgomery on her way out with a loaded trolley. "Oh, hello, David" she said, moving out of the way of other customers. "I was going to contact you soon about some work."

"Nice to see you again, Mrs. Montgomery. What are you planning this time?"

You know that porch on the back of the house. A bit dilapidated, and full of old wellies and stuff. I'd like it pulled down and a nice brick and glass one put there, with shelves for plants and things. I've just had a little windfall, so thought this was the time to call you. Are you very busy?"

"Well, things are looking good, but I'm never too busy for my best customers," he smiled. "I'll come round and take measurements and talk about it whenever you're free. Then I can give you an estimate and figure out a date." He looked at his watch. "I could come in about half an hour, if you like. Laura won't be home for a couple of hours yet."

"That'd be fine. Give me time to put this lot away and put the kettle on. I'll see you in about half an hour, then," and she began to push the trolley towards her car while David made his way into the store.

The porch in question was a rather elderly wood and glass affair. They discussed how it might be enlarged a little, and then David set to work with his measures and notebook. When he was satisfied he went into the kitchen. "I'll let you have the quote as soon as I've worked it out," he said.

"Good. Here's your tea," and she put a mug on the table, indicating that he should sit down. "Piece of cake?" she asked.

"Great. Yes please." He had tasted her cakes when he was working here, making this kitchen, and knew they were good. "It shouldn't take too long, once we get started. How's Mr. Montgomery? Will he approve of the door being moved to the side?"

She gave a great, jolly laugh. "Well, he may notice if he tries to go out the usual way. Otherwise he'll say "Oh, Mary, you decide what's best." Then she remembered something. "Oh, I met your sister the other night, the younger one. Such a tiny little thing, isn't she? She was with Mr. Treherne. Are they friends? He's such a lovely man."

"Do you know him, then?"

"I'm on the PTA of Keiran's school, and so is Mr. Treherne. He's rather shy with adults, but the boys have an enormous respect for him, especially my Keiran. Don't you know him?"

David shook his head, then said slowly, "Mrs. Montgomery, can I ask you something? Have you heard this rumour going round about him? Some woman stopped us in the car park at the centre and told us she had complained to the headmaster about it. Dad was with me and well, Dad was worried about Kitty being hurt. Have you heard it? The woman is saying John is gay."

"I have indeed," she answered, "and a load of nonsense it is, too. Yes, I met that woman, too. I went to see the headmaster myself, first thing yesterday morning."

"Were you worried about Keiran?"

"Good heavens, no! Not a bit. I was worried that Mr. Treherne would get the sack for someone's stupidity. But the headmaster had a letter from the woman's father. He's some kind of lawyer, I believe. Anyway, he explained that his daughter was mentally backward, and apologised to the headmaster for the trouble she had caused him. Pity he didn't think to apologise to Mr. Treherne."

"Thanks, Mrs. Montgomery. I can go and put Dad's mind at rest. He and Kitty have always been close and he was worried." He finished his tea and pushed back his chair. "I'd better go and get our meal started for Laura. I'll drop that quote in myself sometime. Bye for now."

"Bye, David, and you tell your Dad that Mr. Treherne is a lovely man, and that I said so. Your Dad always fixes my car for me, so he'll know who said it and that it's true."

David grinned back at her. "I'll tell him. Bye," and he left the kitchen.

The following morning Richard received a large envelope stuffed with papers. Terry had certainly kept his word and done a great deal of research. On the first sheet he had scribbled, "This one has a branch in Oxford. You might get a free demo." But he would read them all first, compare prices and so on. He was quite engrossed in this when there was a tap at the door, and a young woman entered. She was dressed in a neat dark business suit with a crisp white blouse and carried a leather briefcase. Her hair was short, smooth and shining and her makeup perfect. The true epitome of the modern career woman image. "Mr. Treherne? I'm Mary Duncan from Sandlemanns." She had reached him by now and was holding out her hand.

Richard was taken by surprise, but took her hand and shook it. "Hello," he said a little awkwardly. "I was expecting Mr. Holgate."

"I've taken over some of his clients as he is only working three days a week. Winding down, I think you might say, before retirement." After a brief pause she asked, "May I take a seat?"

Richard flushed slightly at his lack of courtesy. "Of course. Please forgive my apparent rudeness. It has been a little while since I conducted my own business, and I think perhaps my mind was elsewhere."

Freddie had given her a little background information on Richard Treherne, and she understood his comment but said nothing. Moving the chair closer to his, she sat down, holding the briefcase on her lap. Richard reached out with one of the odd gadgets Steve had left for him to try, and drew the trolley he used as a table nearer to her. "We can put all the paperwork on that," he smiled. She nodded, and drew out a folder and laid it down.

"There's not a lot to it, really. These are your only outgoings; she handed him a sheet as she spoke. Your hospital charges, which incidentally have been raised quite considerably just recently, with several extra items. Did you know that?" He nodded, and she went on, "Then there is the allowance to your wife. I understand that Mr. Greenwood is currently handling your divorce," she paused and looked at him, and again he nodded his assent. "Those are your only outgoings at the moment. Now," and she handed him a second sheet. "These are your assets. Your fee as a director of Adams & Treherne. Your share assets. The letting fees for the property Fallowfields, and your pension from the Army. You will see that you are well in the black," and she smiled at him. She had a lovely smile, Richard thought. Was there a Mr. Duncan, he wondered. With all this equality, one never knew, but she wore no ring. "Mr. Greenwood says you have a few questions for me concerning possible house purchase and so on. I did a little research so fire away."

He picked up the top sheet of the papers he had been reading. "Before I can leave here there are several things that have to be sorted. This is my first priority," and he handed the sheet to her.

She read it through quickly. "Well," she agreed, "very definitely a priority I should think. You don't want to be anchored in one place, do you? This would certainly mean a little more independence for you."

"Now I've seen the figures you have, I know I can go ahead and buy it. Next priority would be a home of my own, but this is much more difficult."

"Why?"

"Because there are a few things that I cannot do for myself, even if the electronic wheelchair makes me more mobile. I have to think about a live-in help. And a live-in help would require regular wages."

"True, but I don't think that's too much of a problem. You would have to work out just what they needed to do before you could decide how much you pay them, of course. But a fairly generous wage would be no problem to your income."

"The picture might change with the divorce settlement, surely?"

"I don't think it will change too much, you really aren't a poor man, you know. There's the sale of Fallowfields, too."

"And the purchase of a new home. And surely the profit from Fallowfields will add to the divorce settlement?"

"Mr. Greenwood is working on it, and seems much more optimistic than you are. For the moment, go ahead with the purchase of your new chair, and make a start on looking for a home. We'll discuss it again when we have a better picture."

He sat back and smiled. He was really quite good-looking, though pale from so much time spent indoors. He must have looked quite something in his uniform. As she went to speak again, the door opened and a pretty smiling nurse stepped inside. Richard looked up, saw Karen looking at him, and spoke angrily. "Is it important, nurse? We are in conference here."

Karen flushed scarlet, but said steadily, "Not at all, Mr. Treherne, I apologise for interrupting," and stepped back into the corridor closing the door quietly.

"Now you will understand why I am anxious to leave here. It's impossible to concentrate seriously for long, there are always so many interruptions."

She smiled and nodded. Freddie Greenwood had told her the story when she'd wondered why there had been no other outgoings. Freddie had been crisp and cool, as usual, giving nothing away, but she had the distinct feeling that he was not too impressed with Mr. Richard Treherne. And that nurse had been hurt by his rudeness, too. "Well, everything seems perfectly straightforward, and I hope you'll go ahead now with the wheelchair project. It could change a lot of things for you. Mr. Greenwood, of course, will deal with the house purchase business, but if you need my help with anything more, just call," and she laid a business card on the little trolley table.

"Thanks. I'll do just that." He shook the hand she held out to him. "Goodbye, then," and he watched her, slim and straight-backed, as she walk across the room and left him to his thoughts and his papers. Although he hadn't yet made any choice, he picked up the telephone to dial this Oxford branch. Perhaps a free demo, as Terry had called it, would help him decided where to buy. As for Karen – well, how could she come smiling into his room, pretending that she cared? Surely not after hearing her conversation with Jenny yesterday? He had been rude, perhaps he'd humiliated her in front of another woman, but it would make an end of pretending, wouldn't it?

Karen walked swiftly back along the corridor and through the double doors that led into the main part of the hospital. What had she done, or said, to upset Richard so much? She truly couldn't think of anything. When she had last seen him they had talked easily, she'd promised to phone, but he'd already switched it off for the night by the time she came off duty. Now this snub.

Just one more good reason for getting out, she thought bitterly. She'd had enough of arrogant ex-military men.

Terry drew his car to a halt outside Jane's house. He could see her in the window, struggling with a curtain. When she saw him she dropped the curtain onto a chair and came to the door to meet him.

"This is a nice surprise. Are you staying long?"

He shook his head. "I'm really only passing through. Well, detouring through, you might say. But I've time for coffee, if you have." By now she had led the way indoors and he asked, "Where's Maria."

"Play group. We've finally persuaded her that going to school of some kind is what people do." Jane laughed and added, "There's an added attraction. They have toys she hasn't got."

Terry sat at the kitchen table, and after a moment or two Jane put a mug of coffee before him. "So? Why the detour? Something bothering you?"

"Yes," he answered at once. "Have you spoken to John lately?" When she nodded in answer he continued, "Did he tell you about Patricia and the rumour she has put around about him? She's saying that he's gay?"

Jane was horrified. "Oh, poor John. What on earth has she got against him? She never liked him, of course, but that's because he wouldn't pay her attention. So what's happening now? What's he doing about it?"

"Well, according to David Brownlow, her father wrote the headmaster a letter, more or less explaining that his daughter wasn't all the ticket, and that her complaint to him should be ignored. He suggested that the Head keep the letter to show to anyone who might complain, and he apologised to the Head. Mrs. Montgomery, who told him all that, was furious that Cameron hadn't apologised to John, too. But that's not all of John's problems. He seems to be quite taken with David's sister, and she with him, but each time they do get together, something, or someone, upsets things and, according to David, his sister is quite determined that John is the only man she wants, but she can't figure out how to go on next, or something like that."

Jane looked at him, her face serious and full of concern. "Poor John is so shy with women, I can see all sorts of things would upset him. What's she like, this sister?"

I've only met her once. The first thing you notice is how tiny she is; She must be well under five feet tall, I should think, but with such a bubbly personality, you can't help smiling when she talks to you. Pretty, but fragile looking, although David says she's quite tough really. But that's only a one-off first impression. I only spoke to her for a minute or two."

Jane thought you could trust Terry to pick the good points in any woman. "So what is she going to do?"

"She doesn't know yet, but she hasn't given up on him, according to David. Have you any ideas?"

"Not immediately," Jane said slowly. "What they need is time and space to be together without anyone else around, like a holiday. But I shouldn't think that's possible there." She sat staring into her coffee mug as if the answer might be there, her brow wrinkled in thought.

"Something else I want your opinion on," Terry went on. "Richard wondered why I didn't move my office to somewhere central like Oxford. I'm not actually struck on the idea, I work pretty well from where I am, but I did wonder, seeing as you know him, whether you thought he was trying to help. People on the weekend conferences seem to like the rural area around Hallinford. It makes a break for them. But then, so would Oxford, I suppose. What do you think?"

She hesitated for only a moment, and then said, "Richard has all the financial backing he has ever needed. If you sold the barn conversion, that's not just moving your office, but finding another home, too. It could be quite costly. If I was selfish I'd say you should go ahead, then I'll always have you around when I need you, but that would be wrong." She broke off for a moment, and sipped her coffee. "Terry, you know that I grew up with the Treherne boys, they are more like brothers. I am fond of them both, but if Richard suggests something, you can be sure that it is for Richard's benefit, too." She saw his surprised look and added, "No, I'm not being mean, but even Andrew, his best friend, always said the same thing."

Terry smiled at her. "You couldn't be mean, could you?" he teased. Then he was serious again. "Yes, I do understand, though I can't see how moving my business would benefit Richard, can you? And as I said, I'm not ready to move out of Hallinford. Not yet," he added with a knowing smile. She laughed back at him, and he suddenly changed the subject. "What were you doing when I arrived?"

"Trying to hang a curtain."

He looked at the chair she had been standing on, still in the window. "Don't you have any steps?"

"I think so. I think there are some in the garage, but I didn't have the time to run up the street and fetch them back."

He went to the window of the sitting room and picked up the curtain. Stepping carefully onto the chair, he threaded the hooks into the runners. "There, is that the only one?"

"Yes, I've managed the other, but that one was left-handed. Thanks Terry, I didn't know you were so domesticated."

"Ah," he smiled, "is that a point in my favour? Seriously, Jane, you shouldn't be balancing on chairs."

"OK. I'll give you a call each time the curtains need washing." She realised that he wasn't smiling back at her, and added, "Sorry, Terry. I'll fetch the steps from the garage. Sometime. The curtains are done now."

"Time I was on my way, much as I love you," he said lightly. Put that mind of yours to work and see what we can do to help poor old John out of his dilemma and into some kind of love life. Take care, now." He kissed her on the cheek; "See you," and he left the house and drove away to his next appointment.

The following morning she was startled by a ring at the doorbell as she prepared the children's breakfast. "Sorry to wake you," Terry teased her, "I can't stop, though." By now the children came tumbling down the stairs to see what was happening. "Just delivering something for your Mum." He went back to the car, opened the boot, and drew out a big plastic bag.

"What is it what is it?" the children were jumping about and asking together, but Terry handed the bag to Jane. "No more climbing on chairs, OK?"

She drew out a chrome and blue step stool. "Oh, Terry, that was kind. Thank you."

"Right. I'm on my way. Bye, kids, don't be late for school. See you." By now he had already reached his car and opened the door. "Bye, Jane, see you soon," he called, and drove away.

Jane and the children trooped into the kitchen, with Maria and Debbie arguing over who would sit on the new stool. Jane set it in the corner, and got them organised for breakfast. "I love Terry to bits," Maria announced.

"And I love Terry to bits, too," added Debbie. "He's not like a real grown up at all, is he?" Jane smiled, Terry would be amused at that. Jamie spread Marmite on his toast; love was girls talk, and he wasn't joining in. Terry was OK, though. "I think Terry loves Mum," Debbie said confidentially, taking another piece of toast.

Well, I think Terry loves us all," Jane said, a little smile hovering around her lips. "and I think you'd better get breakfast eaten or you'll be late, Debbie. Maria, drink your juice." She had become firm and businesslike; in a little while there would be the inevitable scramble for lost books, socks and satchels. This was definitely not the time for suspect emotions. She pushed up the sleeves of Andy's old blue sweater she was wearing. No, she thought. Definitely not the time.

Chapter Eight

As she lay in bed that night an idea began to form in Jane's mind. Too late to do anything about it now - why hadn't she thought of it before? Now it would have to wait until morning. She stayed awake for a long time, examine the idea from everyone's angle, and finally drifted off to sleep, convinced that with a little help from various people, it could work.

The following morning, when the breakfast-time scramble was over, missing items found and everyone had gone to school or play group, she fetched the telephone directory, and laid it on the kitchen table. There wouldn't be too many people with that name, surely? "Oh, wonderful," she breathed finding the entry she was looking for; there were only four listed under that name and only one Alan. She copied the number out carefully, put the directory away, and went to the telephone. Disappointment followed this attempt, all she heard was an answering machine, and for this particular call that was of no use at all. Taking the scrap of paper back into the sitting room Jane tucked it under Andrew's picture. "Look after that for me, love," she said to the smiling face in the photograph. "I'll try again this afternoon."

That afternoon, with Maria playing with her dolls in the garden she tried the number again and this time was rewarded when a soft voice answered, "Francesca Chevalier."

"Oh, Fran, it is you," Jane said a little nervously. "I'm not sure if you'll remember me. It's Jane Lawson, Jane Bannister that was. Have I caught you at a busy time?"

"Not at all. Nicky's playing in the garden, and Natalie's at school, so it's fairly quiet. And of course I remember you, Jane. It's lovely to hear from you." There was a little pause and then she added quietly, "and I was really sorry to read about Andrew. He was such a lovely person. But I didn't know what to say, or even whether to say anything, and so kept putting off calling you until, well, it was too late."

"Don't worry, Fran, I understand. It's always difficult to know just what to say, isn't it? And thanks. But listen, I wanted to ask you something about your sister Kitty."

"Kitty? I didn't know you knew Kitty, she was only eleven when they moved."

"No, you're right, I've never met her. But a friend tells me she is getting rather serious about John Trehern, but not getting much in the way of response. You know that I more or less grew up with the Treherne boys? John has been absolutely marvellous to us since the accident, I'm not sure how I'd have coped without him. He's been really good to Richard, too, although I'm afraid it's taken Richard a long while to appreciate it. If there was any way I could do something for John to repay him, I'd do it like a shot, so I wanted to know has Kitty really got it bad over John or is that someone's wrong impression, do you think?"

Francesca chuckled. "Oh, yes, she's really got it seriously bad over him. But she isn't getting very far, and now she's worried because of this stupid rumour. I'm sure you know about that?" When Jane agreed, her friend continued, "He's so depressed and moody he keeps misunderstanding her motives, which frustrates her even more. Evidently some woman put that story about. Kitty wants to help but doesn't know how. Oh, yes, she really is quite serious about him. And she's not the sort to give up easily, I can tell you."

"Great! That's just what I needed to know. John is hopeless at talking to women at the best of times, but my friend is quite sure John feels the same way about Kitty, but he's so withdrawn and tongue-tied where women are concerned. Isn't it odd that he can stand there in front of a class of boys, keep them in order and fend off their awful jokes but can't talk to one woman on her own? Did you know it was Richard's ex-wife, Patricia who is venting her spite on him?"

"Oh, no! What did he do to upset her? I never met her, you know. Alan likes the quiet life, it's as much as I can do to get him to take me to the annual college dinner, and the places she and Richard went to would scare him rigid."

"Falling for quiet men seems to run in the family," Jane laughed. "Now, just suppose that if Kitty had the chance to go away on holiday with him, do you think she would go?"

"Definitely, it's that bad. But she hasn't got that kind of money, she only works for David. And I don't see shy John putting that kind of proposal forward, do you?"

"No, but if she asked him I think he could be pushed into going with her. I'll talk to Terry and see if and how it can be done. But will you ask Kitty if she'd definitely go if she got the chance? Just to be sure we're not all going in different directions."

"Of course I will. Alan's away this weekend so I'm taking the kids down to see Dad; I'll have plenty of time to talk to her then. I'll ring you when I get back. Is that OK?"

"Fine." Jane thought it was time to make Fran feel she wasn't being called just for a purpose. "How old is Nicky?"

"Three. Natalie's six. When she asked Jane told her about the children and they chatted easily for a little while. Then Jane couldn't resist the question. "Fran, did you hear about Richard's wife trying to marry someone else?"

"Did she Really? What happened?"

"This is the reason she's gunning for John." Jane kept the smile from her voice. She was sure Kitty would have told her. "John heard about it, don't ask me how, and stood up in church and objected when the banns were being called."

"He never did! God, that must have taken some doing for someone like John. Did Richard hear about it?"

"Not until much later. For a while Richard sort-of opted out of the world after the accident. But he's picking up now, thank goodness."

There was a loud cry from the other end of the line and Fran said quickly, "Sounds like Nicky's in trouble, Jane. Must go, but I'll be in touch. Bye" and the receiver clattered on to its cradle. Jane replaced her own receiver with a quiet smile. That was the first part of her plan.

That evening Richard telephoned. "Any chance of you and the children visiting this week?" he asked. "I've got something here that might surprise and interest Jamie." When she asked what it was he wouldn't be drawn. "I'd really like to see you all again, anyway." She promised to talk to Terry or John to see if they were busy this weekend.

"Why do you always have to be involve them, Jane," he asked, and there was a sharp little edge of discontent in his voice. "don't you have a driving licence any more?" There was a silence on the line and he spoke again. "Jane?"

"Yes?"

"I said….."

"Yes, I heard what you said, Richard. And yes, I still have a licence, you know my Father taught me to drive when I was seventeen."

"So why do you have to keep asking Terry or John? Why can't you bring the children yourself? It would be nice to have them to myself, not share them with a stranger or with John all the time. Andy had a really good family car that you've driven before."

She spoke in a tight, clipped voice, trying not to sound too angry. "A licence doesn't transport three children, Richard, you need a car for that job. And Terry isn't a stranger any more, and my children adore them both, Terry and John."

And I suppose you are telling me I'm the stranger, he thought bitterly. "But what happened to Andy's car? Don't you have it any more?"

She sighed. He'd been in that hospital far too long, and didn't have a clue about the world outside. He'd always had money to back him in any venture he chose. "I sold it."

"What on earth for, Jane? Surely with three small children it was a necessity not a luxury? It was a pretty decent car, too. Would have lasted a good while."

"Probably," she said abruptly, "but it was that or let the mortgage company reclaim the house. I felt the house was more of a necessity than a luxury." Then she relented and felt a bit sorry for him, it wasn't his fault really. What would Richard Treherne know about making choices in spending? "Let's talk about something else, shall we?"

They chatted about his day and hers, and the children. Finally they ran out of conversation, and said goodnight.

When she rang Terry he was quite happy to visit her that weekend and take them all to the hospital. "He says he has something to show us, but wouldn't say what," she explained. From the smile in his voice and the non-committal way he answered she guessed that Terry knew about it already. "Come on, Terry," she laughed, "Tell me."

"Wait and see," he told her. "Can I come to you Friday night, I'm in that area all day Friday." With these arrangements made, and after some more light conversation they said goodnight. Jane smiled to herself; she would put her plan to Terry on Saturday, see if he'd help, and then wait for Fran to call her on Monday. If only it could all work out right for John. But perhaps she had better tell John about Saturday. She didn't want him to think he'd been pushed out of place by Terry. He was feeling depressed enough, as it was.

When they drew up in the hospital car park on Saturday afternoon it was raining steadily, and they hurried for shelter into the main hall. There was no sign of Richard, and Jane was slightly annoyed; she'd told Richard at their first meeting that she did not want the children visiting him in his room. But there was nothing else to be done, and they set off along the corridor to the private wing. When they reached Richard's door he opened it himself from his wheelchair and began to move out, unaided, into the corridor. "Do you see, Jamie," he said happily, "I listened to what you said and got a powered chair. Great, isn't it?" To Terry and Jane he added quietly, "It's on a week's free trial, but I guess I'll stick with this one, it's good." Turning back to the wide-eyed children he said, "Come on, let's go to the coffee shop for something good to celebrate," and he began to move along the corridor with the children trotting along beside him. Jenny came out of her office and hurried after them. While Mr. Treherne was in the private wing, she was responsible for him, whether he liked it or not.

"Hospital rules," she called over her shoulder. "He has to be accompanied in here." Jane watched them all go, but did not follow. Terry looked across at her raising an eyebrow in question.

"He could have done that eighteen months ago," she said bitterly. "Andy would have done, if things had been different." Suddenly, at the mention of his name, her face crumpled and the tears began to run, unheeded, down her cheeks. She hadn't cried since the news of Andy's death, and now she couldn't stop. Terry put his arms about her, and drew her gently back inside the half-open door of Richard's room. She buried her face in Terry's cashmere sweater and wept for Andy, for her children, for the sheer injustice of it all, and for herself, perhaps. Her whole body shook with convulsive sobbing. He held her close, stroking her hair as her body trembled with the anguish of it all. Slowly, slowly the sobbing subsided, and she grew limp in his arms as if exhausted, but did not raise her face.

"Darling Jane," he said into her hair. "Don't cry any more."

At last she raised her face to look at him. "I'm so sorry, Terry," she said. "I don't know what started that off. But it all just seemed too much. I'm truly sorry," she said again.

"Don't be. It might even help. Now," and he held her at arms' length and his voice was calm and practical, "Go and wash your face and tidy up. The kids will wonder where you are. OK now?"

She gave him a watery smile in gratitude. "Thanks, Terry," and went across to the tiny bathroom in the corner of the room. She splashed the cold water over her face and it made her feel fresher. "Lucky I never wear mascara," she smiled, attempting to reassure him, "I would look so hideous you wouldn't come near me." Then she rummaged in her bag for sunglasses. "Will I do?"

Terry put an arm around her shoulders, "For me, you'll always do," he said softly. "But don't worry, about it Jane, I can wait, I'm a very patient man." He grinned at her, "Come on, I could murder a coffee," and together they left Richard's room, closing the door behind them.

That evening, as Jane prepared a meal for them all, the children chattered happily about Uncle Richard's new chair, and how it had been Jamie's idea, and Maria had wanted to ride on his lap and that nurse had so no, it wasn't allowed. Terry sat quietly, watching their Mother and noting any reaction. Jane was still vulnerable, that was clear. But he could wait, build up the business and keep an eye on them all and just be around. She caught his eye and smiled. "It won't be long," she said. For a fleeting moment he wondered if she had read his thoughts, but she continued, "Are you hungry?"

"Starving!"

"We are too, Mum," said Debbie, "will you be quick?" Jane laughed and began to pile food on to the plates she had taken from the oven. Soon the only sounds in the kitchen were the clatter of knives and forks. Jane seemed quite relaxed and happy; perhaps the weeping had done her some good after all.

Much later, when the children were asleep Jane settled down on the sofa beside him, and Terry laid aside the newspaper he hadn't really been reading. "Terry," she began rather tentatively, "could you do something really deceitful?"

He rolled his eyes in mock alarm. "Oh, lord, what have you found out now?"

She giggled. "Nothing, idiot! But could you? Could you do something that wasn't quite honest, if I asked you to?"

"It has been known. Why?" For a moment she didn't answer and he continued, "come on, Jane. Are you going to tell me about it, or is this a guessing game, or another of your devious plans?" What on earth was this all about?

"I've had this idea. Kitty can't make any headway with John, though Fran says she desperately wants to. Something, or someone always seems to get in the way when she's with him, and often he misjudges her or misunderstands. It's probably that rumour Patricia is on about, it's getting to him. I thought if they could go away together, just for a few days, say, there wouldn't be anyone around to interrupt or spy on them. Fran is going to ask Kitty if she'd do that if she got the chance. She's visiting her father this weekend."

"But she can't afford that, surely? And she couldn't ask John to go with her and then pay the bill. And where does my being deceitful come into it?"

"I know all the snags. But if Richard could be persuaded to fork out, and Kitty pretended she had won a holiday for two and invited John, I don't truly think he would refuse her. So," she said, looking at him appealingly, "I hoped you might persuade Richard to pay."

"How? He's not all that appreciative of John, is he? Would he care whether they sorted themselves out or not? And I don't think he's all that keen on me, either."

"But you are useful to him, and that counts with Richard. And no, he wouldn't care, because he would never understand John's shyness. But he would care about his pride. If you told him of the proposed arrangement and that you and David Brownlow and his Father and possibly me were all going to chip in so that it could be done, he'd hate being left out, and my guess is that he would make the grand gesture and say he'd pay."

Terry looked into her face and said softly, "You haven't much opinion of Richard, have you? But yes, I think it might work. He'll probably remember John's his brother and all that. I've got a genuine reason to call and see him anyway, so I'll bring it into the conversation somehow." He gave her a wry smile and added, "I wouldn't like to be on the opposition to any of your plans, Jane Lawson."

She kissed his cheek. "Thanks Terry. And you're wrong, Richard was someone quite different before all this opting out. Maybe he will be again when he leaves that wretched room and comes into the big wide world. But he'll never, ever understand anyone who lacks money or confidence, because he's always had both in very large amounts. Daddy's blue eyed boy, always. It made him just a touch arrogant." They sat in silence for a few minutes and then she asked, "Why have you got to call on him, anyway?"

"He asked for some information on computers. He's considering buying a laptop. But he also wants info about desktops as well."

"And did you have it?"

"I downloaded it from the internet. I did this for him before with the wheelchairs."

"So in a way, you pushed him into life."

"No, I think Jamie did that. I just found the information, that's all."

The mention of Jamie reminded her. "I think there's something bothering Jamie," she said. "I've tried to talk to him, but he just shrugs me off and says there's nothing and to stop fussing."

"He seemed OK today and this evening. Perhaps he's fallen out with a friend or something."

"Perhaps." But she didn't seem convinced.

They sat quietly together for a long while both deep in their own thoughts, and then Terry asked, "Did John know about today? Did you tell him I was taking you to the hospital? I don't want to make him feel he was being pushed aside. He's always taken care of you until now."

"Don't worry, John will always be part of whatever we are doing, but he's away with some school trip. I did telephone, but only got the answering machine. Then I remembered he wouldn't be back until…..oh, about now I think. I'll tell him all about it in the morning."

If Terry had hoped that Jane's fit of weeping had changed things between them, he now was disappointed. They'd spent a quiet evening together, talking like any other couple but when the time came for sleep Jane had, as always, made him up a bed on the sofa. So, he thought sadly, she isn't ready yet. Andy is still here. But as they drank their hot milk in the kitchen she said, very quietly and without looking at him, "Terry, do you want babies of your own sometime?"

He was startled. "Is this an invitation," he joked to hide his surprise.

"No, a serious question. One that I need answering before I let myself get too fond of you." She still wasn't looking at him, and he felt a little uncomfortable, as though something was wrong, there was something troubling her. He stayed silent and let her continue, if she would. "You see, when I had Maria there were complication and, well, I can't have any more babies. It didn't matter then. That's why I asked you."

"Well," he said slowly, praying for words that wouldn't hurt and wouldn't spoil what they already had. "I've never really thought about it much. I guess it's something you think is sort of automatic when you marry, or something like that."

Now she was looking at him. "It's OK, Terry. You don't have to try and be kind. If you found someone who could, I'd understand and we'd still be friends."

"No." he said, suddenly decisive. "I want us to be more than friends, Jane, you must know that by now. Let's think about what is here and now, and not what might or might not have been. OK?"

She nodded, but he could see she wasn't convinced. Deep down, neither was he. This needed thinking about. He took his mug to the sink and stood it there. "Time for bed, it's been a long day." He kissed her lightly on the cheek and went back to the sitting room to his bed on the sofa. For a long time, once he had put out the light and settled down, he lay staring at the ceiling. He had always pictured himself, at some far off point in the future, holding his new baby son or daughter. Now, if he waited for Jane to need him, that would never happen. But he did want Jane. And surely, Jane was more important than any new unknown as yet baby. And didn't he have a ready made family who cared for him, anyway? That would be enough to work for, surely? He thought of the little ones and wondered what was troubling Jamie. Perhaps he'd find a way of talking with him tomorrow maybe it was something he couldn't take to Jane about. Jane. How long would he have to wait until she was ready for love? He drifted into a troubled sleep with his mind full of unanswerable questions.

Jane woke him with a mug of tea, and he heaved himself into a sitting position. "Where are my tormentors," he grinned. "Do I have a reprieve as its Sunday?"

"Eating their breakfast under threat of no sweeties today," she laughed. "But I wouldn't hang about too long there if I were you."

He drank his tea and headed for the shower as the kitchen door flew open and the two little girls burst into the room. "Too late," he called as he ran up the stairs. Half an hour later, showered and dressed, he sat at the table buttering toast as Jane poured their tea. "If Jamie's got football practice this morning, I'll pick him up afterwards, if he wants," he told her.

She caught his glance and held it. "Thanks, Terry," she said simply. He might just tell Terry what was wrong – he certainly wasn't telling her.

As the small boys streamed off the pitch later that morning Terry spoke to the master in charge. "Terry Kennedy," he said. "I've come to pick up Jamie Lawson."

"Fine," said the master, and Jamie came running towards them. "I don't think he was quite with us today. Not his usual good play today."

"Do you want to go straight home, or shall we drive to the common?" Terry asked. I watched a bit of a really duff football game up there just now? It was so awful it was comic." Jamie shrugged, but then said they could go to the common if Terry liked. For a while they drove in silence and then Terry asked, "Was it a good game today, then?" Jamie shook his head. "You feeling bad?" Again, the boy shook his head, and Terry said no more for a while. They stopped at the edge of the common, watching people with dogs throwing sticks, and children rushing about.

Jamie muttered something he didn't catch, and Terry raised an eyebrow in question. "Are you going to marry Mum?" the boy asked in a small, muffled voice.

So this was it. He thought carefully before answering and then said, "I don't know yet. I would very much like to marry your Mum, but not for a while. Would it upset you if I did?"

"No. Why don't you want to marry her now?"

"Because I don't think your Mum wants to marry anyone yet. And because I don't earn enough money to look after you all yet."

Jamie nodded. "But if you did marry her one day, would I have to call you Dad?"

So this too was worrying him. "No. Not unless you really wanted to. You remember your Dad, don't you? He'll always be your Dad."

"So what would I call you? Stepdad?"

"No, that sounds awkward, doesn't it? You call me Terry now, why change anything?"

The little boy was obviously relieved and gave him a big smile. Then he began to laugh and pointed to a dog behaving rather oddly. "Oh, Terry, just look at that crazy dog."

Terry laughed with him. The moment was over, and Jamie was himself again. "Shall we go and face the womenfolk now, do you think? I'm a bit hungry."

"Me, too, I'm really starving. Come on Terry, let's go. Terry started the engine; he felt he'd solved one little problem anyway, if not the biggest one.

He made excuses about work and left them after lunch. As he drove home, he thought over the several conversations he'd had that weekend. But nothing needed deciding immediately, and things could go on as they were for a while. Wait and see what developed. He remembered the errand he had to do for Jane in the week, and decided, on impulse, to call in on John as he drove through Ledminster. After that school trip he might be glad of some adult company.

As always, there were books and papers over John's desk, and an empty glass too. "Are those still David Brownlow's books?" Terry grinned. "I did warn you."

John laughed. "No, I've sorted them for the time being, and Kitty is taking over gradually. These are Mrs. Jennings from the sweet shop. She's selling up and wants everything neat and tidy. But there's very little for me to do, she's kept them well since I sorted them last year. Are you stopping long enough to have a drink?"

"Only coffee, thanks. I've just come from Jane and the kids. Richard wanted to show off his new toy, his electronic wheelchair. I made sure everyone recognised that it was Jamie's idea, and he really thought he was great. Jane was a bit upset as she watched Richard going off down the corridor under his own steam. She thought Andy wouldn't have wasted life like that. She said Richard could have done that eighteen months ago."

"And so he could have." John's face was set, and his voice was flat. "So what's his great master plan now?"

"Search me. I don't think he altogether approves of me, though I do have my uses. Like surfing the internet for him."

"Ah, yes. My brother is good at finding uses for people. What is it this time?"

"Computers."

"Computers? Can he use one in a hospital. Won't it foul up the communications system?"

Terry grinned. "I've no idea, but if that serves to make him move his butt into a place of his own, so much the better. Think of the time and petrol it will save you. I've got a whole ream of papers for him to browse through, though. That should keep him quiet for a while. So how was the trip?"

John pulled a face, but then smiled. "Not too bad, really. There's always someone who gets lost, or loses something, that's par for the course. No, this was quite a good trip, even the boys thought so." They talked on about other things whilst making and drinking their coffee. Then they both fell silent until John asked, "Terry, is something bothering you?"

His friend looked surprised, but answered quietly, "Not really." He was silent again for a moment or two and then asked, "John, have you ever considered asking Jane to marry you?"

John looked genuinely startled. "Jane? Well, no, of course not. It would be like marrying my sister, in a way. In any case, she wouldn't have me. We're quite different temperaments, you must be able to see that. Oh, no, whatever gave you an idea like that? Jamie?"

"No, not Jamie. But, well, oh I don't know. I suppose I just wanted to be sure in my mind that's all. You know, didn't want you to think I was muscling in, like."

John stared at him blankly for a moment; he had never heard this rather flamboyant friend of his struggling for the right word. Then a slow smile spread across his face. "Ah, I see what you're getting at. No, Jane and I have known each other for so long, we'll always be the best of friends, but nothing more. OK?"

Terry looked a little embarrassed and took his empty cup to the kitchen to hide his feelings. He was laughing when he came back. "Don't you ever wash up, John?"

"Not till I can't find a clean cup," his friend grinned back at him. And in that light-hearted mood, Terry remembered that he still had work to do and left for his own home. John sat back in his chair, thinking over this last conversation. And then his thoughts turned to Kitty and he sighed – if only he had Terry's way with people. On the last occasion he'd spoken to Kitty Keith Samways, that lout of a carpenter, had slammed his way into the office, interrupted their conversation with all manner of remarks and innuendos. When the lout had eventually left them John had been too embarrassed to talk to her properly. Now of course she must think him an absolute wimp, what woman wouldn't? He wasn't sure which was worse, always being interrupted, or being with her and not knowing what to say. No, he corrected himself moodily, it wasn't a case of just looking like a wimp, it was really being one. If she thought that of him, then there wasn't much hope of ever really getting to know her and that was totally depressing.

CHAPTER NINE

It was Wednesday of the following week before Terry could call on Richard. As he was about to knock on the door, it was opened and he came face to face with Jenny. Her smile was instant; "Hi Terry. Haven't seen you for ages."

"You haven't been looking in the right places," he grinned. Then he asked, "Jenny, Jane asked me to give you her phone number. She hoped you'd ask Karen if she could ring her. Is Karen still about?"

"Yes, till the end of next week. It's a shame, really, her leaving is all for nothing now." She waited as Terry scribbled the number on a slip of paper, took it from him and tucked into her pocket. "Sure, I'll pass the message on right away. See you later, maybe," and she stepped aside, leaving the door open for him to enter.

Richard looked put out. "What was all that about? Why does Jane want to speak to Karen," he asked sharply.

Terry had closed the door and crossed the room. Now he sat beside Richard and smiled widely. "Don't ask me, Richard, I'm just the messenger. Jane knew I was coming today and asked me to pass on the message. Mission accomplished. Now," and he pulled a pile of papers from the briefcase he was carrying. "I've divided them into bundles, one for laptops and one for desk jobs. You wouldn't be able to use the desk one in here, and you wouldn't be able to use the internet, either, I shouldn't think. Mess up the machinery."

"I don't want to use either here," Richard said stiffly. "I just need to study them, see what's the best for the stuff I need to do. See who gives the best deals and maybe offers tuition, too." He riffled through the first pile of papers and grinned, "there's enough to keep me occupied, I'd say, for a while."

"Well, it's always worth studying the market. What's happening about the house sale?"

"That's going ahead, the insurance company currently renting it want to buy. Tell John if he wants to search the attics for that picture, he must speak to Freddie about when and how. Have you seen him lately, John I mean."

Brilliant, Terry thought, he's brought the subject up himself, no problem for me now. "Sure, at the weekend. He's a bit depressed. You know John, tongue-tied with women, and mad about Kitty Brownlow. Every time they do get together, someone interrupts and gets John all flustered and embarrassed, or calls one of them away to do something else. Jane and Fran Chevalier have come up with a plan to send them on holiday together, just the two of them, in the hope they can sort themselves out. Fran and David and Ray are going to chip in to pay for it, me too. That way, John will either sink or swim. I guess I just have trouble figuring out why he can't talk normally to women. He talks easy enough to those teenagers at school, but it doesn't work out that way, somehow."

Richard was frowning. "That's not on, he'd never let anyone pay for him like that. He's much too proud. And what does Kitty think about all this?"

"Oh, she's all in favour, now that Fran has put her in the picture. Jane's idea is to say that Kitty has won a holiday for two in Spain, and asks John to go with her. Fran made sure Kitty knew what was going on and asked her if she'd go. She jumped at it – I think she's as frustrated as John, but can't think of a way to push him."

"Well," said Richard shortly, "if you all think it will work, fine. But there's no need for you or the Brownlows to put money into it, I'll pay for the holiday. John is my brother, after all."

So you've noticed at last, Terry thought sarcastically, but all he said was, "Well, that would be great. I'll tell Jane when I ring her next, and she'll tell the others, I guess."

"No," said Richard firmly, "I'll tell Jane myself. I'll ring her tonight."

Terry kept his face straight – he knew Richard would question Jane about her wish to speak to Karen. "Right," he said, "I'll leave this lot with you, then. I have a meeting before lunch, so I'd better get moving. See you again, Richard You know, I think Jane has a good idea there. If John makes a mess of a holiday together, then he deserves to be on his own. Bye for now," and he left the room letting the door close after him.

Jenny was crossing the corridor, and came towards him. "Karen will ring Jane this evening, when she comes off duty. OK?"

"Fine. Thanks Jenny, I'll tell her. Now I have to get to a meeting. See you," and he turned and walked quickly away. Jenny watching him go a little enviously. Men like Terry Kennedy, with his good looks, expensive clothes and easy manner never seemed to come her way. She sighed again, and turned back into the office; she'd better get those notes up to date before someone came checking.

When she took Richard his coffee later he seemed preoccupied with his papers, but as she turned to go he asked as casually as he could manage, "Jenny, why did you say that Karen's leaving was unnecessary and a waste?"

She stopped and half turned. She had no real liking for this arrogant man and the way he had treated Karen because he'd another woman with him simply increased her feelings. What did it matter to him, anyway? But he was her patient, she must be professional and polite. "It was unnecessary," she said shortly. "The major has been moved to a desk job somewhere else." She crossed the room quickly and would have left but he spoke again.

"I don't quite understand. What has the major to do with Karen?"

This time she turned completely to face him. "He fancied her, chased her around the hospital and made life awkward for her. Didn't you know? Everyone else did. So she gave in her notice."

Richard recalled the conversation between the two nurses. "I reckon he fancies you." "Oh, do me a favour!" And they hadn't been talking about him at all. Why had he jumped to that conclusion? Jenny watched him, and saw realisation dawn on him. Serves you right, she thought grimly, military men like you always think they were God's gift to women. Karen's too good for you, anyway. She left the room quickly after that and the pager in her pocket began to buzz. He wouldn't call her back, surely? But thankfully the indicator was flickering over old Mrs. Lawrence's door, and she pulled a face and set off to hear yet another complaint from a querulous old lady.

Richard stared for a moment at the closed door and realised that something about Jenny had changed lately.

Oh, there was nothing he could complain about, she was efficient, polite and friendly to a point, but the warmth had gone. That was the way women were, he reminded himself, when they didn't get quite what they wanted out of life. His thoughts returned to the question, why did Jane want to talk to Karen? Was she part of the plan for John's holiday? He gave a wry smile, poor old John, having to have the women organise his love life, or whatever they thought his love life should be. But why Karen? Perhaps he'd ring Jane now and not wait for the evening. He reached for the phone and dialled, but there was no reply. Angrily he slammed the phone down- why didn't the silly woman have an answer-phone?

Something Terry had said in conversation came back to him now. He had thumbed through the print outs Richard had asked for, and said, "Wouldn't you be better looking around estate agents first. Have somewhere to put the computer." At the time he'd been sharp, he didn't need smart-Alec Kennedy's advice on business, that was certain. Now, on his own and thinking logically again, he knew it was the sensible thing to do. He picked up the phone again and dialled the biggest estate agent in Oxford, the one his father had always used. By the time he replaced the receiver, he had set the ball rolling in his search for a home. There was still the unanswered question of who would care for him, but he'd talk to Jane about that tonight. He had had a brilliant idea. If he bought a large enough house, Jane and the children might move in with him and thus solve his problem. Financially, it might solve some of Jane's too. He was sure she could do the same job as these nurses, and there would be lots of space for the children. He might even get Jamie into his old school –

but that was going too fast and much too far ahead just now. It was a good plan though, and he was convinced it would work. Surely Jane would see all the benefits he could provide for her and her children. Yes, he felt rather pleased with this new idea.

Sitting in his car outside the hospital, Terry took out his mobile phone and pressed Jane's number. There was no answer, so he wrote a brief note, "Richard will pay! I'll try and call you tonight." He was about to sign it when he stopped and thought, then wrote, "love, Terry," and drove round to the little house that he was beginning to know so well. After he'd dropped the note through the letterbox he drove off to his meeting. It still seemed rather comic to him that John should have all these women organising his romance for him. But he liked John a lot, he deserved a bit of a break and if it worked, as Fran and Jane were sure it would, then what did it matter who organised it?

That evening Richard rang Jane again - this was his third attempt and he was growing impatient. "I've been trying to get you all day," he grumbled. "Have you been out?"

Jane smiled at the receiver; same old Richard, why don't you do what I want? Why aren't you there when I decide to call you? "Yes," she said. "The teachers were having a one day strike here, so Fran came over with her two and we all went out." She paused, thinking he might ask after Fran, but he didn't and she continued, "Did you call me for something special?"

"I've had a rather brilliant idea," he began. "I am starting to look for a home of my own, as everyone keeps suggesting, and it occurred to me that if I bought a big enough house, you and the children might move in with me. I'm quite sure you could do what these nurses here do for me, couldn't you? I'm having special equipment built in to help in that direction, anyway. And there'd be lots of space for the children, we'd have a big garden, too. It would save me from some dreadful nurse woman, and maybe help you financially, too. I've already asked the estate agent that Father always used. There should be some details for me in the morning's post. What do you think, Jane? It would make things easier all round, wouldn't it? And the children would benefit, too. It's something I could do for Andy."

Oh, no, Richard Treherne, she thought. You don't dangle the easy money, or the children's welfare as a carrot to get your own way. Or bring Andy into it, either. She was silent for a moment, thinking of the best way to approach this. "No," she said carefully. "No, Richard, I don't think that would work out at all well for any of us. I'm not a nurse, for a start. Children are rather noisy, disruptive creatures, you know. They would probably drive you mad within days. No, it wouldn't work, truly it wouldn't."

"But I don't need nursing as such, just a bit of physical help with dressing and so on. And I love the kids, you know that." It was fortunate, thought Jane, that he couldn't see her raised eyebrows. He had met the children occasionally for short periods – what did he know about loving them? And it needed either a professional help, or someone who loved him, to cope with dressing and undressing and showering him. She would have done all these things for Andy, of course, if it had all been different. But not Richard, oh no, that wasn't for her. "Surely you could take a bit of time to think it through. I'd choose a good area, with lots of space for the children and so on. Think about it, Jane. Don't turn it down without considering it carefully. I'd buy the house outright, no mortgages for you to worry about. You could sell or rent out that little house of yours as an investment for the children. It would make life much easier for you."

He would choose the house, and he would choose the area, where did she come into it except as a replacement nurse? "No,! she said firmly. "It just wouldn't work, especially after all those months in hospital alone. I'm sorry, Richard, I know you thought of the best for us, but I also know it wouldn't work out." And what of the future, she added silently. What if I wanted to marry again. What would you say then? She didn't want to leave the little house she and Andy had bought together, anyway. And she didn't want the children growing up with Richard's influence, either.

"Well," said Richard, "I am very disappointed. It seemed such a good, sound idea to me. Everybody would have benefited. I shall keep the house brochures; when you've had time to think it through properly and see the advantages, you might change your mind. Sleep on it. Now let's change the subject. Terry was here telling me about your scheme for John to go on holiday with his girl."

Jane was relieved to be let off the subject at last. "Kitty? Yes, I had the idea," feigning innocence of his offer, "but couldn't see how we could work it as a surprise. Then Terry and the two Brownlow men chipped in with an offer, and so did Fran. So it can be done. I'm sure it will work."

"I've told Terry that there is no need for outside financial help, I'll pay for this trip if that's what will get poor old John motivated."

"Oh, Richard, that's really great."

"Well, he is my brother, after all. Who's doing the booking and so on?"

"Fran and Kitty have all the brochures, so I guess Fran will do the booking. Shall I ask her to call you?" She knew he'd agree to that at once.

"That's a great idea. It would be nice to talk to her again, anyway. Yes, please Jane, if you'd pass the number on."

"I'll do that, and thanks, Richard."

"And you'll still give my idea some more thought?"

"OK. Yes, I'll do that, too." Trust Richard to think in terms of owing favours, she thought, but this one is a real non-starter. "Time I was getting things organised for the morning," she said. "It's been a long day. Goodnight, Richard." When the line was clear she quickly dialled Fran's number, but only got the answer-phone. She left her message, and Richard's number; she was sure Fran would do the rest.

She had only just replaced the receiver and turned away when the phone rang again. "Jane Lawson."

"Hi Jane. You sound exhausted."

She felt a small surge of comfort that someone had noticed and care. "Terry! You did it! You are an angel! I got your note, thanks."

"So what's up? Had a bad day?"

"Oh, a great day out with Fran and all the kids. But I've just had Richard on the phone with some scheme he's cooked up about buying a great big house and me and the kids going to live with him and look after him. As I knew he'd agreed to pay for the holiday, I had to be a bit careful how I said it, but had to squash this idea flat before he got too carried away. He still doesn't quite believe I mean it. Says I'd be financially better off."

"And would you?"

"Of course not. I'd be completely beholden to Richard Treherne. And that's not my way at all. Richard should know that. And I'm no nurse, anyway. Oh, sorry, Terry, getting carried away. How's things with you?"

"Oh, you know. Busy, but nothing exciting."

"When will we see you again?"

Terry paused, collecting his thoughts. But he knew he couldn't stay away from her for too long. "How about Friday, after lunch? Can I stay?"

"Oh, Terry, what a question, of course you can. The kids would be so disappointed if you didn't."

And would you, he wondered. Would you be disappointed. And yet, yes, he thought she would. "Only the kids?" he asked lightly, trying to make his voice teasing.

Jane heard the underlying pleading in his voice. She supposed it was different for people like Terry to know he was really wanted; she and Andy had loved each other from the age of fourteen, with never a doubt or misgiving. She smiled, making her voice reassuring, "No, not just the kids, me too, Terry."

"Great!" This time she heard pleasure in his voice. "see you Friday lunchtime then. What were you doing all day today, I called a couple of times?"

"You, too, I had a sort of reprimand from Richard for not being around when he called. She told him about the teachers' strike, and Fran bringing her children and all going out for the day. "It was great. Fran's two are the same age as Maria and Debbie, and Jamie put on the older brother act. It was enormous fun. Fran hopes we all might get together when you and Alan are both here in town at the same time. What do you think?"

"I'd like that, if you would. I'd better push off now though Jane, I've a couple of phone calls to make before it's too late in the evening for business."

She giggled, "Is it ever for tycoons like you? OK, Terry, I'll let you go and we'll see you Friday. Bye for now." She waited until she heard his receiver click into place, and then replaced the telephone in its cradle. It rang again immediately. Would she ever get the evening chores done? "Jane Lawson."

"Jane, it's Fran. I called Richard as you said, and it's all more or less fixed, I just have to make the booking tomorrow. Five days in Spain at half term. Kitty says if this doesn't work she'll enter a convent." Fran giggled at the thought. "Even shy John can't spend five days with my sister without getting somewhere, surely?"

"It'd be pretty difficult wouldn't it," Jane laughed. "That's great, Fran. We'd make a good team, wouldn't we?"

"You bet! What's the next assignment?" Ah, no, thought Jane, the next one's just for me. Aloud she said, "Oh, we'll think of something. But whatever, we'll stay in touch now. Thanks for letting me know the score."

"No problem. I'd better go before the kitchen is taken apart in the search for biscuits. Talk to you again soon, Jane. Bye," and with the click of the receiver Fran was gone.

Much later, as she tidied up before going to bed, the telephone rang again, and she snatched it up quickly, not wanting any of the children out of bed just now. "Jane Lawson," she said softly.

"Jane, it's Karen. Jenny gave me your message. I'm sorry it's late but I've just come off duty. Is there something wrong?"

"Karen! Oh, no, nothing's wrong, it's just great to hear from you. I didn't know when you were leaving the hospital, and I didn't want to lose touch. I didn't want you just drifting out of our lives. Are you working this weekend?"

"Only half of Saturday. Why? What's on?"

"Oh, nothing important. We just wondered if you'd like to come over for the day, or as much of the day as you could put up with my three." She hadn't asked Terry, but he wouldn't mind.

There was a slight pause at the other end of the line. "We?" Karen queried, and there was a cautious edge to her voice.

Jane heard that note of suspicion; oh, lord, she must tread carefully here. "Me and Terry, he's here for the weekend. And there's the kids of course. Oh, Karen, do come over for a little while at least. Come to lunch on Sunday. It would be so nice to meet up again."

Karen seemed to relax a little. "Yes, I'd like that. Lunch would be great. How are things with you and the children, anyway? And John, too, I miss seeing John." After a very slight pause she continued, "And Richard, have you seen Richard lately?""

"Oh, Richard," said Jane dismissively. "He dreamed up a ridiculous scheme for buying a big house and me and the kids moving in with him, and me acting as nurse housekeeper. I soon squashed that idea, I can assure you. But we'll tell you all about everything on Sunday. You must be really tired right now."

"A bit," the other woman admitted ruefully. "Maternity Wards are no easy option. Anyway, can I bring anything on Sunday? How about something really squidgy and exotic and messy for a dessert? The children would like that, wouldn't they?"

Jane laughed. "Not just the kids, me too. That'd be great, Karen. We'll see you on Sunday, then. Have you decided what you're going to do after you leave the hospital? Any plans?"

"Take a bit of time for myself first. Then I'll look around. But I'll tell you it all on Sunday, OK. It's been a long day. Goodnight, Jane, and thanks. Bye." And she ended the call. Jane sat for a moment, wondering, and then said aloud, "Oh, well, It could be one step forward."

Karen put down the receiver and went into her kitchen. If Jane was trying matchmaking, then she was in for a disappointment. When Richard had been immobile and inarticulate, she had felt something for him. But once Jane had got him motivated, he'd become a rather different person, and she knew it wasn't her kind of person at all. John was different. It was quite surprising just how different two brothers could be. She yawned, it really had been a long day.

On Sunday, when Karen's car drew up at Jane's house, all three children rushed to welcome her. "Help me unload the car," she said as she hugged them in turn, and handed Jamie a box. "You take that, Jamie, and carry it carefully, no tipping it up or we won't have any pudding today." She handed Debbie a box of fruity yoghurts and Maria a bag of apples. Jane smiled as she watched the little procession of children walking carefully into the kitchen followed by Karen. "It's good to see you again," she said, as she hugged her friend. "Coffee?"

"Oh, yes, please. Where's Terry?"

"He's just gone to put petrol in the car, he'll be back soon." She turned to the children who were all talking at once, bombarding Karen with questions; "Now, let Karen drink her coffee in peace. Off you go to the garden or somewhere. Go on, shoo!" They scampered away, pushing each other and giggling. Jane sat down at the table with her mug of coffee. "You didn't think of taking back your notice? Jenny told Terry that it was all so unnecessary."

"Well, yes, in a way it was. The major who was causing all the havoc got moved to a desk job that would keep him in one place and, hopefully, quiet. But even so, I felt it was time for a change, anyway."

"And nothing to do with Richard?"

Her friend didn't answer at once, but sipped her coffee thoughtfully. Finally she said, "Is that why you invited me, Jane? To find out how I felt for Richard?"

Jane laughed out loud. "No, honestly it isn't. I told you I wanted to stay in touch, and that's the truth. I'm also nosy, as well. But if you don't want us to talk about him, that's fine by me. OK?"

"OK. Sorry, Jane, but I knew you were all close and I wondered, well, you know. How's John?"

"Oh, John! He's fallen for someone but can't bring himself to talk to her. You know what he's like and how reserved he is. Luckily for him Kitty's made of sterner stuff, I think, and won't give up that easily. I haven't seen him for a couple of weeks, but Terry usually drops in on him when he's in Ledminster. Kitty's sister Fran and I were at school together."

Jane's bubbling enthusiasm and small talk made Karen relax at last. There really was no need to be on her guard with this family. "I gather from Jenny that Richard is turning his room into some kind of office, with stacks of paper everywhere."

Jane chuckled, "That's partly Terry's fault, Richard asked for information on computers and Terry printed out everything he could find. It will take Richard months to read through that lot. Still, it will keep him out of mischief."

"Computers? He can't have a computer in the hospital, surely he knows that?"

"That's what Terry told him. So he dreamed up this scheme I told you about for me to live with him and look after him. He got all the big house details from the estate agents, which just added to the pile." Then she became serious and spoke firmly, "but it's not on. I don't want to be his nurse and he'd soon get tired of my three running around. And I don't want to leave here, either, Andy and I chose this house together. OK, money's not flowing like water here, but things will ease when Maria's settled at school and I can get a job. Truly, I am fond of both the Treherne boys, but I know them well, too. I couldn't live with either of them! They'd both drive me mad in a few weeks!".

"No," said Karen thoughtfully, "I don't suppose Richard's the easiest of men to live with."

Jane saw what she read as a faraway look in her friend's eyes, and felt hopeful. "But I'm hoping that you'll be able to help me with a scheme," she said. Karen looked at her sharply. "Don't worry, it's not matchmaking, I promise you. But if I managed to find a house for Richard, a proper sized one and all that, will you view it with me to see if it is suitable for, well, for whatever aids and equipment he may need to live as independently as possible in the outside world?

You'd know what was possible and what wasn't. If I could do this, will you help me?"

"Oh, Jane, of course I will. But would he let you, or me?"

"I think, quite honestly, he'd be a bit relieved, though he'd probably grumble at me for organising him. And then he'd have to advertise for a nurse companion, and I think he might need some help there, too. He's so afraid he'll get one like someone called Brenda."

Karen burst into a peal of laughter. How pretty she was when she laughed. "Oh, Brenda! She has a heart of gold really, but I do see his point there."

Jane laughed with her. "You know, I think Richard is terrified of her. We won't be able to suggest anyone who looks remotely like her, you know, however well qualified she might be."

Just then, Terry appeared in the doorway. "Any coffee left for me? Oh, hi, Karen, you look as gorgeous as ever." He kissed her lightly on the cheek and sat down with them at the table. Truly, Karen thought, he must be the most good-looking man for miles around, and such style, too. No wonder Jenny fancied him. So why was Jane holding him off? Was she still in love with Andy after all this time? Or perhaps it was the other way round? Was it Terry who kept it all light hearted and no commitment? It could be, he could easily be the no commitments type. They were obviously on easy terms with each other but..... The children came running at the sound of Terry's voice, and any adult conversation was at an end for the time being.

"So what are you going to do now, Karen?" Terry asked some time later. They were in the sitting room, just the three adults. "Have you got a new job to go to?"

"No. I'm taking a bit of time for myself first, and then I'll look around. Luckily, I've never lived in the Nurses' Home, so there's no problem of moving out."

"Well, don't tell Jane you're not working, or she'll organise you into something. A real pocket organiser is Jane, every man should have one." He neatly fielded the cushion Jane hurled at him, and Karen laughed. "The secret is to keep moving. She can't organise a moving object."

"I'll remember that," Karen laughed. After a little while of such conversation, she stood up to go. "It's time I made a move," she said. "I've one or two jobs to do before work tomorrow. Oh, roll on Thursday."

"Is that when you leave?" Karen nodded at Jane's question. "Jenny will miss you."

"Maybe. Jenny loves nursing. She's not keen on the private wards, but you'd never know it, would you? She's a real professional."

"And so are you, surely?"

"No. I like nursing as much as any other job I've done. That's not the same thing, though. Anyway, till Thursday, its what I'm paid for, so I'll do it properly. Thanks for a lovely afternoon, and a lovely lunch. It was good seeing you all again."

"But you'll come again, we must stay in touch, Karen. I'll ring you after Thursday, anyway, to see how things are going. OK?"

"Yes, I'd like that. And now I really must go." She picked up her bag and turned to the door, calling goodbye to the children as she left. Jane sat back in her armchair, a half smile on her face.

"Jane. What are you thinking up now?" Terry dropped on to the sofa, and she got up and sat beside him.

"Nothing." She said innocently, "but I can tell you this much. I'm sure She's still cares for Richard. Goodness knows why."

Terry smiled - a gentle, thoughtful smile. "And you think you can hold the two threads together until you can join them up?"

She looked away from him then. "Something like that," she said, almost to herself.

CHAPTER TEN

That same afternoon Kitty and Fran had settled down quietly at the kitchen table with mugs of coffee and a plate of biscuits. Ray had taken the children to the park, and this was their first chance of a real chat together. Francesca smiled at her sister over the rim of her mug. "Listen, Kitty," she said, putting the mug down carefully, "you don't seem to be getting far with John, and Jane and I were wondering if you'd like a bit of help in that direction. We've had an idea."

Kitty was obviously troubled by her sister's suggestion. "What sort of idea? You know John, he'd be all mortified if you or Jane tackled him about it. What sort of idea is it, anyway?" She wasn't sure that she wanted anyone else organising her love life.

"Of course we wouldn't tackle him, Francesca said scornfully, "But what if you went on holiday together, away from all interruptions from John's pupils and all the folks you knew? Just the two of you in a different place. Couldn't it make him talk to you without worrying about others, just as the person you are?"

Kitty gave her sister a wry smile. "And how would we do that? Can you see him asking me? And could he afford it, he's much too much of a gentleman, for want of a better phrase, to let me pay for myself, even if I could. It's a great idea but a definite non-starter, Fran."

"Listen. Jane knew all that when she suggested it. But what if we said you'd won a competition for a holiday for two and wanted him to go with you? That would solve the problem of his pride. And then Jane roped Terry in, and he dropped the hint to Richard Treherne that we were all clubbing together to give you a few days to yourselves. It worked, just as Jane said it would, and he put on that "he's my brother and I'll pay" bit. So, what do you say now? Will you give it a go? He still may say no, of course."

Kitty was silent for a while, sipping her coffee and gazing into space. If she had John all to herself, well, she'd be stupid to turn it down. Then she said, "Well, what have I got to lose? But where will we go? It would have to be in the school holidays, I suppose."

Fran's face was wreathed in a huge smile as she searched in her bag and produced a brochure. "What about Spain? If the going got tough you could always call and see the relatives. Look, this one is five days, and it's in half term, I've checked." She handed the highly colourful pamphlet across the table. "After five days you'd surely know if you were wasting your time, wouldn't you?"

Kitty took the brochure, but already her face had lost it's doubtful look. "And Richard Treherne would really pay for us?" she asked a little incredulously. "Have you spoken to him yourself? Why should he do this for us?"

"I have, and he will. As for why, Richard always liked to make the big gesture, and in truth Kit, he owes John an awful lot. I'm not sure he'd admit it, but who cares? So you think you'll give it a try?"

Suddenly Kitty was full of excitement. "You bet."

"Will you ring John and ask him?"

Her sister thought for a moment and then shook her head. "No, I'll wait till I've got all the bookings and tickets and stuff. Just to be on the safe side. Now, what happens about the booking? Do I do that? How can I pay if it's Richard's money?"

"Don't worry, about it, Kit, it's all arranged. I shall make the booking for you and pay, and Richard will put the money back into our account. No problem. So that's settled. My goodness, Kitty, you must be nuts about this guy to go to all this trouble."

"I thought it was you and Jane who went to all the trouble," Kitty laughed. "Are you trying to get rid of me?" Then she became more serious. "I really am grateful, Fran, I couldn't think of anything to get John motivated my way. Will you thank Jane for me, too?" They finished their coffee, and talked together of family affairs for a while, until they heard the key in the lock, and Nicky and Natalie burst into the room, demanding attention. Fran quickly tucked the brochure back in her bag and Kitty squeezed her sister's hand before they abandoned their quiet moment together. "Thanks, Fran," she said softly. Fran smiled, blew her a kiss, and turned to her children.

Later that evening, in their home in Hallinford, the Camerons had just finished dinner. "Let's take our coffee through to the sitting room," Isobel suggested. Charles had come home late, and was looking very tired. It was time for him to relax for a while She began to put the cups and saucers on a tray.

"Not for me, Mother, thanks" Patricia said, standing up from the table. "Jonathan will be calling for me in a little while. There's a new club opened up just outside Ledminster, and I want to try it out." She smiled at them both, and left the dining room.

"Who's Jonathan?" Charles asked.

"One of the Farman boys I think. Go and settle down while I make the coffee." He nodded, rose wearily and left the dining room, too. Isobel filled the coffee pot, picked up the tray and followed her husband into the sitting room. This room overlooked the garden, but the light was already fading, and the trees and shrubs were casting deep shadows across the grass. Charles had put her favourite Rachmaninov cd on the player, and the room was filled with the beautiful sound of the piano. She poured his coffee, set it beside him and settled down in her chair, gazing dreamily out over the half-hidden garden. They heard the front door open and close, and the sound of a car moving out of the drive. Patricia had gone out for the evening; they could relax and enjoy the peace and the music.

When he had finished his coffee Charles heaved himself out of his chair. "I'd better put the car away before I get too comfortable," he said. "I won't be a moment, so stay where you are and listen to the rest of the cd." He left her, but was back in just a few seconds. "Izzy, the car's gone. It's been stolen. I'd better ring the police at once."

She stood up and crossed the room to him. "it couldn't have been taken while we were at dinner, Charles, or we'd have seen it, so they can't have got far. I have the number" She followed him into the hall, watching as he dialled the number and gave the duty sergeant the necessary information. But she was troubled; something wasn't quite right, and she couldn't bring her mind to focus on it. When they were back in the sitting room she tried hard to concentrate - what was it that was niggling her? But it was no good, she couldn't work it out.

Mick Carter swore under his breath as he drew the car onto the grass verge where it stuttered and came to a halt. He'd been hoping that the last of the petrol left in the tank would get him to the garage, but it hadn't worked out that way. He switched off the ignition and climbed out. Taking the empty can from the boot, he was just locking the doors when he heard the sound of an approaching car. The garage at the crossroads was only a quarter of a mile away, but he might just be able to get a lift there, if he was lucky. As the big, powerful car topped the rise, the headlights caught an animal in their long, straight beam – it looked like a large black dog, but he couldn't be sure. "Run for it, you stupid animal, don't just stand there," Mick muttered. "Get out of the way." He expected the car to slow down but instead it accelerated, heading straight at the dog. The animal suddenly came out of the panic-stricken trance the bright lights had caused and fled across to the safety of the far side of the road. But to Mick's astonishment, the driver of the car swerved across the road, tyres screaming, giving chase to the frightened creature. There came the terrible sounds of tearing metal, shattering glass, what sounded like wild, hysterical laughter and the sickening sound of an animal screaming in pain. Then silence. By now Mick's mobile phone was already in his hand, and he punched out the emergency numbers, giving his message as he ran across the road. He had to try to help before the petrol tank went up.

Patricia had seen the dog in the headlights. It would be fun to chase it. She had seen her father's car keys on the hall table, and knew he'd come in late and hadn't put the car away. It had been simple to invent a night out with the boring but rich Jonathan Farman. This would show them that she was not a child to be punished by them. how dare they forbid her to drive? They had taken away her car keys and locked up her car, just because she had frightened some silly stupid woman and her stupid kids on a crossing. Why did they have to walk so slowly, mothers and children, anyway? She wasn't some silly teenager, she was Patricia Cameron, she'd always done what she wanted and Daddy had always let her have her own way. No one now was going to stop Patricia Cameron when she wanted to do something important. She smiled happily; yes, she would be Patricia Cameron again, soon, her divorce from that boring Richard would soon be through and Daddy would see to it that she would be rich. Then she could do anything and no one could stop her. For a moment the dog left the beam of her headlights as it ran across the road, but she turned the car to pick him out again. She reached it on the grass verge, laughing wildly as it screamed and disappeared beneath the front wheels. Then came the terrible noise, and she remembered no more for a while. She knew nothing of the blood pouring down her face, the pain in her leg, the efforts of a strange man who was trying to release her seatbelt to get her out of the car, and the arrival of the police and ambulance. For a short while, her world was dark and silent.

"Can you tell me exactly what happened?" One of the policemen was talking quietly to Mick. He had already written down Mick's name and address and phone number. "You weren't in the car, too?" It seemed unlikely by the look of him, but you had to ask all the questions, get the facts right, for he was new on this beat.

Mick shook his head, pointing across the road to his own car, with the empty petrol can still standing on the bonnet. "Not me," he said, and there was a note of relief in his voice. "That woman must have been mad. She was driving like a maniac. No, I reckoned I had enough petrol to get me to the garage. I didn't. I was just about to start walking when she came haring over the rise like a bat out of hell." He shook his head in disbelief; "I dunno, these young people."

The policeman nodded, and then continued with his questions. "So what happened then?"

"There was a dog in the road. She caught it in the headlights, put her foot down, and chased it. She went after it right across the road and over the verge and well, here. I thought I heard her laughing and then I heard the dog crying, so it must be under the car now." They both bent to look. "Poor thing it must have been petrified." The paramedics had lifted the inert body into the ambulance, and as it began to pull away from the verge, he added, "Can I go now? It'll be late before I get home, and the wife will be worrying."

The second policeman had left their vehicle to join them. "The car belongs to Charles Cameron, the lawyer," he told them. "It's just been reported stolen." They all looked at one another in surprise. "There should be a tow truck along shortly, and then we can get back to the station." The medics say it's not a fatal case"

"Right. I'll start walking, if that's OK with you," said Mick. "I just want to get home." He'd had enough; it had been a long day and he was tired. It wasn't his problem any more. He turned to cross the road again.

"If you want to hang on, we'll give you a lift to the garage when the truck comes," one of the policemen offered.

But Mick shook his head; with a brusque "No, that's OK. Cheerio, then" he crossed the road, picked up the petrol can and began the walk to the garage.

After Charles had finished the call reporting the theft of his car he and Isobel returned to the sitting room. But Isobel found she couldn't settle again, something was still niggling away at the back of her mind. But what was it? After a while she put the empty cups on the tray, prepared to take it through to the kitchen. As she passed through the hall she saw the polished teak plate on the table in its usual place. They all put their car keys here as they entered the house. There was only one set of keys there now - hers. That was what had been different. She put down the tray and went quickly back to her husband. "Charles, did you leave your keys in the ignition?" she asked in surprise.

"Oh, Izzy, when have I ever done something so foolish? No, of course I didn't, I put them in the usual place. Why?"

"They are not there now. Come and see for yourself."

Together they stared at the plate with its one set of keys, and then at each other. "Have you left the kitchen door unlocked?" Charles asked accusingly. But Isobel was searching through the pages of the telephone directory and didn't answer. "What are you doing now?"

She had picked up the receiver and was dialling. He watched her without speaking again, but listened carefully as she talked. "Good evening, is that Mrs. Farman?? Isobel Cameron here. I wonder, was it Jonathan who just came to collect my daughter Patricia? Oh, I am sorry. Poor boy, I hope it clears up by the morning. No, there's nothing wrong, just curiosity, that's all. Yes, I know, we never stop, do we? I'm sorry to have bothered you.

Goodnight, then," and she gently put the receiver back on its cradle. "Jonathan Farman is in bed with some kind of food bug after an office lunch," she announced. "Charles, I am thinking perhaps Patricia….." but she was interrupted by the ringing of the telephone.

This time her husband snatched it up impatiently. "Charles Cameron."

"Hallinford police station here, Mr. Cameron. Your car has been found. A young lady was driving and has crashed it in Gypsy's Lane, not far from the garage at the junction. It will be towed there in due course."

"Thank you," said Charles. "Is the young lady injured? Do you know her identity? It now seems likely that my daughter may have borrowed the car without my knowledge."

"The young lady has been taken to Ledminster General, sir. I have no information of her identity or injuries as yet, but the hospital may be able to help you there."

"I see. I'll contact them at once. But if it should be that the driver is not my daughter, I trust you will pursue the matter further?"

"Of course, Mr. Cameron. Goodnight, sir," and the duty sergeant hung up. He wasn't interested in spoilt little darlings, and he didn't need the mighty Charles Cameron to teach him his job, either. What he did need was a cup of coffee right now.

Isobel already had her own directory open on the table. "Ledminster General?" she asked, and when her husband nodded, she began to dial the number. How calm she stays in emergencies, Charles thought as he watched her. Then she spoke into the receiver, "Casualty? Sorry, I mean A. & E. I am making enquiries about my daughter, Patricia Cameron, who may have been involved in a road accident and brought to you. Oh, I see. Yes, if you would, thank you." She looked across at Charles. "The reception desk has no information of Patricia; she's checking with A. & E. now." He nodded but said nothing, and she turned again to the telephone. "Yes, this is Isobel Cameron here. She has? Can you tell me the extent of her injuries? Yes, I understand, we'll come at once. Thank you for your help. Goodnight," and she hung up. "They cannot give too much information as yet, but Patricia is in no danger. I said we'll go at once. I'll get some overnight things from her room for her." She hesitated a moment, seeing the tired lines of his face; "Do you want to come with me? I can go alone if you'd rather."

"Oh, Izzy, of course I'll come with you. You go and get her things and I'll lock up the house. We'll be there in no time, and find out for ourselves." She smiled across at him, then went up the stairs to Patricia's bedroom.

The accident department at Ledminster General was busy. A group of young people, gathered around a wheelchair, were making a great deal of noise and confusion. A young nurse hurried past them, and another was trying to pacify a screaming child. But eventually Isobel made her enquiries and they were directed to a cubicle. Patricia lay quietly on a trolley, and a woman doctor was just putting instruments back on to a small trolley beside her. Isobel introduced herself at once and the doctor said, "Your daughter has been lightly sedated; there were glass splinters on her face and head. They had to be removed and she didn't want us to touch her hair. I'm afraid she became quite agitated." She smiled apologetically, "She also has a broken leg, and we'll set that and then admit her. But she's very lucky, really. It could have been much worse."

Isobel looked down at her daughter. The doctor had spread small gauze strips over parts of her face. "Will she be scarred, do you think?" she asked quietly.

"The cut on her hairline might leave a scar, I think, but probably not the others. She began to move the trolley. "If you'll excuse me," she said, "It looks as though we have a busy night ahead. Good evening," and she disappeared through the curtains.

Charles moved closer to his wife. "What do we do now?" he asked.

"Wait with her here. When she has had the leg set, we'll see her to the ward." She looked into his exhausted face. "Charles, why don't you go home? There is nothing whatever that you can do here but wait. It's impossible to know how long it will all take. You heard the doctor, they are in for a busy night. Go on, Charles, go home now." He wanted to argue, to stay with her for some kind of moral support, but she was right. There was nothing to be done. Isobel watched his face as the thoughts ran through his mind. "You'd better take a taxi, though," she added. "I may not be able to get one in the small hours."

"Oh, Izzy," he said and his voice was full of relief and remorse, "If you're sure."

"I'm sure," she said, and kissed his cheek. "Now, go home." Then she added, with a smile in her voice, "If you want to be useful you could put the dinner things in the dishwasher."

She had been teasing, but the light-hearted remark seemed to have motivated him. "Oh, yes, I'll do that, Izzy," he said. He pulled his mobile phone from his pocket, but she took it before he could dial.

"You mustn't use them in hospitals, Charles," she said quickly. "It interferes with the paging systems and things. There's a call box in the entrance hall." He looked at her in surprise, and she laughed. "I do a voluntary job here twice a week, Charles," she said gently. "Now, go and see if you can get a taxi, there may be a queue." He kissed her cheek, ducked out of the cubicle and strode away. Isobel sighed and sat down on a chair beside her daughter. It was going to be a long evening, or maybe even a long night.

In her home not too far away from the hospital and it's drama tonight, Kitty sat brooding over the day's events. She had been filled with wonder at Fran's suggested plan – she didn't even know Richard Treherne. Or Jane Lawson either, well not as a friend, anyway. But it seemed that Jane and John were friends from childhood, and Jane was really trying to help the shy, schoolmaster she had grown up with. Kitty had been sure that if it all came about she could make it work. But what if he refused to go? It would all be wasted. That would be dreadful. On impulse she picked up the phone and dialled John's number. "John, it's Kitty," she said when she heard the familiar voice, and tried to sound calm and ordinary.

"Kitty? Oh, hello Kitty. How are you?" Terry, who had been sitting opposite him now stood up, mouthed "coffee" and left the room quietly closing the door behind him.

Suddenly she felt depressed. It sounded as though he were talking to a colleague or a neighbour. Was this a mistake? But if she wanted him, she had to try. "John, listen. I entered a competition a few weeks ago for a holiday in Spain. The results should be out next week and I was wondering, if I won it, would you come with me?"

"Me? Wouldn't you rather have one of your girl-friends or your sister or someone?"

She rolled her eyes in mock despair but said calmly, "No, not really, I thought it might be more fun to go with someone like you. It's only for five days. I probably won't win anyway, I bet there were loads of entries, but if you didn't want to come with me, I might opt for the second prize instead, or something. Going on my own wouldn't be much fun."

He tried not to smile. She sounded just like a little girl being given a Christmas present. The chances of her winning were pretty long, so it wouldn't hurt him to say yes, and make her happy. He'd love to spend five days with her, anyway, if only he could stop being boring. "Well," he said, "if you're sure it's me you want to invite, then I'd love to have a holiday in Spain with you. If it's not in term time." He added hastily.

She sighed happily, forgetting for a moment that he could hear her. "Oh, that's great then. Let's both keep our fingers crossed. Wouldn't it be lovely if I won?"

This time he didn't hide the smile. "It would," he said. "Let's keep our fingers crossed. What sort of competition was it?" He didn't really care but wanted to keep her on the telephone.

Fran had already thought of this. "All about make up," she said quickly, knowing John would know nothing of such stuff. "You had to choose the ten most important beauty items for your holiday."

"Did you find that difficult?" He was floundering now, and thought perhaps he'd let her go, not knowing just what to say next.

She saved the situation for him. Poor John really wasn't a telephone chatterbox. "It's one of those things where everyone's ideas will be different, and you just have to hope the judges think the same way as you do. Anyway, I'd better go now and see what Dad wants. I'll be in touch, whether I win or not. Bye, John," and she hung up quickly. She was going to have to work hard in those five days, but she'd do it – just watch her! All he needed, she thought, was a bit of encouragement and backup. And she'd be there with it.

When John had replaced the receiver, Terry returned with two mugs of coffee. He set them down, and John reached for one immediately. "That was Kitty," he said.

"Oh, good," Terry grinned, "I was beginning to think you two had fallen out."

John coloured, and said gruffly, "Nothing of the sort. We're just friends."

"John?" Terry's voice was steady. "Don't you fancy her at all? She's a pretty little thing, to my mind, and intelligent with it."

John stared at the empty fireplace. "What's the use," he said at last. "I just don't know what to say to her. She needs someone lively and interesting, with lots of chat. Like you, really."

Terry kept his peace. The plan was OK, and when it was over, Kitty would know whether she was wasting her time. But somehow, Terry thought, even if it failed, she won't give up. So he changed the subject and talked about other things, and watched John relax a little. Time would tell.

CHAPTER ELEVEN

Patricia was sitting in bed, propped up with many pillows. It was a beautiful day, and the sunlight poured through the windows of her room. There were flowers and fruit on the bedside table, and all her favourite fashion magazines within reach. It had been over a week since she had crashed her father's car and ended up here, but of course, in a private room - and one of the best of them, too. Daddy hadn't been too angry with her, although her mother had been quite po-faced for a while. Well, she would, wouldn't she? But who cared what she thought? There was a nervous tap at the door, and after a moment a very young auxiliary came quietly into the room. This was her first day in her new job, and Sharon felt a little nervous in the private rooms; in the wards people had given her advice and whispered to her when she'd got things wrong. But in the private rooms they just looked or even ignored you. "May I take your tray now, Miss Cameron?" she said politely.

"In a moment. But before you do that, could you fetch my handbag? They've put it over there, and I need to comb my hair." The girl obeyed at once, put the bag down on the bed and moved to pick up the tray. Patricia opened the bag and took out her mirror. She had no idea that her mother had warned the nurses about her vanity and her possible reactions to her looks. She had warned them also of her violent temper.

They had listened carefully, and put the mirror out of reach, at least for the time being.

As the young girl turned with the finished tray, Patricia took her first look in her mirror, and screamed. The startled girl quickly put down the tray just as Patricia hurled the mirror at the opposite wall.

"Miss Cameron, what is it?" She reached to take Patricia's hand as her patient took up a magazine and hurled that, too, screaming again. As Sharon tried to hold her back, Patricia dug her long red fingernails into the flesh of the girl's arm and dragged them down leaving three red, raised lines. As Sharon cried out in pain Patricia laughed hysterically, grabbed the bowl of fruit and began to hurl it's contents against the wall, too.

Sharon was very frightened, but as Patricia's hands reached out with the fruit, she ducked behind her and pushed the emergency button over the bed. Then she stepped back in fear as Patricia turned on her again, trying to reach her other arm. Giving that attempt up, she began to fling flowers, make-up, books, anything, within her reach at the wall, all the time raving hysterically and screaming. Oh, God, Sharon wondered, what on earth is going on.

The door opened quickly and Sister entered. Patricia began to throw chocolates at her, but Sister took in the situation quickly. "What happened, Sharon?"

"She asked me to fetch her handbag. I did and before I could take the tray away, she started screaming and shouting. I don't know why, and when I tried to stop her," she trailed off and held out her arm.

By now Patricia had run out of all ammunition within her reach. The floor at the foot of the opposite wall was piled with broken crockery, flowers and fruit. "Stay with her, but out of reach," Sister instructed. "I'll be back in a moment. The girl moved to the window, warily watching her patient. Luckily she had a leg in plaster, so couldn't move out of the bed. Patricia contented herself with screaming insults first at Sharon, then at the hospital and her parents and for some reason Sharon couldn't understand, at "that bloody dog." She just hoped Sister really would be back quickly. What a way to start a new job. She looked down at her arm, Four red lines scored quite deeply, and hoped it wouldn't leave a scar. Scar? The patient's face was scarred. There must have been a mirror in her handbag - well, of course there would be. Oh, God, what had she done?

Patricia was still raving when Sister returned with a young doctor, although a lot of what she screamed was now quite unintelligible. But she didn't fight as the doctor gave her the injection which would make her quiet again. Sharon looked at the patient, and then at Sister. "It was my fault," she began. The doctor excused himself and left the room, anxious to get back to his duties. "She asked me for her handbag. I should have known there'd be a mirror in it. But I didn't know that she hadn't found out about the scars. I am very sorry."

But Sister made no real comment. "Go now and wash your arm carefully with antiseptic. Pull your sleeve down over the marks and then continue with clearing up the trays as you've been told. Then we shall have to clear up all this mess." She turned away to her patient, and Sharon picked up the tray and hurried from the room. Sister watched as Patricia grew quieter and more relaxed, and then she turned to go. In the doorway she met Mr. And Mrs. Cameron. She explained, as succinctly as possible, what had happened, but Isobel had taken in the scene for herself.

"Sister," she said quietly, "if you can send someone with the equipment, we'll clear this lot up. We came to sit with Patricia, so we'll stay a while and make ourselves useful." When the nurse began to protest a little, Isobel smiled. "Come on, Sister Margaret," she said, "you know that I've often cleared up much worse messes than this around the place."

Margaret Tennyson allowed herself a tiny smile, and a nod of acceptance. She would be off duty in an hour and would need to leave everything in order. "Thank you," she said, "I'll send Sharon with the equipment. It's her first day, and she's had quite a shock, too." She left the room and after a while Sharon knocked timidly on the door, and entered, carrying buckets and cloths and dustpan and brush. Isobel smiled at her. "Sister tells me it's your first day," and then, seeing the girl's arm, "Oh, Sharon, did my daughter do that? I am so sorry."

"It's OK, it doesn't hurt. I just didn't know about the mirror. Was Sister angry?"

"Not with you. Probably with herself for not telling you. Now, leave that with me, I'm sure there is plenty for you to do out there and this will have made you late. I'll see to this." When the girl hesitated, she added, "I work in the hospital two days a week, so I know what it's like. Off you go now.," and she began to clear up the broken flowers and glass on the floor. Sharon hesitated again, but only for a second, and then left her to it. Charles stood for a while in the middle of the room, watching his wife expertly clearing the mess, then went to sit beside his sleeping daughter. Still under sedation, she lay calm and still and he wondered just what they were going to face when she woke up.

Richard sat at the French windows of his room, moodily watching as the rain fell steadily outside. He saw Steve striding from one building to another, his dog at his side. He had been right, they had all been right, the do-gooders and the friends alike. It was time to get out of here, the room was beginning to give him claustrophobia. But the brochures from the estate agent his father had always used were not encouraging. The houses were big and expensive. Not that the cost mattered, but since Jane had refused his offer to buy one big enough for them all, there was no point in such a property for him alone. But not entirely alone. For the first time in his life, he was finding decision hard to take - how he needed someone to talk to. How he wished that Jane would visit without the children to distract her, so that he could discuss this with her seriously. He didn't want to speak to John of these thoughts, though. He had asked Jenny for news of karen, but Karen had gone, and Jenny seemed reluctant to discuss her. Who, then, could he talk to? Not Terry, that was for sure. Terry just made him envious, he had so much going for him. But who else was there? It was all very depressing.

He must have fallen asleep in his chair, for he was startled into wakefulness by the ringing of the telephone. Sighing, he reached for the receiver; "Treherne," he muttered, sleepily.

"Oh, Richard, did I wake you?" Jane's voice wasn't so much concerned as surprised. "I'm sorry, but I have some really interesting news for you." Without waiting for his reply she went on. "Do you remember the bungalows at the very end of our road? It was just a patch of scrub when we moved here, but it was cleared and bungalows built there. Do you know where I mean?"

He'd never taken much interest in the place. He remembered being surprised when Jane and Andy had bought such a small house, and in such a quiet neighbourhood, too. "Yes, I think so," he lied. "Why?"

"One of the bungalows is up for sale. The notice board went up this morning. The old lady has gone into a home, poor thing. I wondered if you'd be interested, that's all. It's a bungalow, no stairs and all that."

"How big is it? How many bedrooms?" It might be a small place in a quiet area, but being in the same street as Jane might have its advantages. "Do you know who is selling it?"

"That's another thing. Do you remember Malcolm Taylor? Used to play rugby. A year ahead of you, I think."

"Yes, of course," he lied again. Then a memory came to him. "Oh, his father is an estate agent. Is he handling the sale of this bungalow?"

"His father retired some years ago, and Malcolm runs the business now. Would you like me to take a quick look around it, and tell you what I think, or will you get all the blurb first from the agent? I've got his phone number here."

"Both," said Richard, now wide awake and speaking decisively. "If you can look around and I contact Malcolm for the details, we can then talk together about it, and soon. I'm beginning to need to stretch and move about a bit."

Fortunately for Richard, he couldn't see the look on Jane's face, or hear her mutter under her breath "and not before time, either." Then she said aloud, "Fine, we'll do just that," and gave him Malcolm Taylor's telephone number. "I'll be in touch again, Richard. Bye for now," and when he had acknowledged she hung up quickly. Mr. Treherne was feeling a little sorry for himself, and she wasn't going to sympathise with him. Instead, she picked up the phone again, and dialled another number. "Oh, blast," she said as the answering machine gave its message. "Karen, this is Jane. I think I've found a place that Richard might like. Will you come and look with me and give me your professional opinion? I don't know just how much space his special needs equipment will take up. Talk to you later, perhaps?" She thought for a moment, pressed the button to disconnect and then dialled another number. "Is that Malcolm Taylor's office? Oh, hello Malcolm, Jane Lawson here. I wonder if I could look over the bungalow at the end of our road, Stephens Lane, just to see if it's suitable for a friend of mine? Yes, that's right, has he contacted you already? That's great. Can I pick the keys up, or will you need to come with me? Thanks, Malcolm, I'll do just that. See you soon. Bye." But she thought again for a moment, wondering if she should tell Richard, then replaced the receiver in its cradle. That was as much as she could do for the moment. The children would be in soon anyway.

—∞—

That evening Karen rang back. "Sorry I was out all day and only just picked up your message," she explained. "Tell me all about this place you've found. Does Richard know about it?"

Jane explained about the bungalow, and that Richard would have all the details first thing tomorrow, so hadn't seen it yet. The place had only come onto the market today. "I can go and view it for him," she said, "but I need some expert advice as to how much space any equipment might need. Like the bathroom, for instance. Could you manage to come with me and see what you think?"

Karen didn't seem very enthusiastic, Jane thought, but agreed to meet up next day and have a quick look around the place. "I might just be a bit late," she added. "I have to go and see someone first thing tomorrow. But I'll be there, don't worry."

"Are you working, Karen?" Jane asked. "Is it awkward for you?"

"No, it's OK. It's a job interview but I'll tell you more if I get it. See you tomorrow, Jane," and saying a quick goodbye, Karen hung up. Jane sat for a moment, thinking over the call. Now what was that all about? Karen hadn't been unfriendly, but, well, something wasn't right. She'd find out tomorrow.

Walking to the bungalow next morning, she was surprised to see a car parked outside. It wasn't Karen's. Malcolm Taylor, smiling broadly, stood in the open doorway of the house. "Good morning, Jane," he greeted her. "Richard will be joining us in a minute, he's arranged some kind of special transport from a local charity. Come on in and see what you think while we're waiting. It's a nice little place, and in good order, too." And she followed him into the house.

"Needs a few windows opening," she grinned, wrinkling her nose. "But this room is much bigger than my sitting room. Can I look around?"

"Be my guest, I'll hang around in case Richard needs help. There's only one front step, will he manage?"

Jane had watched Richard at the hospital. "Oh, yes, he'll be OK. Don't, for goodness sake, fuss round him, he hates it. If he wants to live on his own, he may as well start now." He gave her a questioning look, but said nothing and she left him and wandered into the kitchen. He watched her for a moment, wondering if being a widow had made her hard, or whether she might have blamed Richard for it. But she was obviously trying to help him, so it must be OK. It wasn't long before they both heard a commotion at the front of the house, and knew Richard had arrived, too. Jane went back into the sitting room to wait for the two men.

"Hello Jane," said Richard with a smile, manoeuvring his way towards her, "so this is where you think I should spend my days, is it?"

For some reason his words made her angry, but she said simply, "I thought it was worth a look. You haven't got very far with your search yet, have you? Do you notice that this room is much bigger than my sitting room at home."

Malcolm was doing his estate agent best, pointing out several features of the room and giving dimensions when a voice called from the front door, "Jane, are you there?" and seconds later Karen appeared in the doorway. On seeing Richard and Jane together a look of anger flashed across her face, replaced almost immediately by her cool, professional half-smile. So that was what it was about really, Jane trying her best at matchmaking. Too bad she wasn't interested any more. "Hi, Jane. Richard." She paused and Malcolm quickly stepped forward, his hand outstretched.

"Malcolm Taylor," he said, smiling down at her,. "estate agent."

This time Karen's smile was warm and friendly. "Karen Anderson. Glad to meet you, Malcolm." She had allowed him to hold her hand for a fraction longer than introductions demanded. She would let Richard Trehern know that some men knew how to treat a woman. She half-turned to Jane and added, "I don't have a lot of time. Can we look to see what's needed first?" Turning back to Malcolm and smiling up at him, she explained, "I'm a nurse, and evidently my opinion as to whether Mr. Treherne's needs would fit in here counts with Jane."

God, Jane thought, Karen really is having a go and rubbing it in. But they all moved together and toured the bungalow, with Karen approving and pointing out what might be needed all the way. Jane noticed, and wondered if Richard had, that Malcolm stayed as close to Karen as he reasonably could. When they were once again back in the sitting room Karen turned to Richard. "From a professional point of view, this place would suit you well. So now the rest is up to you, your choice. But it's a nice place, though." She turned as if to leave, but then stopped; "Have you found anyone as a live in house-keeper yet?"

Richard's sombre face lightened a little; was she inter-ested, after all? It would be so good to have someone he knew and trusted around him. "No," he said, "not yet. I only heard about this place yesterday, and finding a house seemed to be the first priority. Why?" He looked at her hopefully.

"I think I know just the person. Her name is Mollie Hardaker. She's a nurse, but prefers live-in jobs now that she has no family living with her. You've met her nephew, Steve, the physiotherapist. Would you like me to ask her to ring you?"

Richard looked doubtful. Perhaps, Jane thought, events were moving too fast for him. "Well," he said, after a pause, "perhaps you would give me her number. It might be a while before everything is sorted." Then he added, rather hopefully, "Are you working now, Karen?"

She was already writing something on a pad taken from her bag. She handed the paper to him. "I start my new job the day after tomorrow, that's why I'm a bit pushed for time. Here's Mollie's number, but try and contact her soon as her current job is almost over. Now, I must be going there's such a lot to do before I go away." Seeing Jane's questioning look, she added "I'll tell you all about it this evening, OK?"

Malcolm stepped forward. "I'll see you to your car." He fell into step beside her, and together they left the house, still talking easily together.

Suddenly Jane felt really sorry for Richard. The one thing he hated was people standing around while he sat, but in an empty house, there was no option. And Karen had made it clear that he'd upset her. And Malcolm had made the best of it, too. "What do you think, Richard?" she asked. "Is the house big enough for you? Certainly it needs decorating, but then, if you take it, you've got building work to do, too. Tell me what you think."

He looked about him, as if seeing it for the first time. "Oh, Jane, I don't know. I feel a bit..." but whatever it was he felt, it had to wait. Malcolm had returned, and was probably hoping for a decision.

"So," he said. "What do you think, Richard?"

"It seems fairly suitable at first look. But can I think it over and discuss it with Jane here, and probably my brother too, and let you know?"

"Of course. It's a big decision. Any queries, though?"

"No, I don't think so," But as he spoke there came a sound of a horn from outside. "I guess that's my transport," he said. "I'll ring you with a decision soon, Malcolm," and he began to manoeuvre his chair towards the door. Malcolm moved as if to help, but Jane took his arm and held it. Together they followed Richard and watched as a ramp was lowered and he made his way into the waiting van.

"Bye, Richard," Jane called after him. "Ring me this evening, but make it later after the kids are in bed, then we can talk it all through."

"I'll do that. Bye, Jane. Bye Malcolm, and thanks for your help. I'll be in touch," he said as the doors of the van closed behind him.

Terry was sitting in his car, wondering what to do with his afternoon. The appointment he was here to keep had just been rescheduled for next week. Perhaps he could follow up the number that a friend had given him for a possible lecture. He reached for his mobile phone, but as he picked it up it began to ring. Jane's number flickered on the screen. He hadn't seen her for a couple of weeks; last weekend he'd been tied up with a business school. "Terry Kennedy," he said as he sat back in his seat. There was a hoarse, whispering voice at the other end of the line. "Sorry," he said, "I can't quite hear you. Who is it speaking?"

The voice came a little louder. "I can't talk loud, Terry, I'm in the loo 'cos I don't want Mrs. Porter to hear me. Please, Terry, can you come?"

Terry knew the voice at once. "Jamie," he said, "What's up?"

"Can you come, Terry? Mum's at the hospital and

Mrs. Porter is looking after us, but she's got to go to work. Oh, Terry, can you come?" The voice had begun to tremble a little.

"Course I can, and I'm not very far away, either. I'll be about ten minutes. Can you hold on till then?"

The relief in the young boy's voice was unmistakeable. "Oh, thanks, Terry." Then after a little pause he added, "Could you pretend you'd just come to see us. That I didn't ask you?"

"Of course I can. Now, go back to the others and I'll get moving. See you soon," and he clicked his telephone off and started the engine. It had been better to wait and see what was wrong when he got there. He had no idea who Mrs. porter was, and was concerned that Jane was at the hospital but knew Jamie wasn't a kid to make a fuss without reason. And he felt a little warm glow that Jamie had thought to ring him; that made him feel good. Luckily the traffic hadn't yet started to build up for the usual Friday afternoon rush to get away. He'd be there in no time.

When he rang the bell a few minutes later, a small grey-haired lady opened the door just wide enough to look out. "Yes," she said, "who is it?" But the children were behind her, and Debbie cried out to him.

"Terry, oh it's Terry." She pushed past the woman, whom he took to be Mrs. Porter, and threw herself into his arms. "Terry, Maria's ill. Mummy's at the hospital. Oh, Terry," and she turned her face into his sweater and began to cry.

"Easy now, Debs," he soothed. "It'll be OK, you'll see." He looked to the woman. "I'm Terry Kennedy. I was coming for the weekend." By now Jamie had joined them too, and explained to Mrs. Porter that

Terry was a friend of Mum and Dads. She looked relieved, and opened the door wide to let them all back in again.

"I haven't quite known what to do, Mr. Kennedy," she said as she led the way to the kitchen. "I have to go to work soon, and Mrs. Lawson is still at the hospital."

Terry smiled down at her. "If you will take the children's recognition as my reference," he said, "I'll be happy to take over now, I'm here till Sunday night. Well, that was the invitation, I'm sure Jane would understand that you have to work, too."

She hesitated only momentarily. "Thank you," she said. "We are already very short staffed at the hospital, and it did worry me that I might not be able to go. I can call and see Mrs. Lawson and Maria on my way in, so that's fine. Will you be OK getting their tea, and so on?"

By now Debbie had dried her tears and was smiling again. "anyone can make beans on toast," she said with a grin, "even Terry." She ducked away as he pretended to tap her arm. But the woman had already began to put on her coat and gather her belongings. "Will you tell my Mum not to worry, Terry's here."

When Mrs. Porter had gone Terry made a pot of tea, Jamie found some biscuits and they settled around the kitchen table. "Now," he said, "tell me what has happened." Between them they explained that Maria had been ill at school, the headmistress had sent for an ambulance, and Mum had gone there to be with her. She'd asked Mrs. Porter to keep an eye on them, but she had grumbled a lot because she thought she wouldn't get to work. Jamie had said nothing about the phone call, so Terry guesses he hadn't told Debbie, either. "Right,"

He said after a while, "what is there to do? Home-work?"

"Terry, it's Friday," Debbie said patiently. "We have all weekend to do that. Can I watch television now?"

The rest of the afternoon passed quite uneventfully, then he made their supper and finally tucked them both into bed. As he was leaving Jamie's room the boy said, rather gruffly, "Thanks for coming Terry."

"No problem. I would have come tomorrow for a while, anyway. Now go to sleep, we'll see how things are in the morning, eh?" and he switched off the light but left the door ajar, as he had seen Jane do. She had left a news-paper on the sofa, so he settled down to read, wondering if she would contact him tonight. Some time later the phone rang and he picked it up quickly. "Hello," he said.

Richard sounded a little put out. "Oh, hello Terry. Is Jane there?" Terry explained briefly what had happened. "Oh," said Richard, "is it some childhood thing? Will Jane be home soon?"

"I have no idea." Terry was trying to keep his voice level. "It does sound rather more serious than an ordi-nary childhood thing."

"So who is looking after the other two?"

"I am. I guess Jane will stay there with her for as long as she's needed. Is there anything I can help with?"

"No." Richard's voice was flat now. "We looked at a property together today and I wanted to talk to her about it. If she does come back tonight, tell her she can ring me, I don't sleep much. OK?"

Arrogant, selfish sod, Terry thought savagely, but aloud he said, "I wouldn't wait up for her if I were you. Goodnight, Richard," and put the phone down without waiting for a reply.

CHAPTER TWELVE

It was Saturday morning, and John stood in his bedroom regarding the clothes he had just selected for his holiday. But he'd really have to go into town and buy some new shorts; these were fine for school trips, but he needed to look a bit smarter if he was out with Kitty. Kitty. Why had he agreed to go with her? What would he find to say? It was always difficult, even when he took her to a concert, or the cinema, he was always conscious that it was Kitty doing all the talking while he just felt dull and inadequate.

When she'd first told him of the competition it had been so easy to say yes, he'd love to go with her. Well, it was true to a point, anyway, he did want to be with her. But he hadn't believed in her winning, especially when she'd told him the competition was all about makeup and such things; she hardly used any. Then, some time later, a very excited Kitty had telephoned again. "Oh, John, guess what? I've won the holiday! Isn't it marvellous? You will come with me, won't you, you haven't changed your mind?"

He had stared at his reflection in the mirror above the little telephone table. A startled, worried-looking face reflected back at him. He must try to match her enthusiasm. "Hey, that's great, and I haven't changed my mind. Tell me all about it now." He couldn't disappoint her. But he couldn't help feeling that she'd end up disappointed with him, if not the whole holiday, when it was all over. Now he sighed, put the offending shorts back into the drawer, left the packing for the moment and went into the kitchen for coffee. Perhaps he'd buy a new shirt and some different aftershave while he was in town, too. Of course he wanted to go; of course he wanted to be with Kitty, and not have to meet his pupils each time he went out with her, but, well, he just wasn't any good at talking to women. Not even Kitty, and she was someone special. He was committed now though - sink or swim.

Jane hadn't come home or phoned by Saturday morning, so as soon as the children had finished breakfast, Terry began to organise the day. "First of all," he told them, "I need your help. Debs, we must sort out some clean things for your Mum, and Jamie can find Maria's favourite storybooks, and maybe a teddy bear, or something. Then we'll all go to the hospital and leave the stuff there for your Mum. Then I'll ask her if it's OK to take you to my house while I pick up some stuff for me, too. That's if you want to come with me, of course." He looked at them for an answer and they both smiled and nodded. "Then I think we'd better go to the supermarket, there's no more juice or milk and we can get a few other things, too. How's that for a plan?"

The children seemed happier to have something to do organised for them. Upstairs in Jane's room Terry found a small weekend case on top of the wardrobe, and told Debbie to look in the drawers for clean underwear, tights and a sweater for her Mother. These were put into the case, and Jamie came and added two books and a furry animal of uncertain shape. "What is it?" Terry laughed, as they tucked these items into the case.

"Maria calls it Gonkie," Debbie explained. "She only ever has Gonkie in bed with her at night. He's awful, isn't he?"

They all left Jane's room together, and went downstairs. "We'll stop off at the paper shop," Terry said. "Anyone know what sort of magazine Mum reads?"

"Mrs. Thomas will," Jamie said practically. "Can we buy her some chocolate, too? She only likes the dark coloured sort."

They left the house and as the children climbed into the car, Terry thought he heard the telephone ringing. Should he go back, it might be Jane. But before he could open the front door, it had stopped. Somebody impatient, he thought. Not Jane. The children were arguing over who should sit in the front seat with Terry. "Right," he said. "Jamie on the way there, Debs on the way back. OK?" To his surprise they simply climbed into the car as he had said. When they'd bought the chocolate and magazine, They set off for the hospital. In the entrance hall they met Mrs. Porter, just coming off duty and looking rather tired. "Now," she said, "they won't let visitors in at this hour of the morning. And probably not the children, anyway."

"Do you think you could get this case to Mrs. Lawson for us, then," Terry asked, "or could you tell us where to take it? It's only some things for her. I really wanted to speak to her, if I could."

The woman took the case and asked them to wait where they were. Jamie and Debbie had begun to look worried again. "Hospitals have to have rules," Terry explained. "You can't have people wandering in and out all the time, when would they get the work done and the beds made? That's sensible, isn't it?"

"We haven't made our beds yet," Debbie, giggled.

"Then I think I had better make rules, too," Terry laughed. As long as the children were distracted, the worried looks vanished. "Oh, look, Mrs. Porter is coming back."

"Mrs. Lawson was so relieved to get the clothes and things. She is going to ring you on your mobile phone when she has a chance. But she can't come to speak to you just now. Is that OK?"

It would have to be. Terry thanked her for her help and she went off along the corridor. "Come on, then," he said, shepherding the children out into the car park. "We'd better go buy some food, I think. Now I really do need your help, don't I?" He thought he was probably going to be taken for a ride here, but it didn't matter. Keep them occupied, that's the answer.

It was about an hour later that Terry's mobile phone rang. "Oh, Terry, that was really good of you," Jane began. "But will you hold on at home for a while longer? Mrs. Porter seems to think that you had come for the weekend. Can you really stay that long?"

"I'll stay as long as it takes," he reassured her. "But I wanted to ask you if it's OK to take the children down to my place this afternoon. I think I can arrange for my secretary to be there, you know, a sort of chaperone, but I do need to pick up some gear and a few papers and so on. Would that be OK?"

"Of course it would, they'd love it. And I'm not bothered about your secretary being there, though if it makes you more comfortable, go ahead. I'll ring you if and when there's any news, but I must go back now. Bye' Terry," and she rang off.

As he returned the phone to his pocket Terry felt rather surprised that Jane hadn't wanted to say hello to the kids. Perhaps she felt it would upset them. She hadn't said anything about Maria, either. Again, perhaps she had a good reason. He'd already decided for himself not to mention the little girl's illness to John; they were off to Spain tomorrow and he felt Kitty deserved a holiday without any extra agitation. She had put such an effort in to getting John to go with her, she must really care for him and he hoped it worked out for them. John needed someone to care. But Terry would never understand John's shyness with women, not as long as he lived.

When they reached the barn conversion later, the children were delighted and set about exploring. Mrs. Paget was in the kitchen wearing a big white apron, which was a surprise to Terry. On the table lay a baking tray of goodies. "What's that?" asked Debbie, always interested in food.

"Gingerbread men," said Mrs. Paget., "Would you like one?" While the children were occupied she said, "Terry, I'm glad you called me. I have a bit of news for you. I've decided to go to Brussels to be with my daughter. You know her husband's been posted there, and she gets a bit lonely, I think. So I need to give you notice. I've put it on your desk, but I didn't know when you'd be in, so it's good that you came today."

Terry groaned. "This place will fall apart without you. When do you want to go?"

"About a month should do, it will take some sorting out at home as well as here. Do you want me to draft an advert for the paper? I could do the interviews if you wanted me to." She handed Debbie another cake and said, "Just one more, that's all, or you'll be poorly in Terry's car. You can take the rest home with you." Turning back to Terry she repeated her question; "Do you want me draft the advert?"

"No, it can wait a few days. Might be good time to have a rethink, anyway. This place is empty too often, time I sorted out what's best for the business. And for my bank balance," he added, with a grin "I'll just pick up the papers on that Briscoll account. They rescheduled for Tuesday at half an hour's notice, would you believe? And I need a few clean things, and then I'll take these two back home. Thanks for your help, Mrs. Paget. It's much appreciated."

She gave him an odd look. "I hope Mrs. Lawson is as appreciative as you," she said, but there was no smile with her words. Terry raised an enquiring eyebrow, but she shook her head. Now, he thought, what was that all about?

Jane rang late that evening, after the children were in bed. "There's no change," she said bleakly. "I'll stay on here if you can manage, something might happen."

"You do that," he said, "we're managing fine." Again he was struck that she didn't ask after the children, but let it go. Worry took different people in different ways. "Is there anything you need?"

"No," she answered flatly. "Look, I've got to go. I'll try and ring tomorrow," and the line went dead. He sat for a while, brooding on the change in Jane. But there was nothing he could do about it now. Now his concern should be what he was going to do about the business, and he didn't know the answer to that, either, not right at this minute. And then the telephone rang again.

"Hello," Terry said quickly. It was how Jane always answered her phone, no names, no numbers, no help to the phone hoaxers.

"Oh, Terry, are you still there? Where's Jane?" Richard's voice sounded surprised.

"She's still at the hospital, has been there since Friday afternoon. Maria isn't responding to treatment, and Jane won't leave her for a moment."

"Oh. I didn't realise the child was that ill. So you are still looking after the other two?"

"That's right. Is there any way I can help, or was it just a chat you wanted with Jane?" Terry thought he knew the answer to his own question, but waited to hear what Richard had to say.

"No, not really. Will you tell her I called when you next ring her? Better still, can you give me a number where I can reach her?"

"No, sorry. We can't contact her. She slips out occasionally but she isn't supposed to use the hospital phones and there's no call box near. I'll tell her you were asking after Maria when she rings next time." He heard Richard's muttered thanks, and then hung up. Richard Trehern was the most self-absorbed person he knew.

Sunday morning was bright and sunny and the children seemed to be in good humour. When they had had breakfast and tidied the house up, Terry offered to take them to the common. It was a good move, they quickly shrugged themselves into coats, found a football and were soon on their way. It wasn't long before both children met friends, and Terry was left to his thoughts for a while. He'd always thought of the barn conversion as being useful for holding seminars and so on. But the last two occasions, while being good publicity, had been a loss, financially. His accountant had suggested using a slot at other seminars, rather than run the whole thing himself. Well, Mrs. Paget had done most of the organising, anyway, and now she was leaving. Perhaps this was his catalyst for moving on.

He checked his watch and realised with a smile that other men, probably fathers or uncles, were all doing the same from time to time. Sunday morning on the common, Dads giving Mum a break he thought. Did Andy do this? Twice today he had caught himself thinking of Andy - perhaps it was because he was doing just what Andy would have done in the circumstances. He became aware of the man who had stopped beside him. "Sorry," Terry apologised, "I was miles away."

"Your boy," the man repeated. "Very clever with his feet. Make a great footballer one day."

Terry smiled, watching Jamie running towards them, dribbling the ball all the way. The man had already moved on, calling to a little girl as he went.

After a while both children came back to him. "I'm starving," said Debbie. "Can we go and have something to eat, and then come back?"

"We'll go and have lunch," Terry promised. "But I'm not sure about coming back, though. Just look at those black clouds." They raced ahead of him to the car all worries forgotten, their faces rosy from fresh air and exercise. Could this sort of life ever be his?

By the time they had eaten lunch and tidied up afterwards it was raining steadily, and the children settled down to a board game which seemed to involve a great deal of arguing. Terry fetched his laptop and spent a little time reading the Brit-Col files again, making quite sure he knew what he was talking about. True, the appointment was not until Tuesday, but he thought he'd snatch this quiet time to sort it out. With these two to look after, who knew when the next quiet time might be.

They were all in the kitchen, making tea, when they heard the front door open and close. "Mum!" said Jamie, and the children rushed into the hall to meet her. But she pushed past them, walked into the sitting room and flung herself into the armchair. The children stood in the doorway, staring at her. Her hair was tousled and uncombed, her eyes were red-rimmed, with great dark shadows beneath them, and her face was blotchy but pale. She'd obviously slept in her clothes, too. No wonder the children were worried. She stared, hollow-eyed at Terry. "She's dead," she said flatly.

"Oh, Jane," Terry began, moving to kneel beside her chair and putting a hand on her arm. But he got no further. She pushed him off roughly. "She's dead," she repeated. Debbie began to cry. "Oh, for God's sake shut her up," Jane said, and turned her face away from him.

"Jamie, take Debs into the kitchen, will you? She hasn't finished her tea yet. Go on, both of you," and Terry shepherded them towards the kitchen door. "We'll make some fresh tea for Mum in a minute."

"Tea" said Jane. "Who wants tea? Maria is dead, do you hear me? Dead. Stop going on about tea."

"Jane," Terry said carefully, "they are only children. Don't hurt them."

"They are not your children, are they? Do you think you have just stepped into Andy's place, just because you looked after them in an emergency? Well, you didn't. They are my children, mine. You can go home now, if you like."

"No," shouted Jamie from the kitchen door. "No, Terry, don't go." Behind him Debbie was crying noisily. "Mum, you can't make him go away."

"What have you been saying to them? You've alien-
ated my kids while I've been caring for Maria. How could
you do that to me, Terry? Just go away and leave us alone
so that I can undo whatever it is you've done. Go on, go.
This is my house, after all. I decide what goes on here."
This was a Jane he did not know. What should he do?
Suddenly remembering the incident with the chocolates,
how she'd hurled them out of the window after him, he
quickly picked his laptop from the table. Debbie took this
as a sign that he was leaving, and began to cry even
louder. "Debbie, stop that row at once," Jane's voice was
harsh. "We don't need anyone else here, just the three of
us, OK? Goodbye Terry. Thanks for the help."

There seemed to be nothing more he could do or say.
Arguing only seemed to make her more angry with the
children. He was quite sure she wouldn't hurt them, and
they were sensible kids. He crossed the room to them,
knelt in front of Debbie and said, "Now dry your eyes,
and try to help Mummy, because she's very tired. I have
to go now, but I'll come back soon. Bye, Debs, Bye
Jamie," and he hugged them both and then made for the
door. "Bye, Jane, you know where to find me if you need
me," but she made no answer, and carrying just his
laptop, the Briscoll file and his jacket, he left the house.
He wondered if he should tell anybody what had
happened, but who? Not the social people that was for
sure. With a really heavy heart he put his things on the
passenger seat, started the car, and headed for home.

Kitty had chatted happily on the plane journey; she
had already told him how she loved travelling, and her
enjoyment was almost infectious. Almost. From time to
time he glanced sideways at her, when he thought she
was engrossed in something else, and wondered why she

should choose a dull person like him. It seemed too good to be true. He was really fond of Kitty – perhaps he even loved her, but that was an emotion he was afraid to explore. Surely he was bound to be hurt in the end, she was soon going to find him dull company.

They had collected the key of the apartment from the reception hall, and now Kitty stood expectantly, waiting for John to open the door and lift their luggage inside. It will work, she promised herself. I shall make it work, make him believe that he's the man I want to be with. How can a person who teaches all those teenage boys that we keep meeting be so unsure of himself with me? But I'll change that - just watch me. Together they wandered through the apartment; a sunny lounge with doors leading to a tiny patio with tubs of flowers at one side, a minute kitchen which made Kitty laugh. "No one was ever meant to cook here," she said.

"No one's going to cook here," John told her solemnly. "We're on holiday."

They continued their exploration. Two small bedrooms and a very large bathroom. But her high spirits faltered a little as he asked, "Which bedroom would you like?"

Don't rush him, she thought, you have five days. She did a bit of quick thinking; he would never come to her, she was sure of that, so sooner or later she must go to him. "You take the double one," she said. "I can use one of these twin beds to spread my clothes about."

He looked a bit dubious; "Are you sure you wouldn't like the double room, it has a better view."

"Goodness, John, I shan't spend enough time in there to worry about the view. No, I'll have this room, OK? Now I'm going to change out of this travel gear and maybe unpack - no I'm not going to bother with that just now. I'll be with you in about ten seconds."

He left her, took his case to the other room and then wandered into the lounge. There was a bowl of fresh fruits on the table and, in the tiny fridge in the kitchen, a bottle of wine. She would be delighted. He went out on to the patio, blinking in the bright sunlight and a few moments later she joined him there, wearing tiny white shorts and a pretty loose top. She'd let her hair down, and it fell over her shoulders in dark waves which made her look impossibly young. "Oh, you haven't changed," she said. "Aren't you hot?"

"Sorry," he apologised, "I was just looking around. Won't be long," and he went into his bedroom and closed the door. Kitty sighed, stretched her arms above her head and breathed deeply. It was good to be back in Spain. Settling down on the canopied swing, she wondered if they might fit in a visit to her old great-aunt, but they'd think about that later. Just this moment she wanted to soak up some real sunshine. On his way to join her, John paused in the doorway and stood looking at her, so relaxed and at home. She really was lovely. If only he could say and do the right things to make his dreams reality. He crossed the tiny patio and sat down beside her. At first he thought she was sleeping, she lay so still with her eyes closed, so he simply sat quietly, watching her in companionable silence. After what seemed a very long while, or perhaps he too had slept, he couldn't be sure, she yawned, stretch and turned to him. "John, I'm starving, let's go and explore and find something to eat." She stood up, taking his hand and pulling him to his feet. "Come on, aren't you hungry too?"

John gave her an enormous smile, it was all so natural and special. "I am, but I didn't realise it. But can you really walk in those?" and he pointed to her pink sandals, which only seemed to have one tiny strap.

She laughed back at him. "Course I can, come on, let's go," and she led the way back through the apartment.

They had wandered through the town a little, found a restaurant they liked and had a long, leisurely meal. Now they were back on the patio in the warm, scented dusk. Kitty sighed deeply; "It's good to be back, Spain will always be home to me."

"Yes," he said thoughtfully, "I can tell that. But you didn't live here, well not for long, did you?"

"We used to come every year for a long stay with my grandmother. She spoke no English, so we all had to speak Spanish." She laughed softly and added, "Except Dad. He just got one of us to speak for him. Then my Mother died, and our visits got a bit difficult."

"How old were you then?" Was he asking too many questions? But he wanted her to go on talking, telling him about her life.

"Eleven. Dad couldn't bear to stay in the place after Mother went, so he sold up and bought the garage in Ledminster. Fran was doing exams, so she stayed on with Granny Brownlow, but David came with us to Ledminster, he was only fourteen." She was silent for a while, and John was afraid to ask another question. Would she think he was being nosy? "Tell me about your family, John," she said at length. "Is it just you and Richard?"

"Yes. Our Mother died when I was thirteen. I never got on with my father. I was a disappointment to him and he made it very clear." He stopped, did he sound self-pitying?

"Why?"

"I didn't want to do the things he had planned for me. Like joining the army, or going to university."

"And Richard did. He was in the army, wasn't he?"

"Oh, yes, Richard did everything that father wanted, but only because it was what Richard wanted." Now he was sounding bitter and grudging, and that wasn't what he wanted. "But it all worked out the way I planned it, with or without his help, so what does it matter?"

Kitty was quiet for a long while. She remembered her Dad, always there for her, always ready to listen. It was as if he felt he had to double the love he gave her, once he was on his own. She knew David felt the same way about him, though of course men didn't say. It didn't sound as though John's father cared too much. "So who looked after you, after your mother died?" she asked.

Keep it level, he told himself. No playing for sympathy. "We had a housekeeper when Mother was ill. Gradually she took over, and stayed on with us afterwards."

Kitty thought about coming home from school, either to the warm back room at the garage, or to the house where Dad always had something cooking or at least a hot mug of tea and a biscuit. She pictured John coming in from school. Would a housekeeper think of things the way Dad did? She doubted it. "Was she nice?" she asked.

"She was OK, but she thought the kitchen was no place for the sons of the house. She laid a tray in the dining-room." He half smiled to himself at the memory; Mrs. Gutteridge laid a plate of scones, or fancy cakes on a spotless white tray-cloth, along with a gleaming metal teapot and delicate cups and saucers – for two lads of thirteen and sixteen! As if he had spoken all this aloud, he added, "She did her best," he added defensively, "she had no experience of young boys."

Poor John, Kitty thought as she finished the wine in her glass. No wonder he's so tongue-tied. She yawned and stretched her arms above her head. "Gosh, I'm tired. It's been quite a day." She stood up, "I'm off to bed," she said, "What about you?"

"I'll stay for a while longer." He wasn't quite sure why he'd said that, but if she was disappointed, she didn't show it.

She walked across the patio and turned in the doorway. "Goodnight, John."

So that was it. She didn't expect him to follow her. He wasn't sure whether he was relieved or rejected. He lingered for a while longer, and then he, too, went to bed.

CHAPTER THIRTEEN

Monday morning, and Terry was glad to be up and about; he had spent the evening trying to work, but found it hard to concentrate. Jane's change of character and rough words bothered him a great deal. And he wondered how the children were copeing. After a restless night, it was a relief to slip out of the house for a good long run – that would clear the cobwebs. It was a fine morning, still quite early so there was no one about. He began to relax, letting the rhythm of his run clear his mind. But when he turned back into his driveway forty minutes later, he was sharply jolted out of his good humour. There in the drive was a police car, with two policemen obviously waiting for him. Oh, God, what now? He slowed down and drew level with the car as the men got out. "Terry Kennedy?" the older, man enquired.

"Yes," said Terry. "Is something wrong?"

"May we come in and have a word?" the police officer asked. "You ought to cover up, anyway, after a run," Without waiting for an answer, they all walked towards the door. Terry unlocked it and ushered them inside. He led the way to his office.

"Now," he said quickly, "tell me why you're here. Is there something wrong with the children? Or Jane?"

"Do you mean the Lawson family?" and when Terry nodded impatiently, the policeman continued, "We were hoping you'd tell us that."

"Oh, for God's sake," Terry exclaimed. "Just tell me what's happened and why you are here."

"Do you have Jamie Lawson here with you?" When Terry looked at him in utter astonishment he added, "His Mother thinks you do."

"She isn't well. No, I left Jamie with her yesterday afternoon. She asked me to leave and although I wasn't happy, I knew the children would be OK. I'd given them their meals. I was trying to work out who I could tell about them, without causing her any more pain. So what has happened to Jamie now?"

"He's disappeared. Run away perhaps. Do you mind if we look around?"

The question made him angry, but he understood the reasons. "Go ahead," he said. "I'll find some clothes while you look."

They were all back in the office quickly and the policemen looked as though they were ready to leave when the phone rang. Terry raised his eyebrows in question, and the two men nodded. "Terry Kennedy."

"Terry, can you come and find me? Please, Terry," Jamie's voice was uncertain.

"Jamie!" Terry exclaimed, and the two policemen moved closer, trying to hear. "Where are you?"

"Hallinford bus station," came the reply. "Can you come and meet me? Mum got so cross last night that she hit me, so I've run away. Will you come, Terry?"

"Listen, Jamie. Do you see the seat by the door of the café? Good lad. Go and sit there and wait, don't wander about, OK? I'll be there in five minutes. OK? " After another moment he put the phone down. "Will you let me go and meet him? He might be scared if you picked him up."

They looked at each other, and then the older one agreed. "OK, but we'll follow you. Let's go."

In the bus station, one forlorn-looking little boy was sitting rigidly on the seat by the café door. As Terry approached he stood up and ran to him, "Oh, Terry," and his lower lip began to tremble.

Terry put an arm around his shoulders. "It's OK, you're safe now. But listen, Jamie, your Mum has reported you missing, so these two policemen will need to talk to you in a minute. OK?"

Jamie looked fearful. "Will I have to go to the police station?" Please, Terry, can I stay with you and talk to them?" Terry looked enquiringly at the policemen.

"I think we should go back to your place, sir, and find out just what is going on. Then we'll have to take him back to his mother."

"No," said Jamie. "No, please."

"Let's go home, have a cup of tea, and sort it all out," Terry said and taking Jamie by the hand, began to walk across the bus station. The policemen followed – it was all a bit irregular, but they didn't want to frighten the kid even more.

Back in Terry's kitchen, the older policemen very gently began to question Jamie. "So why did you run away then?" he asked as though it was the most natural thing to do.

"It's Mum," his voice was almost a whisper. "She's not the same. She's like someone else in Mum's skin. She got angry and hit me. She never hit me before. I don't want to be with her the way she is. And she wouldn't let Terry stay and look after us, and she can't she's too tired and cross and keeps crying."

The older of the two policemen ruffled Jamie's hair. "Don't worry, we'll soon sort it all out. But we have to take you back, you know."

"Will you come too," Jamie looked imploringly at Terry.

"Yes," said Terry without consulting the policemen. Then turning to them he asked, "Do you know the background? Jane was at the hospital for three days with her sick daughter. Maria died, and Jane fell apart. I'd been there all weekend with the kids, but she told me to go away. I'll come back with you and Jamie if I may, and see if I'm needed."

The policemen hesitated; it wasn't usual. But the kid was looking at them, and obviously the bloke was trusted at home. "OK," said Dave Sinclair, the older man. "We'll all go together. That OK, Jamie? Ready for a ride in a police car then?"

He nodded, but as they all stood up to leave, he stayed close beside Terry. I really need to take my car," Terry thought, but the look on Jamie's face told him that he couldn't follow on in his own car. Oh, well, perhaps he might be able to borrow one somewhere. The younger of the two policemen busied himself, strapping Jamie carefully in the back seat. The older one drew Terry aside. "A quiet word. When we get there, I may need to speak to Mrs. Lawson quite off the record. Completely, not even Colin there. OK?"

"No problem," said Terry. "I'll follow whatever you say." The policeman smiled, opened the rear door for Terry to join Jamie, and as he climbed into the front seat Colin started up the car and they were away. And within ten minutes of their journey, Jamie was fast asleep in his corner.

When the car drew up outside Jane's house there was little sign of life, but when they rang the bell, the door was opened by Debbie, who threw herself into Terry's arms, buried her face in his jacket and burst into tears. Jamie moved closer to them both, but said nothing. "Easy, Debs," Terry said, stroking her tangled hair. "It's all right. Easy, Debs. Look, Jamie's here, too." She did not let go or raise her head. "Come on now, we want to come in for a cup of tea. Let us in, Debs," and he tried to unlock her little arms from around him. Carefully he eased her and Jamie along the hall, and the two men followed closing the front door behind them.

In the sitting room Jane sat at the table looking as though she had been there all night. She was still wearing the same clothes and her hair was dull and untidy. She looked up at them without any apparent interest. "I knew you'd turned the kids against me," she said in a dull, lifeless voice. "You think you take Andy's place, don't you?"

"Mrs. Lawson," Dave Sinclair's voice cut in firmly, "we have brought Jamie back." She said nothing, so he turned to the others. "Colin, take Mr. Kennedy and the children to the kitchen and see they have a warm drink. OK?"

"Will do. Come on kids," and as Terry moved towards the kitchen, the children went with him. "Let's put the kettle on...." The rest was lost with the closing of the door.

Dave sat down at the table beside Jane. "Look," he said, "I understand how you feel."

She turned to stare at him. Maybe she was pretty in normal times, but the face that looked at him now was ugly in its grief and neglect. "Understand," she repeated, her voice rising sharply. "Understand! How could you understand. Yesterday morning I had three children. Today I have two. Can you understand that?"

His voice was firm but quiet. "Yes," he said. "Six months ago I had five children. Now I have four. Next year it's possible I will only have three. So, yes, I understand. But the kids don't."

"You mean, you know a child might die?" her voice was incredulous. Then she put her head down on the table and began to cry. Her whole body shook with the great gulping sobs. "You're just deadly tired," he said. "But just listen to me a moment longer. If you send Mr. Kennedy away again, I shall have to make out a report that the children are in need. And if they see you like this, they'll take them away and put them in care. If Mr. Kennedy stays until you are yourself again, I can report that the kids are being cared for at home. Do you understand me? This is between you and me, and of course its up to you its your home. Your decision."

She lifted her head and looked at him. Now she truly was ugly, he thought. "They wouldn't take them away would they? I'm their mother for God's sake." Then she stopped. "Yes, OK," she said tiredly.

He stood up and crossed to the door. "Right, Colin, time we got back to the station," he called. "We'll leave the kids with Mr. Kennedy for the time being, anyway." When Terry joined the two policemen in the hall to see them out, he added, "You may get a visit from a Social worker but don't worry; if everything's OK she won't look for problems. Good luck," and he walked out to the waiting car.

Terry watched it drive away, and then returned to the kitchen. The children sat at the table where he'd left them. "Right," he said, "Let's take Mum a cup of coffee and see what we can do to help her." They watched him make the coffee and take it through to the sitting room. They stood in the doorway looking a little fearful. Terry put the coffee down and laid his hand on Jane's shoulder. "Come on, Janey," he said firmly, "here's some coffee, and then I think you should go to bed. Do you want me to call the doctor?"

She lifted her head from the table and looked at him. He waited quietly, and the children looked nervous. "No," she said at last, "I don't need a doctor. And I'm sorry, Terry."

"Drink the coffee while it's hot," he advised. Then to the children he said, "Debs, go upstairs and put on some proper clothes. Jeans and a tee shirt, please. Then brush your hair and wash your face, OK?" She nodded and scampered away. "Jamie, can you go and run a nice hot bath for your Mum, and find a big clean towel from somewhere? She'll be up as soon as she's finished her coffee." Jamie gave him a grin and disappeared up the stairs. Jane sat staring at the empty doorway. She looked dreadful, Terry thought. Her eyes were still red and puffy, with those great dark shadows beneath them, and the skin on her face was even more blotched than before. Her mouth sagged with tiredness. "Come on, Jane, let's get you a bath and some sleep. Then we'll work out what's to be done." She said nothing, but allowed him to help her from the chair and guide her upstairs. Her mind was a blank, she simply followed Terry's instructions. Debbie, now looking much better, was sent to find Mum's nightdress and dressing gown, and then both children were despatched to pick up all dirty laundry, leaving Jane in peace. Half an hour later she was in her own bed, propped up on the pillows. Terry drew the curtains across the window and came to stand beside the bed. "Sleep, Jane," he smiled down at her. "Don't worry about anything now. Just sleep." He bent and brushed her cheek with his lips but before he could straighten up again, she had put her arms out and pulled his face to her. She kissed his mouth, held his face between her hands for a long moment and then, as if this had exhausted her, let her arms drop back on to the bed. Her eyes closed and almost as he watched her, she fell asleep.

While Jane slept, Terry and the children busied themselves tidying the house, shopping, making meals just the routine things that told the children everything was back to normal. Terry just hoped it would be. In the afternoon the phone began to ring, and Terry snatched it up quickly, he didn't want Jane to wake before she was ready. "Hello," he said quietly.

"Terry?" Richard's voice was questioning. "Isn't Jane there?"

"She's asleep, she's exhausted," and he explained very briefly what was happening. He made no mention, though, of Jamie running away and the police being called. Jane could tell if she wanted to.

"I rang yesterday," Richard said. "She was in a bit of a state then. So you are looking after them all?" He sounded a little aggrieved.

"I am. Who else is there?"

"That's true. She'd probably have called John if he'd been around. Trust him to be absent when he's needed."

Terry had been controlling his anger until now. He took a deep breath, let it out and snapped, "Honestly, Richard, you are the most selfish, arrogant sod. Who was always around when you were wallowing in self-pity? Who worked with your solicitor on your behalf for a company in which he had no part? Who worked with him again letting his old home, which was left to his brother? Who can't have any visitors to stay, because his spare room is filled with your clothes, your books, your hi-fi and God knows what else of yours? And all you can do is sneer at him. God, you make me angry."

There was a long silence at the other end, and Terry was about to replace the receiver when Richard spoke. "It seems to have been my time for home truths," he said bitterly. "First Karen, then Jane and now you." He didn't add that the words "selfish" and "arrogant" had crept into all three conversations. He had called Jane about the house he might buy, but she had almost screamed at him in her rage. "It's your bloody life, and your house," she'd said. "You want me to decide for you? You'll want me to come to the boardroom next and tell you how to vote. For goodness sake Richard," and there had been a pause before she added "make up your own mind." She had been going to say "stand on your own feet" but had managed to stop herself just in time.

"Sorry," said Terry briskly, "but I think John has had a rough ride. Everyone needs someone to care for him for a change, and until now, he never had anyone. So don't begrudge him this. Do you want me to give Jane a message when she wakes?" The children were peeping round the door, hearing Terry's angry voice.

"If you would," said Richard coldly. "Just tell her that I've bought the house, well, set the wheels in motion anyway, and that I'll wait for her to contact me when she's feeling better," and with that, he hung up.

Jane slept soundly until early evening. Terry had given the children their tea and they were watching television when she came downstairs, wrapped in her old dressing gown. Suddenly the children looked nervous again; it was going to take a real effort to get back in to the old ways and happy routines. She sat on the sofa, and Terry came and sat beside her. "What about something to eat, or maybe just a drink?" he asked.

Jane's voice was still husky with tiredness. "I'd love a coffee, and perhaps some biscuits if there are any. I don't remember," she said apologetically.

"We bought lots," said Debbie. "We went shopping this afternoon, didn't we Terry?"

"We did. And you ate lots of them, too," he laughed.

Jane smiled. "That's Debs, always hungry. Come and sit with me and we'll share the biscuits when Terry brings them." For a moment the little girl hung back, afraid, but Jamie got up from the floor and went to sit beside his mother. She put a tentative arm around his shoulders, and it encouraged Debbie to join them. "I'm sorry," Jane said, looking from one to the other, "I am really, really sorry. I was upset and angry. I really didn't mean to shout at you both. Can we still be friends?"

Terry came back into the room carrying a tray, and Jamie moved a little table in front of Jane. Terry set the tray down "I brought lots," he said, grinning at Debbie. He lifted the little girl up, sat down beside Jane, and sat Debbie on his knee. "here, how's that Debs? You can reach the plate from there."

She giggled, and took a biscuit. "We are just like a family," she said. "Aren't we, Jamie?" Her brother nodded but waited to see if Mum got cross again. She didn't. But he wished it was true; he wished Terry was his Dad and didn't have to keep going away again. Everything was OK when Terry was here.

Jane sipped her coffee and then began to look worried. "Terry, what about your work," she said turning to look at him. "Are you missing appointments and things?"

"Don't worry, it's all sorted. But I may have to go to Hallinford sometime to pick up the car and my laptop. But that's for later, let's just relax and worry about today. Richard rang, by the way."

"Oh, lord, did he tell you? I think I raged at him, too."

" No, but he said it had been his time for home truths because I told him what I thought of him. He was sneering at John and that always gets to me. He said Karen and Jane had told him what they thought of him, too." He grinned at her. "Don't even think about it, Jane, it won't hurt him. And anyway, it must have done some good, because he's buying the house, wherever that is."

"At the end of the street," Jane said. "One of those two bungalows." She turned to the children and said, "Uncle Richard is going to buy Mrs. Blake's house." But she had caught the look on Terry's face and asked him quietly, "What's wrong?"

"Nothing" he lied. Would Richard have Jane and the children running around after him like errand boys? He was arrogant enough. "Now he'll have to find someone to housekeep for him."

Jane had understood. "Karen has recommended some-one she knows. She has a new job, and isn't interested any more. Somewhere along the line Richard must have hurt her, I think." She tried to stifle a yawn but failed. "I think I'll go back to bed, if you don't mind, Terry." She hugged and kissed both children, and went slowly from the room. "Come and say goodnight to me, all of you, when it's bedtime," she called over her shoulder.

Richard hadn't moved since speaking to Terry. He sat with his hand on the bedside table which held the phone, and stared into space. "Everyone needs someone to care, and until now John had no one" repeated itself in his mind. Was it true? And a long-forgotten memory surfaced - it had been at his Mother's funeral, and Father and the two boys had stood beside the grave. When the service was over, Father had said simply, "Come along Richard," and together they had walked to the car parked at the cemetery gates. And thirteen year old John, now motherless too, had walked behind them, unnoticed and probably very unhappy. Had it always been like that with Father? But although John had been quiet and studious, he had never let Father stand in the way of what he wanted to do, quietly but firmly he had stuck to his ideas, and so they never got on well together. Yes, he had to admit, Terry was right, though what business it was of his Richard didn't really understand. And Karen? Karen had called him arrogant, too. When she had come to see the new house to give her opinion on his equipment needs he had been hopeful; perhaps she would come and care for him after all. So he had called her that afternoon, but she was crisp and formal until something he said made her angry. Then once again mentioned Molly Hardaker. And then there was Jane. But he knew she was under stress, so he didn't want to remember the things she had screamed at him down the phone. Poor Jane - first Andy and now Maria. He hoped she had got his message, and that she'd be glad he was moving so near to her. But if Terry was going to be a permanent feature in her life, would that change things? Perhaps. He made up his mind to ring Molly Hardaker that evening – he had put it off in the hope that Karen might change her mind, but with her new job he knew now that she wouldn't. Everyone needed someone to care, but who cared for Richard Treherne?

The children were washed and ready for bed. As they sat together Terry saw Debbie's eyes half-closing. Poor kid, she hadn't got much sleep last night by the look of her. "Time to go and say goodnight to Mum," he said gently. She made a half-hearted protest, but then they went willingly upstairs to the door of Jane's room. "Yes, I'm awake," she said sleepily, and the children ran to her to kiss her goodnight. She hugged them both, then let them go. "Goodnight Debs, goodnight Jamies. Sleep well. Everything will be fine tomorrow, you'll see." She watched them go through half-closed eyes, still quite exhausted.

Terry tucked them into bed and left both their doors ajar as he knew Jane did. Then he went back to her. "Can I get you anything, Janey?" he said, sitting on the edge of the bed. She shook her head but murmured something he couldn't hear. He bent closer and asked "What did you say? Something you want?"

She reached up to touch his face. "I said, you were truly special, and I love you," she said, then turned her head into the pillow and closed her eyes. He sat there wondering if he had really heard those words, but she didn't stir again. He couldn't tell if she was really asleep but after a while he gave up wondering and slipped silently out of the room.

Charles Cameron walked into the kitchen where Isobel was preparing their meal. She looked up from the vegetables she had been chopping and slicing and was startled by the look on his face. "What is it, Charles? What's the matter?"

"I've just been talking to that psychiatrist fellow at the hospital. Patricia is ready to be discharged, but he is concerned about her mental state."

"What does he mean? Exactly?"

"Well, it seems that even though those scabby cuts she took for scars have now disappeared, and even though they have encouraged her to use a mirror, put on some makeup and so on, she just says she's ugly and won't bother. You know that. She said it when we were there last. He wondered if she should be sent home or to a - well - rehabilitation place. Privately, of course," he added quickly.

Isobel waited, but Charles said no more, just sat looking at her almost helplessly. "Of course she should come home," she said decisively. "She'll soon pick up where she left off if she's among her own people and possessions."

"She'll need looking after, Izzy. Will you be able to manage her?"

"She's my daughter, Charles, of course I can manage her." She wished she felt as confident of that as she sounded. But Charles was looking quite unwell these days, since the accident, and she wanted to ease his worries. "There are quite a number of mirrors in our house, too, she'll probably end up looking in one by accident and knowing she's fine." But not, she thought, if in her mental state she is convinced she's scarred. They would just have to work it out, one day at a time. "Will you tell Dr. Phillips?"

"He said to discuss it with you, and he will ring me again in the morning. Shall we eat in the kitchen tonight, and save ourselves a lot of work?"

She looked at him in surprise; Charles had always wanted everything done properly, dinner in the dining room, coffee in the sitting room and Isobel to fetch and carry everything about. Eating in the kitchen was something quite new. "Yes," she said, "it would be nice, so much easier too. Thank you, Charles," and she began to set the table. "Do you want wine?"

He nodded and stood up. "I'll fetch glasses from the dining-room."

Isobel continued with her preparations, but after a while became concerned. Where was he? She hadn't heard the phone, but perhaps he had remembered a call he had to make or something. She went across to the dining-room. Charles had sat down and was slumped across the table. She ran to him, feeling for a pulse, taking in all the details of his appearance. Then she reached for the phone on the sideboard, and dialled the emergency services. Charles was a big man, and the dining room was awkward. She knew she couldn't make him more comfortable, but fetched a blanket and covered him gently. Then she went to the kitchen and dealt with the food, putting it in the cool oven for the moment. She fetched her jacket, and handbag, and waited in the hall for the paramedics, who arrived only minutes later. "Will you follow us in your car?" they asked. She knew them both well.

"No, it will take too long to find a parking space. I'll come with you." They were working as they talked, checking her husband over, although all the signs were there, moving him on to a stretcher and after only another few minutes, the ambulance was on its way, siren blaring. Please, God, she thought, please let us get there in time.

Terry woke to find Jane standing beside the sofa, holding a steaming cup of coffee. She was already showered and dressed, looking her usual self again. He moved a little so that she could sit down, and took the coffee from her. "You're up bright and early. Feeling better?"

She smiled at him. "I'm fine now, Terry, thanks. But now I'm back to thinking normally, there's a few things to be done. Phone calls and arrangements be made. At the hospital," she added, in case he didn't understand.

"Yes, I know. I thought about it all yesterday but there wasn't anyway I could do it for you."

She leaned across and kissed his cheek. "You've been great. But listen, there's something I don't understand. Mrs. Porter said you told her we'd arranged for you to stay the weekend. But we hadn't, had we? Do you have second sight, or something," she laughed.

"No, sorry nothing interesting like that. Jamie rang and asked me to come. I'd no appointments that afternoon, so it was no problem. But I do have one this afternoon."

"Jamie asked you to come," she repeated. "Oh, lord, Terry, no wonder he ran away when I made you leave."

"Well, none of it matters now you're well again. What can I do to help with these arrangements?" He drank his coffee, his eyes never leaving her face.

"Can you keep the children out of the way while I tell Andy's parents and my brother and then ring the hospital. And the undertaker," she said sadly.

"Of course. I have to go to Hallinford sometime today. I'd been thinking of hiring a car and taking us all there. Leave the hire car in a garage to be collected, and drive my own back. I've an appointment to keep late this morning. Would you like me to do that this morning - I'd hoped to take you with us so that you can see the barn conversion before it's too late."

"Too late! Why?"

"I'm considering selling. Haven't quite made up my mind yet, but it seems the best option. Mrs. Paget has given notice, she's going to Belgium to live with her daughter for a year. And the reason I kept it on was for the seminars, but the accountant says the last two made a loss. So...."

"I'd love to come and see it. I'll get everything sorted this morning and we'll go this afternoon. You could take the children out, get some shopping and go and organise the hire car, and maybe take them to a café, or something, for a little treat. You're already their number one best friend, anyway." He searched her face, was she being bitter. But she was smiling back at him, it was OK.

"Janey," but he stopped, not sure of what he wanted to say.

"Oh, Terry, it's OK. I'm not concerned about it, truly." She stood up and took his empty cup. "Anyway, number one best friend had better get up before we are overrun with marauding children." She smiled at the thought. "So is that plan OK for you?"

"Fine."

She left him and went into the kitchen where he could hear her setting out the breakfast dishes. He grabbed his clothes and headed for the shower.

"Where's Terry?" said Jamie in a worried voice as he came into the kitchen. "Has he gone away again?"

Jane laughed. "No, he's in the shower. How about 'Hello, Mum instead?"

"Hello, Mum," said Jamie. "I'm starving." Jane smiled and put two boxes of cereals on the table; it would take a day or two before they completely trusted her, she supposed, but she wasn't going to get uptight about it.

Terry and Debbie came in together, with Debbie yawning and rubbing her eyes. "Will you have cereals, Terry, or shall I cook something?" Jane asked.

"Cereals will be fine. Not sure there's anything to cook, anyway, we didn't do much shopping yesterday, my two helpers were dragging their feet and grumbling about being tired." He grinned at Jamie, whose face was now all smiles.

"Well, perhaps the three of you could go shopping this morning," suggested Jane. "I've got one or two things I have to do, but I could write you a list so that you know what to buy. How about that, kids?"

While the children washed and dressed, the adults washed up and tidied the kitchen. "Will you stay with us for a while, Terry," Jane asked tentatively. "I don't think the children trust me yet."

"As long as you like, Janey."

She hesitated, flushing a little. "Permanently?" The question took him by surprise, and he didn't answer at once, and Jane looked more flustered. "Sorry, Terry, I didn't.....I wasn't...."

She had turned away in embarrassment but he took her shoulders and turned her back to face him. "I'd like that," he said, "but if I do, can we bring the sofa from the barn conversion? It might be more comfortable."

She put her arms around him and whispered into his sweater, "Oh, I think we can do better than that." He held her close for a long moment, and then they broke away at the sound of Jamie's great whoop of delight from the doorway. Jane gave a soft little laugh and murmured, "It's going to be a courtship for three I think."

Isobel woke as the first hint of daybreak crept through the Venetian blinds at the window. Remembering immediately where she was, she looked across to the monitors at the end of Charles' bed; a flood of relief went through her – they were all winking steadily, just as they should. She yawned and stretched, stiff from her half-sleep in the armchair. Reaching for her handbag, she stood up and moved silently to the door. She would find the bathroom and make herself look presentable before a member of the nursing staff came to check on their patient. She could see that the colour had returned to his face, and he seemed to be breathing perfectly regularly. She would tidy herself up and come back and wait for, hopefully, reassurance that all was going well for him.

It was some time later before she was able to get a real opinion. The nurses were not prepared to commit themselves. "You will have to ask Sister or the consultant," they said kindly. But they did bring her a tray with tea and biscuits, for which she was grateful. The room was one of the hospital's best, and she stood at the window, watching as people arrived and night staff left, and delivery boys with flowers, and the postman. Finally, the night sister came to do her last check before going off duty. "I think it would be safe for you to slip away home for a while," she said practically. "He won't wake for some time yet, and the real danger is past. Go and have some breakfast and maybe a little walk, and then come back if you want to. How does that sound to you?"

"If you are sure the worst is over," Isobel said.

"Well, nothing in this life is ever certain," smiled sister, "but I think he'll be fine for a little while. Stretch your legs a bit and have some food."

Isobel thanked her, put on her coat, and stood by the bed for a few minutes more. Then she turned and left the room. She had a bigger problem than breakfast on her mind, but common sense said that she must eat if she was going to be any use to either of them. From the front entrance she called a taxi, and was soon home. She made herself a pot of coffee and some buttered toast, and took them through to Charles' study. Here she could put the tray on the desk in front of her while she used the phone. She dialled and waited, sipping her coffee as she did so. "Oh, Iris, it's Isobel. Sorry did I disturbed you?" She listened and then smiled. "Oh, that's OK then. Look, I'm wondering if you could help me out with a problem." Briefly she explained about last night's trouble, and that Patricia was due to be brought home from hospital today. "I can't look after her and stay with Charles as well," she said. "Do you think Patricia could come to stay with you for a while?"

"Of course she can." Her sister's voice was firm and practical. "She lived quite happily with me for a while before she was married, didn't she? She can have the same two rooms as before, and I'll make sure she eats regularly."

"But you do know about this phobia she has, and that she's almost reverted to being a fourteen year old altogether now. The psychiatrist isn't particularly hopeful that it will all settle back to normal again."

"Isobel, of course I know, you told me. But I don't see it as too much of a problem for me. She liked living in the town here, too. And, well, it'd be a bit of company perhaps."

Isobel wasn't too sure that Patricia would be good company, but she said nothing. It was true Patricia had liked living with Iris, who lived almost in the centre of Ledmister. "We'd have to come to some arrangement about money, you know, board and lodgings" she said practically. "She has her own allowance for her personal spending."

"Well, yes, it would be good if we could arrange something. Her sister sounded rather embarrassed. "I hate to ask, but….."

"Oh, Iris, don't be silly, of course we will. Let's arrange for two weeks just now, and see how we all get along."

Iris was relieved. Harry was back to gambling again and it always worried her. Perhaps Isobel had sensed something like that, the two sisters had always been close. When they were younger, Iris had often wondered why Isobel had married Charles, who was so formal, so serious and worked so hard all the time. Harry had been dashing, and exciting and flamboyant and he still was really. Now, though, she could wish he was more like Charles, who gave Isobel no worries and such a comfortable lifestyle. "Shall I go to the hospital and fetch her?"

"Let me talk to her first, and then perhaps you could pick her up this afternoon, unless something goes wrong, in which case I'll ring you. Is that all right with you?" They talked about Charles for a few minutes longer, and then said goodbye. Well, thought Isobel, that's the first hurdle over. Now to tell Patricia. But she allowed herself to relax; she didn't think Patricia would mind at all. She finished the pot of coffee, but left the toast untouched. After a quick shower and some fresh clothes, she was soon on her way back to the hospital, to her husband and her daughter.

As Richard sat in his room that morning, it occurred to him for the first time; if - no, when – he moved into his own place, he could get up in the mornings whenever he pleased. Well, he supposed he could here really, but didn't like to put the nursing routine out too much. Last night he had telephoned Molly Hardaker, and made an appointment to see her this morning. He hoped it would all work out, but he wasn't making too many plans just yet.

There was a light tap at the door, and a small neat woman stepped into the room. She had dark hair, just beginning to show signs of grey, clear blue eyes and a big wide smile. "Mr. Treherne?" When Richard nodded agreement she crossed the room quickly and held out her hand. "Molly Hardaker. It's a lovely morning, isn't it?"

She had the sort of face you couldn't help smiling back at. "Do you know," he said with a smile, "I hadn't really noticed. That's the trouble with being shut in, isn't it?" She had drawn up the spare chair beside him, and now sat down. "There should be coffee soon."

"Yes, I just saw Jenny preparing it." She slipped off her jacket and hung it over the back of her chair. "So, tell me about the house you are buying. Where is it?"

"Stephen's Lane, do you know it?" She smiled again, and nodded. "I have a friend living in Stephen's Lane, and she told me about it. Karen, the nurse who used to care for me before all the changes, looked it over to see if there was space for equipment for me, you know, hoists and bathroom stuff. She approved, so I bought the house. Well, I've started the wheels turning, anyway. Ah, here's Jenny.""

Molly leaned forward and drew the small table towards them. Jenny put down the tray saying "It's good to see you again Molly. Still as busy as ever?"

"Oh, you know. The old lady goes into a home at the end of the week, so here I am, back in circulation. I'll do the pouring, Jenny, don't worry about it." The young nurse smiled and thanked her, then turned and left the room.

Having enquired how he took his coffee, Molly poured and handed him a cup. "So it will be a few weeks before the house is settled," she said.

"It will, I'm afraid. Some rooms need redecorating, and there's the other stuff to install."

She sipped her coffee, and seemed to be weighing up what to say. "Look, Mr. Treherne," she said after a while. "My present post finishes at the end of next week. But from what I've gathered here, you won't need me in an, well, official capacity for a while. But I was wondering. How far have you moved about by yourself from here?" Richard looked puzzled, so she continued, "Are you simply planning to move from this room to a room in your new house and stay there? Wouldn't you like to go to the stores, choose your wallpaper and paint and stuff like that? Go to the post office and buy your stamps, or even just go down to your friend's house for coffee? Surely leaving here is the beginning of something better?"

He was silent for a while. She had, in the few minutes that she had been here, made him see just what could be done. Why hadn't anyone else been so positive? Why hadn't he? She was like a breath of fresh air. "You're right," he said, and this time his smile was much more than just polite. "I have been here too long. It has addled my brain." He reached forward and put his cup on the tray, aware that, unlike others, she didn't try to take it from him. "So what do you think?" He grinned at her almost boyishly, "for it's obvious you have it all planned."

She burst into a peal of laughter. "Well, let's just say I have ideas. But listen, if you wanted professional help from a mobility officer...." She stopped as he held up his hands in mock supplication. "Well then, if you don't want officialdom, I could help you, get you orientated, in the weeks while you wait for the solicitors and builders and so one. True, it's in my own interest, I'm out of work next week, but I know I could help, if you wanted me to."

"So what had you in mind?"

"Well, first of all, just going out. Out of the gates, using the pavements, that kind of thing. You can't do it without someone with you, not while you're under the care of the hospital. But I could come with you. If you turn left out of the gates and then left again, there is a small park. If we go the other way, there are a few shops, a post office and a café. Enough to get you wanting something more." She laughed at his expression. "You might even enjoy it. Later I might borrow Michael's van, and get Steve here to help us find the best way of getting in and out of cars. If we can master that, well, we can go anywhere."

She looked almost excited, and he was drawn along by her enthusiasm. They talked for another half an hour, finally coming to an agreement that she would be his carer, on a month's trial "to see if we like each other" she laughed, and after that Freddie could do a proper contract, if she wanted that. Finally she stood up and began to reach for her jacket.

"It's been a real pleasure talking to you Mrs. Hardaker," he said. "I think we'll get along fine, don't you?"

"I do. But I'd prefer you to call me Molly, if that doesn't offend you. It sounds more like a friend and less like an official."

"Good thinking. So we can dispense with the Mr. Treherne, too – it's Richard. I'll see you in a couple of weeks, but I'll be in touch before that. Goodbye for the moment then, Molly," and he held out his hand to her.

Taking his outstretched hand she said, "Bye, Richard." She walked briskly across the room and opened the door. "See you soon," she said, and closed the door quietly behind her.

That morning Kitty had seemed a little depressed and John had begun to worry that she was growing tired of him. There was one way to find out; "Are you bored?" he asked as they finished their breakfast.

She gave him a smile. "No, not at all. I was just wondering how to ask you something. Would you mind if we went to see great-aunt Elena today?" As he shook his head and began to speak she went on, "It's just that they don't speak much English. You might feel left out. But I'd like to see her while we're here. Could you put up with it for a while."

"Oh, Kitty, of course I can. Will we need to hire a car?" How far is it?" Will I manage on Spanish roads, he added silently.

"I think a car would be best. The bus would take forever and we'd have to come home as soon as we arrived, practically. Is that OK? No problems?"

He smiled at her reassuringly. "We'll be fine," he said. The maid arrived at that moment, and she and Kitty talked rapidly in Spanish for a minute or two. Then Kitty turned back to John.

"Right, Rosa explained where to hire a car. Let's go and leave her to get on with her work?"" In just a few minutes they were walking in the sunlit street, but not before Kitty had telephoned her aunt and been invited to lunch. Now they were heading for the garage at the centre of the village.

The drive took about forty minutes, with Kitty pointing out several places she knew. When they arrived John parked the car carefully in the shade, but while he stopped to lock the doors, Kitty was already running up the steps to the house and being embraced by a tall well-built woman who had been waiting at the open door. He steeled himself to walk casually, tried to smile as he too was swept into an embrace and a torrent of voluble Spanish. Kitty freed him from her aunt's embrace, laughing all the while and scolding, he thought, the older woman. "John, this is my aunt Anna," she said, and John smiled and nodded at the woman. "She says you are very welcome here." They all trooped into the house, which was cool and shadowy after the bright sunlight outside. Kitty took his hand and gave it to a small, very old and wrinkled lady sitting in a chair, again speaking in Spanish. Then she said, "John, this is great-aunt Elena."

The old lady turned her head to look at him. She had dark, intelligent eyes and they seemed to take in every detail of him. She smiled and nodded at him, then said something to Kitty. "She says I have good taste in men," Kitty laughed happily. "I told her you have good taste in women."

It was impossible not to feel relaxed and at ease with these smiling people, he thought. So very different from the families he had known at home. He longed to be part of such a family, warm and friendly and loving. The day passed very quickly; the old lady, who John discovered knew a little English, but preferred Spanish, had her siesta after lunch, and John and the others sat out on the veranda in long cane chairs. When she woke she called to Kitty, who ran to her and bent to hear her whisper. She had drawn a small velvet bag from her pocket, and Kitty called to John, "John, come here a minute, great aunt Elena wants to show you something."

He stood up and went to stand beside the old lady's chair. "You have something to show me?" he said, and Kitty translated at once. Elena opened the little bag and drew out a ring. It was of the most unusual dark gold, much darker than he'd ever seen before, with three stones, emeralds, he thought, within an old fashioned curled effect setting. "It is beautiful," he said, turning it in his hand.

Kitty lifted the ring from his palm. "Isn't it lovely?" she said, turning it to catch the light. She began to speak rapidly in Spanish to Elena, and John watched as the colour crept into her face. She was shaking her head and looking, he thought, rather flustered.

The old lady began to speak, pointing to him first, then to the ring, and then to Kitty. She made the movements of putting the ring on her fourth finger. John looked puzzled. "What is she trying to tell me?" he asked.

Kitty became even more flushed and almost shy. "I think she is trying to tell us it should be an engagement ring," she said finally. "I have explained that we are not, well, you know, and she said……" But Kitty couldn't go on. She just smiled and turned away. The old lady put the ring back in its velvet bag, and tucked it into the pocket of John's shirt. She nodded and smiled, tapped her fourth finger again, and nodded again. John was truly moved; he took Elena's wrinkled hand in his and said "Thank you, senora," Then he put his hand over his shirt pocket and held it there. "So," he said cautiously. "So, senora Elena." He hoped it was the right word.

Kitty was very quiet as they drove home, but perhaps she was tired, it had been a day of excitement and much talking. They returned the car to the garage, bought cheese and fruit and wine, and made their way back to the apartment.

They ate their simple supper out of doors on the patio as the coolness of dusk settled around them, and first stars began to prick through the deep velvet of the sky. Kitty sighed with contentment, her head tipped back among the cushions, gazing into that beautiful night sky. "Isn't it strange," she said dreamily, "the stars always seem so much nearer and brighter here. Just like jewels on a velvet cushion."

"Mmmm," John was surprised at such a romantic description. "Do you know the poem called The Cloths of Heaven?"

"I don't think I know any poems at all John. Is it about the stars?"

"Partly, but the sky really. And dreams."

"Can you tell it to me? Do you know it all by heart?"

And softly, in the half-light, John recited the poem to her. He kept his gaze fixed on a particular star, not looking at her at all. She seemed to be staring up at the sky, too. He came to the last line, "Tread softly," he said and his voice grew even lower so that she had to strain to hear it. "Tread softly, for you tread upon my dreams." He felt his face burning and hoped she could not see it in this light.

She had moved closer to him to hear those last few muffled words. She was quiet for a long time and then asked softly, "Do you have dreams to tread on, John?"

"Yes."

"Don't you want to tell me?"

"Yes." She waited, still gazing into the night sky, and after some minutes he said, "My dream is to know the right words, have the courage or the strength or what it takes to ask the girl I love to marry me."

It was the longest personal revelation he had ever made. He couldn't look at her, would she smile, look puzzled, surprised? He almost wished he hadn't spoken, what had made him say all that? "Do you want to know my dreams to tread on, John?"

She sounded gentle and dreamy again. She had moved closer to him, and her hair brushed against his bare arm. "Tell me your dreams, Kitty."

"I have this special dream. In it, I spend a whole year showing the man I love that he is special. He is a true man for me. We will go places together, and I will show him that life isn't all serious. And then, there will be the sort of wedding that my Mother would have loved. But I must be patient and wait for him to ask me to marry him. That's my dream."

As she spoke she turned to look at him, but still he gazed up at the stars - the sky was full of them now. Slowly and rather tentatively he turned to her, slid his arms about her, and held her close. "Oh, Kitty." He could say no more just then, his voice had let him down. She kissed his face, finding tears on his cheeks. Then he kissed her, first very gently and then holding her so tightly she could hardly breathe. At last she pulled away a little and looked into his eyes. He smiled and released her a little as he stood up, pulling her to her feet. "Oh, Kitty," he murmured into her hair. "I love you. Let's go to bed."

CHAPTER FOURTEEN

When Terry and the children arrived home just before lunchtime, Jane was sitting at the kitchen table with a mug of coffee. She made as if to get up and switch the kettle on again, but Terry stopped her. "I've just had one, thanks. We had to hang around a bit." As yet, the children didn't rush to hug Jane as they had always done, but he thought a couple more days of stability would see them back to normal again.

"Terry's bought a really cool car." Debbie pulled out a chair and sat down. "We came home in it."

"He didn't buy it, empty head, he's only borrowed it." Jamie gave his sister a scornful glance. Terry had fetched two large carrier bags from the car and put them on the table. "We got all the shopping, too. Can I have a biscuit, Mum, Terry bought loads."

Jane shook off the sadness that had haunted her after her phone calls. "Only one, mind," she said. "It'll soon be lunch time. But thanks for doing the shopping, all of you." She stood up and began to sort through the bags and put things away. Then she looked across at Terry while the children were distracted, and he raised his eyebrows in question. Jane nodded, and murmured, "All done." It had been so hard talking to Andy's parents. But very carefully and gently she had persuaded them not to fly over for the funeral. She knew they couldn't afford it. Her brother hadn't been at home, and Sylvie had burst into tears and sobbed throughout the whole conversation. Jane had had to keep it as short as she could without hurting Sylvia and sounding hard and practical. Compared with these two calls, all the other arrangements had been easy. On impulse she had phoned Fran as well, who had been amazingly calm and supportive. She hoped that their two families would stay in touch now, Fran was great company.

That afternoon they drove to Hallinford. On the way Jane began to tell Terry of the ideas she had about his business. "If your Mrs. Paget only does two days a week, I could cope with your secretarial work. It might have to be evenings in the school holidays, but it shouldn't be too difficult. We could turn the dining room into an office. You'd be much more central then." After the explosive conversation on Sunday with Richard, and Karen's dismissal of him, she was a little wary of planning for Terry. But he didn't know things had changed just now.

He grinned at her mischievously, raising one eyebrow. "And the sofa?"

She flushed and turned to look out of the window, muttering "No sofa, Terry." After a while she turned back and added, "And I was wondering about the barn conversion; might it be a good idea to let it, rather than sell?" She was remembering the look on his face when she'd told him she couldn't have more children. One day, - well, she didn't know how strong that feeling was. But keeping his home might be a better option until they were sure of themselves.

When they arrived the house was newly cleaned and Mrs. Paget was there to greet them. "Have you made gingerbread men?" Debbie asked, and they all laughed.

"Well, they were lovely," Debbie said by way of explanation to Jane. The children followed Mrs. Paget into the kitchen, and Terry showed Jane all over the house. It was clear from her expression that she loved it. She went to the kitchen to talk to Mrs. Paget for the children had run into the front garden to play, each clutching a cake. Jane explained that she would take over the secretarial work at the end of the month, and the older woman outlined what she did. There was nothing there to worry Jane too much about what she was taking on.

Terry had been packing the things he needed and his laptop and some papers into the boot of the car when the children came running. "There's a posh van coming," Debbie said."

"It's a courier service," said Jamie importantly, having been able to read the word Debbie couldn't.

"Ah, that's Jimmy," said Terry and they all went off to meet him. The two women joined them from the kitchen and Terry made all the introductions.

"You moving out then?" Jimmy asked.

"Well, sort of. Nothing's definite yet, but Mrs. Paget is here till the end of the month, so I'll be coming back. After that, I'm not sure." He looked across at Jane who smiled back happily.

"Thinking of selling, are you?" Jimmy was as sharp as always.

"Don't think so. We thought we might let on a regular lease. Any ideas?"

"You know me, Terry, ear to the ground and all that. I'll listen out for you. Miss you though. New car?"

"No, hired. I needed to come and collect my own today for work tomorrow. I've got to leave it in Macey's to be collected."

"Take it now, Terry, and I'll follow and bring you back if you like."

"Hey, thanks Jimmy, that'll save me asking Mrs. Paget." The older man said his goodbyes and walked back to his van. Terry climbed into the hired car, and followed the courier down the drive and away. Another problem solved. Jane went back inside the house, and Mrs. Paget began to put on her coat ready to leave.

"I hope everything works out for you Jane," she said, taking the younger woman's hand. "God knows you deserve it. And he's a grand man, Terry. I've always enjoyed working for him. I hope you'll make each other happy." Jane's eyes began to fill, and she couldn't speak. Rose Paget swallowed hard, too in an effort to stay controlled. "Take care now," she said, and left, calling goodbye to the children as she went.

That night Terry woke suddenly and realised Jane had quietly slipped out of bed. He heard her cross the room, then stop and turn and come back into bed beside him. She lay with her back to him, and her whole body shook with enormous sobs. He took her into his arms stroking her hair and gently rocking her. "What is it, Janey? Was it a bad dream?"

"I thought I heard Maria call, she often woke in the night. Then I remembered she wasn't there." She turned to him and buried her face in his shoulder. He could do nothing but hold her close and wait for her to grow calm again. Gradually the shaking subsided, and then her breathing became slow and regular and she slept. He lay as still as he could with a cramp in his arm, not wanting to move and disturb her. The morning's calls had been difficult for her, but there was still the funeral to get through on Saturday. Perhaps helping him run the business was a really good idea after all. Something different to occupy her mind, something that had never included Maria. She turned over, releasing his arm, and he settled down to sleep, too. He had to get back into the work routine tomorrow. It seemed that he had only been asleep a few minutes when he woke again. But this time it wasn't a dream, someone, it sounded like Debbie, really was crying. He shook Jane's shoulder gently; "someone's crying," he whispered. She was instantly awake and out of bed. He lay there for a while, wondering what was happening, and then Jane returned. It sounded as though she was smiling as she spoke.

"Debbie crept downstairs because she was hungry," she said and almost giggled. "She saw the sofa was empty and thought I'd sent you away again." She snuggled in to him, "Seems like we're tied together by the children, Terry.

"Sounds great to me," he said. "Just as long as they let us have some sleep, too."

"Welcome to family life," she murmured as they both drifted into sleep.

"Iris," said Harry, as they were preparing for bed that night, "what will happen to that girl's money? Surely there was quite a tidy divorce settlement?"

Iris knew exactly where he hoped this was leading. "It's in trust for her now. The psychiatrist has said that mentally and emotionally she's a minor."

"So who administers this trust? Charles?"

"Of course, who else? Jointly with Isobel."

"And if anything happened to him, if he didn't recover, wouldn't she need a guardian or something. If we are caring for her long term, wouldn't it be proper for us to be her guardians?"

Iris hid a wry smile. Us? "If anything happens to Charles, as you put it, Isobel will continue to administer the trust. Are you going to read for a while?"

But he wasn't going to be deterred that easily. "Is that all legal, or just Isobel being bossy?"

"It's legal, Harry. Charles is a barrister, after all, and he has signed one of those a power of attorney things when he went through that tidying up affairs phase, don't you remember? I think he thought he was going to be ill or something. He showed you how to avoid inheritance tax by splitting the ownership of this house with that agreement. They both signed the attorney thing to each other, I think. Are you going to read, or shall I put the light out?"

This time he gave in. "No, I'm tired. You can put the light out," and he turned away from her and settled down to sleep. In the darkness Iris turned a sigh of relief into a loud yawn, but knew that this wasn't the end of the story. How deeply he was in debt this time she hadn't yet found out. But he had always managed to work things out in the past, and she could rest assured that Patricia's money was safe. The girl was only twenty nine and she'd need it all for her future, whatever that might be.

Kitty lay awake feeling deliciously happy and contented. The room was filled with moonlight, and she could see John's sleeping face on the pillow beside her, relaxed and almost boyish in sleep. One arm was flung across her body, as if to make sure she didn't run away in the night. She smiled at the thought. She'd never run away from John, not ever. Beside her head, on the bedside table, she could see the ring lying on the velvet bag gleaming green and gold in the moonlight. Tomorrow they would find a jeweller who might alter it in time. John had said wait until they returned home, nothing could be done in the two days they had left. He was thinking about English jewellers, who would say "Come back in a week." But she knew that this attitude wouldn't work in Spain. They would find out in the morning. She'd have to handle it carefully though. John wanted to do it all according to the book, buy her a traditional engagement ring, and the memory of his hurt pride and anger after that concert when Dad had given her the money for a taxi was still vivid. She wanted this antique ring for her engagement ring, but she didn't want to hurt John. She sighed, it would work out, she thought as she drifted off to sleep, it always did in the end.

When she woke again, the sun was streaming through the windows and John stood beside her with a tray. "Breakfast," he said, setting it down on the table and giving her a hug. He was dressed in shorts and shirt and had already showered, for his hair was still wet. She sat up and took the tray on to her lap. "Is breakfast in bed just for holidays, or will it be a permanent feature," she laughed.

"Oh, strictly for holidays, I'm a working man you know. What shall we do today?"

She hesitated, but only for a moment. She wouldn't think of it yet as an engagement ring, just a ring that she wanted to wear, now. "Let's take Aunt Elena's ring to a jeweller, see if they could alter it for me in time." He looked doubtful, so she added, "We can ask, anyway. If they say no, we take it home with us, that's all. But I'd love to wear it home. Let's try, please John."

He relented, how could he refuse her when she looked at him like that. "OK. But I'd rather buy a proper engagement ring with diamonds, one like the other girls would choose?"

She shook her head so vehemently that her long dark hair flew all over her face, which made them both laugh. "Look, John," she said more seriously, pushing her hair out of her eyes, "I do understand that you want to buy our engagement ring. But truly, John, I want to wear this one. It's much more beautiful than diamonds and it's a family ring. Wearing it will tell everyone I belong to you, and you belong to my family. It doesn't matter whoever bought it, but wearing it will tell aunt Elena that we love her and that she's part of our life together. Please, John, let me wear this one. There will be lots of other things to buy for me, won't there? Please, John."

She looked so young and lovely that he felt he would do anything to please her. He moved the tray aside and took her in his arms. "If that's what you want, then that's what you shall have my lovely," he said, although his voice was muffled as he nuzzled into her neck. After a while he gently let her go and stood up. "If you don't get up," he laughed, "we won't go anywhere at all, and Rosa will have to clean around you. She's already pushed me out of the kitchen." He grabbed the tray just in time as Kitty flung back the sheets and swung her legs out of bed. He watched, smiling broadly, as she disappeared into the bathroom, and then took the tray back to the kitchen.

And she had been right after all. In the jeweller's shop, tucked away in the corner of the main square, Kitty and the old man behind the counter had talked rapidly in Spanish, with quick translations for John's benefit. The old man had fetched a ring card, and she'd put her finger through different holes until she found the right one. All the time, the old man had glanced from Kitty to John, smiling and nodding. "He says, come back tomorrow morning, and it will be ready," she explained at last. She looked absolutely delighted as she slipped her arm through his. The old man said something more to her, and she smiled and blushed a little. John waited for a translation, so she said shyly, "He says you are a lucky man. I said we are both lucky. Come on, let's go and have some coffee."

When Terry woke next morning Jane was not there, probably already up and about with the children. He showered and dressed and went downstairs to the kitchen. The children were already eating their breakfast, so he pulled a chair up to the table with them. "You look nice," said Debbie "are we all going somewhere special again?"

Terry laughed. "I'm going to work. Don't know where you're going, Debs."

"We're going to turn the dining room into your new office," said Jane. "We might need your help later if there's stuff to go to the tip. Will we need another phone later?"

"Nothing will change until Mrs. Paget has left, we'll sort it out then. Will you be OK, Jane?" The question was casual, but his eyes searched her face. She smiled and nodded. "I'll be back for some lunch, then out again at two."

She wondered if this was his usual routine or whether he was simply checking up, keeping an eye on the children. Then she dismissed such thoughts - Terry wasn't like that. "See you lunchtime, then," she smiled at him and began to pile up the breakfast dishes.

Isobel went first to the room where she had left Charles sleeping, but now his eyes were open and she thought he was aware of her. She took his hand and held it between her own. "Charles," she said softly, "how are you?"

As he made an effort to speak Sister entered the room. "Ah, Mrs. Cameron," she said. "The news isn't all bad. Mother Nature is telling him to slow down or take the consequences. He must rest more. But the consultant feels that we need to make him relax before attempting any operation. He's been lucky this time."

Isobel realised that Sister was telling her all this in a general, not detailed, way for Charles' benefit; she would discuss it with the consultant herself later on. "I'm glad Mother Nature is on my side," she laughed. "I've been telling him the same for months now. Now he'll have to listen to me." She squeezed his hand and smiled at him. "You are listening, aren't you, Charles?" Sister left them, and Isobel settled down to talk or read to Charles for a little while, but soon he had drifted off to sleep again. She stayed quietly where she was, still holding his hand for what seemed like hours. Then very gently she slid her hands away and stood up. Time to go and see Patricia.

She found her daughter sitting in an armchair by the window of her room. She was dressed, and her crutches stood propped against the wall beside her. As Isobel entered she turned her head and greeted her Mother, "Oh, hello Mummy. Why didn't Daddy come with you? Has he gone to work?"

Isobel drew up a chair beside Patricia. "I'm afraid Daddy isn't very well. He's here in hospital. I've just left him sleeping. He was taken ill last night."

"Poor Daddy. He won't like being ill. Shall I come home with just you, then?"

Isobel was rather taken aback by the lack of reaction. "That's what I want to talk to you about. You see, I am spending lots of time with Daddy, here in the hospital and will have to look after him when they let him go home. But you can't stay on in hospital now that you're nearly well. I was wondering if you would like to go and stay with Aunt Iris for a little while. She says she'd like that."

This time Isobel got the reaction she had expected. "Aunt Iris. Oh, yes, please. It's so much nicer living in the town than stuck miles from anywhere in Hallinford. When can I go?"

I should feel hurt, Isobel thought, but all I can feel is relief. "She'll come and pick you up here this afternoon, about two. I'll ring her when I leave you just to make sure. You'll need some clothes, though."

"We could go and pick them up this afternoon." Such enthusiasm, thought Isobel, and no real questions about her father. But then, that was how it was with Patricia now.

"You'll have to tell Iris what you need," Isobel said practically. "You won't be able to go upstairs on crutches, will you?" Iris would sort it out, she thought. Iris was practical and very fond of Patricia, too.

Saturday proved to be a beautiful, early summer day. Jane had arranged for the children to stay the morning with their friends. Terry watched her as she moved about the house, tidying and straightening things that were already tidy and straight. "Jane," he said softly. "It's time to go."

"I know." She reached for the jacket that hung on the back of a chair. "Maria called this my wedding suit," she said. She picked up her bag. "Ready, Terry." They left the house, closing the door quietly as if afraid of disturbing someone.

At the church gates three people stood waiting for them. Terry heard Jane's involuntary gasp and smiled. He'd been asked not to mention John's coming, just in case he had got held up somewhere. John looked tanned and relaxed, though very serious. Maria had always been his favourite, and this wasn't going to be easy.

"John," said Jane, "how lovely to see you here. Hello Fran, hello Alan, thank you so much for coming."

She was being so calm and controlled, Terry thought. Please let her keep it that way for a while longer. "so, John," he said. "Good holiday?" Fran, Jane and Alan were already moving on and Terry and John fell in behind them.

"Brilliant," John answered. "Absolutely brilliant. How has Jane taken this?"

"Pretty well," Terry said. If Jane wanted John to know the details, she would tell him herself. "How's Kitty?"

"She's fine," John smiled, "She's looking after the children just now." They had reached the church and the little group now fell silent. Be brave, Janey, Terry willed. Be brave my darling.

It was over. They had said their goodbyes to Maria and left her in the little churchyard. Jane hadn't cried, though her eyes had never left the small white coffin as it was lowered into the ground. Then she had turned away, the others respecting her need for being solitary for a moment or two.

Jane, with Fran, walked a little ahead of the men. At the church porch they stopped. "You three go on ahead," Jane said. "We'll be with you in a little while." Fran had come from the porch now with flowers.

Terry looked at Alan. "Andy," Alan said, not waiting for the question. They nodded and walked on to the gate and the two parked cars.

Now they were all on their way back to the house, the others following in Alan's car. Terry wanted to speak, but could think of nothing that didn't sound false. And so they made the short journey in friendly silence.

As Fran and Jane busied themselves making sandwiches and coffee, Terry asked, "So come on, John, how was the holiday?"

Fran was just setting a tray on the table, and she laughed aloud. "Terry, you should see my sister. She has suddenly become left-handed, flashing the most beautiful ring you ever saw. I'm quite envious."

"Oh, John," cried Jane, dropping the knife she was using and running to hug him. "Oh, congratulations, John. I'm so pleased. When are we going to meet her?"

John looked a bit embarrassed, but only for a moment. "Well," he said, "We were rather hoping we could come tomorrow. We're staying with Fran and Alan, you see. Kitty's minding the children for Fran just now. She didn't think, well, you know, meeting you first just now, well…"

"I know," Jane said soothingly. "I understand. But come and spend as long as you can with us tomorrow, the children will be delighted to see you both. Come early and stay for lunch. Have you told Richard about the engagement yet?"

"We're going to see him this afternoon. He sounded much more cheerful when I rang him."

Fran and Alan were taking cups and plates to the kitchen. When they returned Fran said, "I'm sorry not to stay longer, Jane, but I think we ought to get back and

relieve Kitty. I bet the kids are running rings around her."
She slipped her arms into the light summer coat Alan was
holding out to her. "But we'll all stay in touch now, all
six of us, OK?"

Jane hugged them all in turn, thanking them for
coming, and reminding John to come early tomorrow.
She watched from the doorway as the car drove away,
with John waving to her from the back. Then she closed
the door and leaned against it wearily. Terry came to find
her and held her close, not speaking, and she leaned
against him gratefully. "Come on," he said. "Let's just go
and sit quietly, just for a while, before the kids get back."
He led her to the sitting room, waited as she settled herself
in the corner of the sofa and then dropped down beside
her, his arm lightly around her shoulders. And there they
stayed, each of them busy with their own thoughts, until
a commotion at the front door and a little voice calling
through the letterbox told them the children were back.
He kissed her cheek, and stood up. "Family life?" he
grinned, and then added, "stay there, I'll let them in."

John was very quiet that afternoon as they drove to the
hospital to visit Richard. Maria's funeral had upset him,
of course, but Kitty also wondered if the mood was to do
with seeing Richard again. Perhaps today would see the
beginning of those dreams, the dream she had told him
about that evening on the patio in Spain. He was a
wonderful man - all she had to do was make him believe
it! That was all, but it was enough. He turned to look at
her for a moment. "What are you thinking about?"

She smiled too. "Just my dreams, John," she
answered. "And how to make them true."

They had at last found somewhere to park, and
walked in the sunshine to the hospital. As they passed

through the double doors into the private wards, Jenny came out of her office. "Oh, Mr. Treherne," she said, "its good to see you again. Have you been on holiday?" Her tone was warm and genuine, all the nurses on the private patients section were fond of the shy schoolmaster.

"We have. Jenny, this is my fiancé Kitty."

For once Jenny the professional relaxed. She said, "Oh, that's wonderful, I'm so pleased for you both," and hugged them in turn. Kitty wasn't sure who was the most startled of the three of them. Jenny stepped back quickly, remembering her position but took Kitty's left hand. "Can I see? Ah, that's really beautiful," as she caught sight of the ring. "It's the loveliest ring I've ever seen, Kitty. Lucky you, a beautiful ring and Mr. Treherne, too." Then she flushed a little and said briskly, "Your brother is waiting for you, I think," and turned away as her pager began to bleep.

John stood looking at Kitty for a moment. She really had quite an effect on people, he thought. She smiled back at him, obviously Jenny didn't usually react in this way and it had taken him by surprise. She was glad. Something had changed already. "Are we going to stand here, John, or shall we go and see Richard?" she asked, still smiling at him.

Richard was sitting by the window. John held the door open and ushered Kitty in. As they crossed the room he said, "Richard, this is Kitty. Kitty, my brother Richard."

Kitty kissed Richard's cheek and took the hand he offered. "Hello Richard," she said, sitting down in the chair beside him. "I'm glad to meet you." John was pleased and relieved; she had avoided the one thing Richard hated, someone standing over him. But then she was so small, would it have mattered? Probably, knowing Richard.

"Welcome to the Treherne family," Richard smiled. "This is all of it. Me and John. You'll make a welcome addition. Congratulations, both of you."

"Thanks," said John, who had drawn another chair close beside his brother. "So how's things, Richard? Jane said you had news but wouldn't say what."

Richard's smile was real this time. He really is quite handsome, Kitty thought, at least, when he smiles. "Yes, I've bought a house. Well, Freddie is doing his stuff at the moment. And I've found a really great carer, too. Things are working out for me at last."

John thought of all the times he had come here, visiting Richard, and sat beside him while his brother simply stared out of the window. No point in telling him he could have done all this months ago. He suspected Jane had told him, anyway. "Good, I'm glad. Where's the house?"

"Stephen's Lane." Richard watched for John's reaction. But his brother simply nodded, so he continued, "there are two bungalows at the end, you will remember. Jane says it was a field when she and Andy moved in. It's a decent size, needs a bit of decorating and some extras for me, but it will suit nicely. And the carer is a great lady called Molly.

She has lots of ideas for my rehabilitation. He laughed a little self-consciously and changed the subject. "Now," and he turned to Kitty, "How was Spain?"

"Great," she said, "but then it always is. It's my second home. I've even taught John some Spanish already." She laughed, "He knows now how to address my great aunt Elena."

"Oh, of course. I was forgetting. You and Fran are half Spanish, aren't you? How is Fran?"

"She's fine." She wanted to make him understand John's quiet mood. "This morning made her a bit sad, though. You know, Maria's funeral."

Richard looked uncomfortable. He had obviously forgotten all about Maria. Jane's children had never meant much to him, and she had always been John's favourite. "Yes," he said slowly, "it must have been upsetting for all of you. I wasn't sure whether flowers were appropriate for a tiny one like that, so I did nothing, I'm afraid. Was Jane very upset?"

"I don't know, I stayed to mind Nicky and Natalie. I haven't met Jane yet."

John now joined the conversation. "Jane was really brave. No tears. Having Fran and Alan there helped, and Terry too, of course. She talked Andy's parents out of flying over, she said it was just too much, too soon for them. She was marvellous."

This was the longest speech Richard had heard his brother make voluntarily. The girl Kitty must be good for him. "So when do you introduce Kitty and Jane?" he asked, smiling at them both.

"Tomorrow," said Kitty promptly. "We are spending a good part of the day with them. We've been staying with Fran and Alan but must go home tomorrow evening, ready for Monday morning."

"Is Terry still with Jane, then?" John knew his brother well enough to recognise the slight contempt in the tone.

Kitty looked to John, who answered, "Yes, I think he's moved in. He mentioned letting the barn conversion."

"Oh?" Richard looked put out. Surely he's not jealous John thought. Or maybe just possessive. Whatever it was, Jane wouldn't appreciate it, that was for sure.

Jenny brought them tea and they talked about their various plans for an hour or so, before John stood up and said they ought to be getting back, as Fran was preparing dinner for them that evening. Kitty hugged Richard again as she said her goodbyes. "We'll keep in touch so that we know how things are going with the house," she said. "And we'll be back before you move out of here, won't we John?"

"Probably, unless Freddie knows of secret ways to speed thing up. Bye, Richard," and he took Kitty's hand firmly drawing her towards the door. "See you, Richard." He called, as they left the room and walked away and out through the big double doors.

CHAPTER FIFTEEN

On Sunday morning Isobel put their suitcases in the boot of her car and with Charles beside her in the passenger seat, they were ready for their trip to Cornwall. They'd call and see Patricia and Iris first to say goodbye and to reassure themselves that Patricia was happy to stay where she was. Isobel knew quite well that her daughter wouldn't want to stay in the Cornish cottage they had bought. She had made it plain often enough. But that had been before the accident; would anything have changed? Somehow, she doubted it.

Harry met them at the front door and ushered them inside. "The women have gone shopping," he explained. "But they won't be long, it's only to the grocer's. They said they'd be back in time for you. Can I get you a drink? Tea, coffee or," as he turned to look at Charles, "whiskey perhaps."

"Not for me, thanks," Charles said. His voice was still a little gruff, but it was improving and growing stronger every day.

"Nor for me, thanks, Harry," Isobel said as she settled into an armchair. "How are things with you then, Harry?"

"Oh, well, you know," he said, "Up and down. But I was hoping to have a word with you both. About Patricia's stay with us."

Isobel looked at him sharply. "Is there a problem? We

can take her to Cornwall with us if she's causing trouble for Iris."

"No, no, nothing like that." Harry looked a little flustered. "It's just, well, the cost of keeping her here. Iris loves having her around, but, well, grocery bills and so on…." His voice tailed away as he heard the front door open and voices in the hall.

Patricia came quickly into the room. "Hello Mummy, hello Daddy," she said with a smile. "Iris says you're going to Cornwall for a holiday."

"That's right," Isobel agreed. "We wondered if you wanted to come with us." She saw her daughter's look of disdain and smiled at her. "I didn't think you would, but I didn't want you to feel left out. Is there anything you need before we go? We'll be away about three weeks or so."

Patricia looked to Iris, who shook her head. "No, thank you Mummy, I've got all I need." Isobel still found it odd that since the accident her daughter's way of addressing her had changed from Mother to Mummy.

The two sisters exchanged glances, and Iris nodded towards the door to the hall. "I've something to show you," Iris said, and led the way out of the room and away from the others. She closed the door behind them and then asked quietly, "Has Harry been talking to you about money?"

Isobel smiled. "Well, he began but you came in just as he got to the point. And you did warn me. Are things bad this time?"

"I don't know," Iris said, "and I don't want to. He'll get himself out of whatever jam he's in, but it won't be with your money or mine. Or Patricia's," she added firmly. "Now go off to Cornwall, and get Charles back on his feet again. But I must say he's looking a lot better than I expected. A bit of sun and sea air will do wonders. For both of you."

Isobel hugged her tightly. "Thanks, Iris, I don't think I could have managed both of them at the same time. But you'll let me know if Patricia needs anything, any help, or if she's just too much for you, won't you?" She thought for a moment and then added, "You are sure that the allowance is enough?"

"Oh, Izzy, it's ample. Don't let Harry tell you otherwise. And you know I've always liked having Patricia here. More so now that she's, well, a bit dependent. A bit clingy and not so, well, hoity-toity. So don't fret over us, go and have a rest, you need it too, you know. We'd better go back in so you can say your goodbyes and be on your way," and she opened the door and led the way back into the sitting room.

"Are you ready then, Charles?" Isobel asked, following Iris into the room. "It's time we were on our way." She watched as he got carefully to his feet. "We'll see you when we get back, Patricia. Goodbye for the moment," and she squeezed her daughter's arm as she kissed her cheek.

They all went to the front door together and the others stood watching as Charles and Isobel got into the car. "Bye, Daddy, bye, Mummy," Patricia called from the doorway. "Have a good holiday," and she turned and went indoors.

"Drive carefully," Iris called, and Isobel smiled, waved and then started the car. It would be so good to get away from everything and just be quiet for a while. Iris was right, they both needed to rest now.

Charles was silent for a while as Isobel negotiated the busier town roads, and then took the roads to the west. Presently he asked, "What kind of trouble is Harry in, do you know?"

"No, but I imagine it's the usual gambling debts. Iris seems to have washed her hands of it all in a way. She says he can get himself out of whatever jam he's in. Apparently he hasn't told her anything, and she wants it kept that way. It's happened so many times before hasn't it? She seems quite distant about it all. I think that's why she's glad of Patricia's company."

"He asked if I could lend him thirty thousand pounds," said Charles. "A bit high for a gambling debt, wouldn't you say?"

"Thirty thousand?" Isobel repeated. "Oh, Charles, what on earth can he need that much for? And why worry you with it at such a time?"

Isobel was delighted to hear a deep chuckle from her husband. "Because he knew it wasn't worth asking you," he smiled at her.

"Iris would be terribly worried if she knew the amount. And if she knew he'd troubled you with his problems."

"Then don't tell her. She has said he's got to sort it out himself, and doesn't appear worried. Leave it at that. She wouldn't tell you she was worried anyway, not just now." He didn't say "with all the worry you've had" but he was aware just how much she'd coped with lately.

"Well, while we are on holiday, I'll leave things as they are. Let's just forget all about them all and enjoy ourselves. Where shall we stop for lunch?"

He knew the question had simply been to change the subject, and smiling, stretched himself more comfortably. There was a restaurant which was her favourite stopping place not far from Exeter. "You choose," he said.

But after a few more miles she asked tentatively, "Could it be some problem at work, do you think?"

"There's no way of telling, Izzy, and we mustn't think of things that he might have done when the answer could be quite honest. And I do believe Iris, when she says she doesn't know. So we'll just have to wait and see what happens next."

"Last week Iris told me that he'd talked about asking to be made Patricia's guardian, but she'd quickly put him straight there. I suppose that was the money again."

"Izzy," Charles said sternly, "we are not going to spend the next three weeks supposing, wondering and worrying, are we? For if we are, we may as well go back home and do it."

She gave him a brilliant smile. "Yes, you're right. I'm sorry, Charles. What do you want to do while we're away – just relax at the cottage, or go places?"

"Both. We must go to that old bookshop again, Izzy, it was fascinating."

She nodded. "And I want to see some more of the paintings. Maybe buy one if there's something I like." Then she became silent as she negotiated some road works, but her mind was still churning over and over, thirty thousand pounds. Poor Iris.

It was just after ten thirty on another lovely morning when John's car drew up outside the familiar house in Stephen's Lane. They just had time to climb out before Jane's front door flew open, and two small figures hurtled down the path. "Uncle John, Uncle, John," they both shrieked, hugging him and telling him their news all at the same time and trying to outdo each other. When he'd finally untangled them all and could make himself heard, John said, "Kitty, this is Jamie and Debs. Come on, you two, say hello to Kitty." When the children chorused hello, John continued, "Now let's all go indoors for coffee, OK?"

Jane and Terry were waiting at the door as the little group approached. Jane held out both hands to Kitty, and hugged her. "You two look well," she said, "Spain surely agrees with you, John. Come on in, Kitty, coffee's ready and waiting."

Terry bent and kissed Kitty's cheek. "Welcome to the mad house," he grinned. "And congratulations, both of you."

"Oh, yes, how could I forget?" Jane exclaimed. "Many, many congratulations, both of you. I'm really delighted for you." Kitty had pushed up the sleeves of her cardigan and heard Jane's intake of breath. "Oh, Kitty, it's beautiful. It's surely the loveliest ring I've ever seen." Jenny's words all over again, thought John. Jane still wore her wedding and engagement rings, and now John could see why Kitty had begged for Great Aunt Elena's ring, the comparison was so obvious. He must trust her judgment on such things from now on.

As Jane went to fetch the coffee, the children reappeared. "I wanted to show you something uncle John," Jamie said, and set a long white card notice on the table in front of him. "We went to Sarah's house yesterday and I thought it would be really boring and horrid with just girls, but Sarah's Dad showed me how to make notices with special pens. So I made this one for Terry's office."

John looked down at the car. "Do Not Disterb" he read. "I spelled it wrong," Jamie explained quickly, "but

Terry says it doesn't matter, everyone will know he can't spell." He turned the notice over to reveal "Closed".

"How did you get the letters all nice and even?" Kitty asked, admiring Jamie's work.

"Sarah's Dad has a brilliant stencil set, well, more than one, and all sorts of pens for different writing. It's really great. If I had one I could make notices for every room."

John smiled at him. "I think there's one somewhere in my house. When Uncle Richard's stuff has gone we will start clearing out cupboards, perhaps we'll find it for you."

"And we all worked hard turning the dining room into Terry's office, didn't we Mum?" Debbie said, not wanting to be left out of the conversation. "I polished and polished and polished the desk, and Terry put his laptop on it."

"He asked us first if we minded him using Dad's desk, though," Jamie added. "And we all said he could, didn't we Mum?"

John caught Jane's eye and she smiled. "Yes," she said, "we all said he could."

"And Mum's going to be his secretary," Debbie added. "But she can't make gingerbread men yet."

"I'm a secretary, too," said Kitty laughing, "and I can't make gingerbread men, either. Are we bad secretaries, Debs?"

"Mrs. Paget made lovely gingerbread men," Debbie said. "But I expect you both could learn if you wanted." John drank his coffee thoughtfully; so Terry was going to start up here. It was certainly more central than Hallinford. And with Jane to help him, too. He hoped that would take her mind off the loss of Maria a little, as well. Perhaps things were working out for Jane, too.

He came out of his reverie to hear Debbie ask, "Is your name really Kitty? I've never heard of someone being called Kitty before."

Kitty laughed and hugged the little girl. "No, really it's Catarina. But at school they shortened it to Cat, and then that changed to Kitty.Cat and then just Kitty. Catarina is Spanish."

Debbie's eyes were round with wonder. "It's a beautiful name. I wish I was called Catarina. I shall tell Sarah I've got a new auntie Catarina." She slid from Kitty's lap and went towards the door.

"Not now, Debs," Jane said firmly. "We're having lunch in a minute, and I expect Sarah is too. Wait till this afternoon, please. Are you hungry?" Everyone laughed, for Debs was always hungry. "Come on then and help me in the kitchen instead." She took Debbie's hand and they headed for the kitchen door.

"What made you decide to move the office here?" John asked. "Was it Richard's suggestion?"

"No. Mrs. Paget gave in her notice and the accountant told me the seminars at the barn conversion were losing me money. Jane wanted to take over Mrs. P.'s job, and, well, the rest was Jane's idea, really. And she does have a degree in business management, so I should be on the up and up from now on."

"Is Richard part of your business?" Kitty asked.

Terry pulled a face. "no way. And not likely to be, even if he will be living just up the lane."

"He might put business your way, though," John said thoughtfully. "Not that he's taken much interest in his own lately." There was no bitterness in his voice; Father had left the business to Richard, and John had never been interested, anyway. He had never wanted to do anything but teach. He'd explained this to Kitty, just in case she might have had plans for him but no, she had understood perfectly. He was so lucky to have had the chance to be with her alone like that, it had made all the difference in the world. Whoever had judged that competition had done him an enormous favour.

They spent a happy afternoon together, talking, planning, laughing and drinking tea until John said reluctantly, "I think we had better think about moving, Kitty." To the others he added, "We haven't even unpacked from Spain, yet, and we both need to be at work tomorrow."

They understood. As they were leaving Jane hugged John tightly again and whispered, "Thank you for yesterday, John." Aloud she said, "It's been a lovely day, and I'm so happy to know you, Kitty. You will come often, won't you?"

"With Richard just up the lane, I guess we'll make double visits," John laughed. "But don't worry, we'll be back and soon, won't we Kit?"

"You bet. Till they get fed up with us," she laughed. She put her arms around Debbie. "Bye, Debs, we'll see you again soon."

"Bye, Auntie Catarina," Debbie answered and gave Kitty a kiss. They all trooped down to the car together, and the little family stood on the pavement waving them out of sight. "Isn't she lovely," said Jane as they went indoors. "And John obviously adores her."

"Well, you should take a bow there, Janey, it was all your idea to get them together." He put his arm around her. "Come on, Mrs. Cupid, I'll give you a hand clearing up. Then I must sort some stuff for tomorrow."

That Sunday afternoon, as promised, Molly arrived looking neat and fresh and smelling of the outdoors. She'd been riding that morning, out with her son, she explained. They didn't often get time out together with the horses. During their previous conversation Richard had learned that her brother, Steve's father, was a doctor, following their father into general practice, and her late husband a chemist, so now he asked, "Is he a doctor, too?"

She gave a little laugh. "Yes, in a way," she answered. "He's a vet. He breeds horses for a hobby. But I only ride Ranger I've had him for a long time now. Do you have a jacket?"

It was something which hadn't occurred to him. "Is it cold out? Do I need one? I haven't got one here." He looked a little distressed. It was obvious he'd become rather institutionalised.

"Oh, I think your warm sweater will do, I only asked because men always seem to want a jacket. No, you'll be fine. But it's something you ought to think about, in case we go out in the rain, or cold, or whatever."

He would ask John to fetch him a jacket on his next visit. That would be another bonus for moving out of here; choosing clothes from his own wardrobe. Now he'd made the first move towards it, he wanted to be gone as soon as possible. They left his room together, and Molly found Jenny to tell her they were going out. Then they set off down the drive, Molly walking just a little behind but beside him. She knew without being told that he would hate someone towering over him.

"Watch out for the slope at the end," she advised. "You don't want to hurtle out into the road." He nodded his thanks, concentrating on keeping his chair nice and straight, as he would a car on the road. "Turn right at the gate," Molly instructed. "We'll head for the park. We can stop for a cup of tea at the tea room there if you feel like it." He had to concentrate harder now, the pavements were so uneven. Thank goodness he'd chosen a motorised model, and wasn't having to push himself all the way. "Right again," Molly said, as they approached a side road. "We'll go along a bit, you'll find sloping driveways you can use it as ramps to cross over. It'll be easier till you've learned how to get up and down steps. OK?"

He stored that away as a useful tip. The sun was warm and the pavements were deserted. It was good to be outdoors again. "Molly, this is marvellous." He had seen two driveways on opposite sides of the road. "I can cross here easily." It was all really a matter of common sense, so why had he put it off so long? But Molly wished there were more people about. She wondered how he'd take it when strangers stared, as they always would, at him in his wheelchair. But it didn't look as though they'd find out today.

When they were back in his room some time later, Molly prepared to take her leave of him. "Well," she said with a smile, "that wasn't very difficult. But not many people to get in your way, or dogs, or kids on bicycles and so on. Still, I enjoyed my tea. Thanks Richard."

"You're more than welcome. So when will I see you again?"

"Can I ring you? It will probably be Tuesday, but I'm not quite sure yet. Still sorting the old lady's house as the daughter is putting it on the market. But listen, Richard, you must get someone to find you a waterproof jacket of some kind. You'll find wet pavements slow you down a bit, and you'll need protection if we go out in the rain. Can't guarantee fine days all the time, can we?" He nodded his agreement, and she moved towards the door.

"I'll ring you tomorrow. Bye now," and she slipped through the door and was gone.

He sat there unmoving for a while. This was how it was going to be, never quite being in complete charge of events, not even now he was mobile. For Captain Richard Treherne this was a very new experience. But it would be a challenge to see just how much independence he could win back for himself. If only he could get started right away. So much wasted time. But he couldn't blame anyone but himself for that. He reached for the telephone; he had to see if John could help him over the jacket problem.

That evening, David Brownlow let himself into the old family home and closed the front door, calling as he did so "It's me, Dad," as he headed for the kitchen. There'd been no light in the sitting room window as he'd passed it. The kitchen was warm and quiet, and he found his father with maps spread across the table. "What are you doing, Dad?"

Ray looked up. "Oh, hello David. There's tea in the pot if you want it. I just got the maps out of the cupboard again. Your Mother and I often used to look at them and plan and argue about the route we'd take to Australia."

David poured himself a mug of tea and sat beside his father. "So what made you start looking at them again tonight?"

"Oh, you know, Just remembering. That sort of thing. Maybe I shall make the journey one day. With Kitty gone there'll…."

"Dad, she's not going yet, she's only just got engaged. And you know darn well she said it will be a year before she marries John." Kitty had telephoned Ray from Spain with the news of their engagement. He was glad for her, of course he was, but he wondered how he'd cope with the loneliness. "She'd be a bit upset if she knew how you were talking. Come on, Dad, put the maps away before she comes in."

Ray smiled at his son, folded up the maps and put them in the box in front of him. "I'm not sure if she'll be back tonight," he said. "They went up to Fran's as soon as they were back. John had to go to the funeral of that little girl, you know, Fran's friend Jane's daughter. She may stay over at John's place from now on, anyway."

David nodded. "Yeah, she may, but she'll still need you around, so don't you go all miserable on her or she'll think you don't approve, or something."

"You're right," Ray laughed, and standing up, pushed the map box back into the cupboard. "Did you come round for anything special? Anything I can do for you?"

David laughed. "No, Dad, nothing's wrong. Laura's giving one of those parties where men are definitely not required. So I came to see if you fancied a pint."

Ray went into the hall for his jacket, and together the two men left the house. But as they reached the gate, John's car drew up at the kerb and Kitty jumped out, almost before it had stopped. "Dad," she called, and ran into his arms. "Where are you going?"

"Oh, we were only going for a pint. OK if we skip it, Dave?" he asked turning his head.

—⁓—

"Course it is, let's go back and they can tell us all the news." David had been behind his father, and already he had his key in the lock and was opening the door for them. As they all went into the house, Kitty chattered away to them all at once. As always, they made for the kitchen and settled around the table. John had brought a bottle of wine, and David fetched glasses. Ray felt so grateful to his son – at least Kitty hadn't found him moping and miserable.

"Here's to Kitty and John," David said, lifting his glass. "Good luck to you both."

"Yes, may you be really happy, both of you," Ray added. "Now, come on, tell us all the news from Spain. And from Fran, too."

David had caught sight of Kitty's ring. "God, but that's beautiful," he said softly, "Laura will be dead envious."

Ray took her hand. She had her Mother's good taste, that was for sure. "It's lovely, Cats, really special. Did you choose it?"

John waited for Kitty to tell them the origin of the ring, he thought as they were family they might even have recognised it, but she simply gave him a brilliant smile. "We chose it together, didn't we, John?" He nodded, but flushed a little at his own ideas about it. He would learn not to doubt her judgment in time, perhaps.

"It's lucky the holiday was free," David laughed, "or you'd be a very poor man right now. Do you want a refill, or are you driving again tonight?" He nodded towards the wine bottle.

John put his hand over his glass. "Not for me, David, thanks. I've a bit of last-minute marking to do before morning school tomorrow, and Kitty wanted to sort a few things with Ray. I'm off home now, if you'll forgive me."

Kitty walked with him to the door. "Pick me up from work tomorrow," she said. "I'll bring a few things with me and leave them at your place. Then I'll make you dinner. OK?"

He held her close. "You're lovely," he said into her hair. "I shall miss you."

She laughed up at him. "Just for one night? Go and get your marking done. I love you, John. Goodnight," but she could say no more as he held her tightly and kissed her.

"Goodnight, Catarina," he said softly. "Sleep well, even without me."

CHAPTER SIXTEEN

The year that followed proved to be an eventful one for them all, but for Richard the first few months frustration seemed almost unbearable. Agents, solicitors and surveyors all seemed to be taking far longer than he had anticipated or believed they should, and he was now impatient to live away from the hospital, to be able to come and go as he pleased. The new regime, even under a new quiet manager, seemed to annoy or irritate him more each day, but slowly, slowly it all began to fall into place. Molly was insistent that he continued to explore the neighbourhood of the hospital, always with her and seeking Jenny's approval, several times a week while he waited. She knew that he had to get used to using the wheelchair in all weathers, and cope with all kinds of people and experience all manner of situations. But she accomplished this so tactfully that he didn't always realise her motives. They visited the local post office, finding that it had a step up to an awkward door. Molly advised as best she could, with a little quiet help from Steve, but wondered aloud, but only once, if perhaps he should really call on the services of a mobility expert. She was taken aback at the vehemence of his refusal, and didn't make the suggestion again. However, she did do a little research of her own, and found useful gadgets to describe to him. Wisely, she left it to Richard to decide whether he would buy and use them.

At last all the paperwork was finished, and the house was his. He'd have liked to have taken Molly to lunch to celebrate after signing the contracts, but he knew he wasn't ready for sitting in public places for long in his chair. The next big hurdle was visiting the house. It was too far to walk, that was certain. One day, he thought, perhaps I'll have a specially adapted car but for the first visit they made use of the local disabled society's van, a special favour for which he knew he couldn't ask every day; sooner or later he would have to research and decide on the best way to solve that problem, too. Still, they used the day wisely, taking measurements for curtains and carpets, moving from room to room together. Richard wrote notes of what needed doing, what could be left as it was and which of the bedrooms would be best for Molly. With the decorating, and the installation of his bed and bath equipment, it was going to be more frustrating time spent waiting around while others got on with the job. When at last they had finished all their measuring and notes and discussion he reached into his pocket for his new mobile phone. "Wait," said Molly. "There's a little treat planned for us for all our hard work. Come on, lock up your new home carefully, and come with me." She was laughing, and it made him smile too. How much younger and boyish he looks when he smiles, Molly thought as she watched him lock his own front door, pushing gently against it afterwards to ensure it was firmly locked. Steve had told her the whole story of Richard, his despair, his refusal of any help and the guilt over the death of his friend. But it had been his friend's widow who had snapped him out of it. And now Molly was going to meet her for the first time.

"What is it?" he asked, looking around him as they moved down the path together.

"Turn right and keep going," she said, "Number twenty seven. Jane has the kettle on ready for a nice cup of celebration tea. She called me earlier, thinking it might be welcome after all that effort back there."

Richard suddenly felt slightly aggrieved. Why had Jane asked Molly and not him, did she think Molly was his minder? Now, too, he also felt rather exposed and uncomfortable, moving down this street on this, his first real outing. Had Molly known he would feel this way and so kept the arrangement from him until the last minute? It was very likely. They moved together in silence down Stephens Lane to number twenty seven, and Molly rang the bell, noting that the pushbutton was well within Richard's reach, should he come alone at any time. I must watch for things like that, she thought. I'm not his minder, just his nurse.

"Richard!" Jane exclaimed with pleasure, "Oh, Richard, it's lovely to see you. I had a nasty feeling you might back out. Come on in, the children aren't home yet, so we can have our tea in peace." She turned to Molly and added, "You must be Molly, it's good to meet you. Richard is forgetting his manners in that hospital."

Richard flushed a little. "Sorry, Molly, I quite forgot. Jane has always bossed us Treherne boys about." He grinned at them both, still a little uncomfortable, but then carefully he began to manoeuvre his chair through the hall and into the sitting room. It was much smaller than his, he noted with a kind of warm satisfaction. "My head is full of figures," he laughed. "So much to decide and I'm not good at it yet."

Jane set a tray on the table and then sat down. She had moved a chair from the end so that Richard could be seated at the table with ease. Molly took a seat opposite Jane, and gratefully sipped the tea placed in front of her. Watching Richard's movements without appearing to notice him was quite tiring, but she felt they had made a great deal of progress with both the house and with Richard's approach to problems. She'd talk to Steve later for advice on getting Richard in and out of cars. He'd know. And he understood why she was asking him, and not the professional in this field.

"So what's next Richard?" Jane asked. "Obviously you won't be moving in for a while, but have you thought about furniture? Have you any in store from Fallowfields?"

"No. Most of it was sold with the house. My father had chosen it all carefully, each individual piece for its special place and it all blended together, you'll remember. No, I'm starting more or less from scratch, with my own ideas. And Molly's advice, of course," he added with a quick smile in her direction. "John has all my hifi equipment, books and clothes stored at his place, so that will have to be moved, too. I'm sure he'll be glad to get rid of it now." He looked across at Molly and thought she looked a little tired; if he was honest, so was he. They finished their tea and chatted about the children and John and Kitty for a while before he took out the phone again. "I think it's time we were moving again," he said. Jane didn't argue. This first visit must be a strain for him, whether he admitted it or not. He dialled the number and made his request, and in ten minutes the van was at the door. "Thanks for the tea, Jane, it'll be a while before I can return the compliment," he smiled, as she bent to kiss him.

"Never mind. It'll be grand to have Uncle Richard living just up the road, especially if he buys that state of the art computer Terry was describing. Take care, both of you. Bye now," and the van door closed behind Richard as Molly climbed into the passenger seat. She waved as the van drew away from the kerb, turned the corner and was quickly out of sight. So, Jane thought, Richard has made a start on his new life. She hoped it would make him happy again.

For John, the year brought many changes. Kitty kept her promise, made that wonderful evening in Spain,. With her beside him at various functions through the school year, such events didn't seem nearly so difficult and daunting any more. But she had not been with him on that first day back at school. He hadn't been prepared for that.

As he walked towards the school gates the Mont-gomery's car was just pulling away. It stopped suddenly with a squeal of brakes and Mrs. Montgomery called, "Mr. Treherne, Mr. Treherne, wait a minute." As she clambered quickly out of the car and hurried towards him. "Oh, Mr. Treherne, congratulations on your engagement. We're so pleased for you, Keiran and me. Such a nice girl, and a great family, too. You're a lucky man." He thought for one moment that she was going to hug him.

John looked startled. "Thanks, Mrs. Montgomery," he said awkwardly, "You're right, I am indeed. But how did you know?"

It was her turn to look surprised. "It was in Saturday's paper of course, didn't you see it?" Naturally he hadn't, he'd been in Oxford. Ray must have put in the announcement and not told them. She smiled at what she took for his usual reserve and unconcern. "I must fly," she said quickly, "I'm already late for work. Bye, Mr. Treherne," and she climbed hurriedly back into the car and drove away.

As he crossed the playground the headmaster's car slowed and stopped beside him. "Oh, John, many congratulations. Myra and I hope you'll be very happy."

"Thanks, Brian." What else was there to say? Yes, I hope we'll be very happy too?

"Down to earth with a bump now," Brian laughed. "9J is waiting for you." John smiled, and the headmaster drove slowly to his parking space beside the front entrance.

9J, well, Monty in particular, were indeed waiting for him. "Congratulations," Monty said as John came through the classroom door. "We all knew you'd make it in the end." John flushed a little at this remark, and some of the other boys added various comments. "She's a cracker," Monty told the boys around him.

That was enough, and John became his usual brisk self. "Thank you all. Now let's get on with the register and then the next section of the maths program, shall we? Page 64." There were groans and mutters, and shuffling through school bags for books and pens as they answered their names, and then the classroom became quiet save for John's voice explaining and questioning. Thank goodness he had survived that hurdle, anyway.

At the end of the term there were various functions from which John had always managed to back out, but Kitty would have none of it. "John," she said, and there was a firm note in her voice which made him look up quickly, "do you want to keep me hidden away? Don't you want them all to meet your future wife? Are you afraid to let them know how lucky we are to be together? I'd love this end of term party, we really ought to go, you know. It will kill the nasty gossip stone dead. Please, John, trust me, I know you'll enjoy it and I'll be there for you all the evening."

Who could refuse her anything, he wondered. Not even the serious schoolmaster, John Treherne. After that there came a few more invitations, and very gradually the quiet schoolmaster began to relax and enjoy himself, just as she'd predicted. It didn't happen overnight and it didn't always work out that way, of course, life never does. And although no one would ever think of John as the life and soul of the party, at least he could now hold conversations, make people smile, and still enjoy being there, just as long as Kitty was with him. For many months, though, he refused to accept any invitations for functions that didn't include her. That kind of confidence would only grow in time.

She had not moved in with him permanently. "There's been just me and Dad for so long," she explained, "I can't leave him suddenly, just like that. I'll have to do it gently, let him get used to evenings on his own." She spent some weekends at home with Ray, and some with John. She had wondered aloud if John might stay with them sometimes, but he didn't think he could. "Your Dad wouldn't accept us sleeping together, he'd be embarrassed, or maybe it would be against what he believed was right," he said.

"He's not that old-fashioned," she argued, but after that nothing more was said on the subject. He wondered whether she'd approached her father and found John had been right, or whether she'd had second thoughts herself. It didn't matter, anyway, she'd be all his soon enough.

When his brother finally moved into his own home and removed all his stored possessions from John's cottage he was left with a rather shabby and dusty spare room. "It needs a good clean and decorating," Kitty said wrinkling her nose in the dusty air. "I want to have a go at painting it"

"You? Why not ask David? He could do it as a wedding present," he laughed. "Save himself some money."

"No. I want to try. It's only the spare room, after all. I shall ask David to get the paint cost price for me, though."

For some reason he didn't understand, John felt uncomfortable about it all. Would she expect him to help? Wasn't it supposed to be the sort of thing husbands did? But she was looking at him again in that funny, pleading way and he gave in. "Well," he said slowly, "if you're sure you want to do it and if you have the time, go ahead." Why she felt the need to do this, when her brother would have willingly done the job for her, he wasn't quite sure. But she looked so determined, and pleased that he'd agreed. Who was he to argue with this adorable little creature?

It took her several weeks, working at odd times and some weekends. He had to admit, though, that the finished job was very professional. She came to him, her dark hair tumbling over her shoulders and her dark eyes shining with pleasure, stood on tiptoe and wrapped her arms about him. "I told you you could Trust me," she said softly. "I know what I'm doing. Didn't Spain prove that to you?" He held her close for a long while and kissed her, gently at first and then much more urgently. She had taken charge of his life, and turned it around, and he had never felt so happy. "I love you, John Treherne," she said huskily, pushing him gently away and catching her breath. "Now we must start on the wedding plans."

It was a good year for Terry and Jane, too. Running the office from her home at first gave Jane a few problems because she wanted to answer every phone call, every query, every request as they came in. After a week or two of this kind of disruption which seemed to leave her little time to run her home and family, she set herself working hours. Instead of running to the dining room each time the telephone rang, she left a recorded message on the answering machine, giving hours at which the office was open. That left her free to concentrate on getting the children ready and off to school and the dishes washed before she started work. And Terry was the first to realise that although Mrs. Paget had kept all his work up to date, she had only been there two mornings a week, and other phone calls had gone unanswered until he had returned to his home. Gradually, there was more business to chase. Although he'd smiled gently when she'd shown it to him, the big desk diary Jane had bought now had many entries for each week. Of course, all the calls didn't always mean more work, and there were slack times, as in all businesses, but then Jane would leave Terry to man the office while she caught up with other jobs, shopping and friends. It was an easy, comfortable working relationship.

As the year progressed, something other than work occupied Jane's thoughts. She and Terry lived happily together but she had hoped fervently that one day they might marry. When Andy had died she had truly believed there could be no one else, but now, well, she felt quite differently. Terry was a great friend, a great lover, and her children adored him and she wanted to be settled, happily married again. But that didn't seem likely now, the subject was never mentioned between them. Her fear of maybe losing him one day came from that conversation they'd had so long ago when she'd told him there could be no more babies for her. He hadn't said much, but had gone very quiet and left early that weekend, as though something was on his mind. Could it be possible that some day he would find someone else who could give him the children he so obviously wanted. And yet she thought he loved her. How strong was it for him? Over the weeks and months she had realised that life without Terry would be rather bleak again, just as it had felt after Andy's death. She pushed the whole problem to the back of her mind, determined to enjoy life as it was just now. Maybe she was just feeling a touch of envy for the happiness of Kitty and John, that was all. She and Terry were happy and comfortable as they were. And yet the little niggly thought would not go away. Eventually, and quite unexpectedly, it was Jamie who solved the problem for her, without realising it.

He had been home from school with a cold, and was sitting on the floor beside the hearth, making a jigsaw puzzle on the coffee table. She had left the office door open to come and sit with him for a while, settling herself on the end of the sofa beside him. Debs was still at school and Terry was out. They talked about childish things until the office phone rang, and Jane went to answer it. When she returned and settled down again Jamie asked, as if it didn't matter at all, "Do you think Terry is making lots of money?"

She was surprised. "Well, I think he's doing quite well. Was there something you wanted. You mustn't ask Terry for things, you know, you must ask me."

"Oh, I know that," he said crossly. "I wouldn't ask Terry to buy things, that would be greedy. I just wondered if he was earning lots of money, that's all."

"Why, then? Why did you want to know that?"

"Because he said that he would marry you and be our Dad when he was earning enough to look after us all. So I wondered, that's all."

She looked at her young son in astonishment. "Jamie, why would he say that to you? Did you just make that up?"

This time the little boy was really cross so that his face went red, and he started a coughing fit. She was concerned for him, and fetched him a drink, but was still puzzled. "Why, Jamie? Tell me."

"It was ages ago when I was a kid. We went to the common after football practice. I asked him if he wanted to marry you, I wanted to know what I'd have to call him if he did. Terry was great, didn't laugh or anything, just talked serious. He said he wanted to marry you, but he had to be earning enough money for us all before he could ask you. And he said I could still call him Terry like always, or call him Dad if I wanted, but he knew I remembered Dad. Terry never laughs at you like other grown ups do. So I wondered if he was earning lots of money yet."

She sat quietly for a minute or two, and Jamie continued with his puzzle, not sure whether he should have told her all that. Grown ups were a problem sometimes. Finally she said, "the piece you're looking for is on the floor by your foot. And thanks, Jamie. Don't worry, I won't say a word about it any more. OK?"

He grinned and nodded. "OK. Are there any more biscuits in the tin?" She went to the kitchen to fetch a fresh supply of biscuits. After talking to Jamie she knew she could wait for Terry to decided, there was no need to fret about it any more.

Richard wasn't the only one to move house that year. Through the autumn it had been obvious that Harry had a great deal on his mind, making him edgy and impatient. From his conversation with Charles in the summer Iris guessed that there were financial problems again, appearing to be big financial problems, too, but this time she did not ask. After so many years of helping straighten out his debts, and endless promises from him to stop gambling, she had had enough – let him sort this one out himself. So she answered his questions, but gave nothing else in the way of help. Yes, the money she received for caring for Patricia was more than adequate. Yes, she had been able to save a little for repairs and decorating in the house. No, she didn't think that Harry should look for a better job, not at his age. Sometimes he looked at her oddly – she had always come up with ideas and solutions for his problems before. Why was she being awkward and unhelpful now? Finally, as they prepared for bed one evening he asked, "Have you ever thought of selling this house and buy something smaller? It's too big for us, and you are looking tired with the running of it and with Patricia to organise, too? What do you think? It would make sense, you know."

They had bought this house long ago with the hope of producing a family to fill it, but that hadn't happened. It was big, that was true. But she wasn't unaware of the real need to sell – he thought he could pay his debts with the extra money after selling this one and buying a smaller house. Suddenly she was angry. Why should she go on sharing her life with this man who obviously cared nothing for what she thought or did, so long as she helped him out of trouble when he needed her. "It's an idea," she said steadily, her anger still under control. "We might even go on a cruise, or something, with the difference in the price." She had no intention or interest in going on a cruise, she just felt like annoying him. "Hmmmm," she continued, as though considering this new idea, "That might be rather nice."

"Well, there might not be that much in the price difference nowadays," Harry said carefully. "But you would seriously consider buying something smaller?" His voice held a note of relief which she now found rather pathetic. "Shall I call in the estate agents tomorrow, then?"

"No, I'll do that myself. I might have a quick look at what's available, too." She would go and talk to Charles and Isobel first, though. Harry had quite forgotten, if he had ever taken any notice in the first place, that when the house was sold the money was paid equally to each of them. But first she had to be sure that this was really what she wanted to do. Yet even as that little doubt crossed her mind her reason asked just how long could one go on picking up the pieces after a man who cared little for anything but gambling. True, he worked well at his job, but where did that get her? She had used part of her own income in the beginning, sorting him out and setting him straight again, but when she saw it dwindling, bit by bit and never a word about paying back, she stopped, saying she had no more money. Whether he believed her or not wasn't important, she had to keep something back. And now he wanted to sell the house. Perhaps this would be the best way to end this one-sided relationship. She could sell the house, take her share, and find somewhere for herself and Patricia to share. She would talk it over with Isobel from the personal point of view, and Charles from the legal angle. "We'll think about the selling first," she said. "We'll buy when we know just where we want to go and what price we will have to pay."

Harry sighed deeply. It was going to be all right. He could get the money back before the auditors did the books. Iris had always got him out of trouble. He switched out his bedside lamp and pulled the duvet around his shoulders. Everything was going to be all right.

Isobel was calm and practical as always when Iris telephoned her the next morning. She had waited until Patricia was in the bath so that the girl would not overhear the conversation. No need for her to worry about it yet. "Have you quite made up your mind to do this," her sister asked quietly. "Sell the house, I mean?"

"Yes," said Iris firmly. "I've thought it over carefully last night and again this morning in the hard light of day. I think his debts are pretty big this time, and although I am going to leave him I won't see him go to prison. I think it's as bad as that, though I've been careful not to ask."

"Have you told him?"

"That I plan to leave him? No, not until I've talked it over with Charles, and with you of course. Can I call round this afternoon? Are you going out?"

Isobel laughed. She and Charles were becoming stay-at-homes these days. "No. We'll be glad to see you. But does Patricia know what's in the air?"

"Not yet, not till I've got all the details straight with you and Charles. We'll find a way to distract her while I talk to Charles about it all. Will he help and advise me?

"Oh, Iris! Do you really need to ask? Of course he will, we both will. But we'll help in any way we can, as long as you are sure of what you're doing."

"I am growing more sure each minute. It's been such a problem, all these years, pretending that everything was fine and bailing him out of debt. Quite honestly, Izzy, I've had enough. Now he'll have to learn to fend for himself. But I won't send him to prison for all that. So yes, I've decided we'll sell the house. Thanks, Izzy, I only needed to talk it out with you to make up my mind. I shall go to the house agent later this morning. When and if Patricia gets out of the bath." She heard her sister chuckle at the other end of the line. "Next problem will be, just how much to tell her. But with Patricia I've always played it by ear. I'll see you both this afternoon. Bye for now," and having heard her sister's reply, Iris put the phone back on its hook. Yes, she had now made up her mind. Definitely.

The estate agent Iris had chosen was delighted to handle the sale of her house. Unconverted large properties in such a good area would sell easily, and of course make a good commission. She had a desultory look at some of the smaller properties he was offering, but decided to leave this side of the arrangement until she knew how things would work out. Patricia, when iris told her what was happening, was rather disappointed that they were going to live in a smaller house, but she quickly forgot and later became quite excited at helping to choose a new house. When it looked as though they might have a buyer, Iris felt it was time to bring her plans out into the open with Harry.

"But you can't mean this, Iris, old thing," he said, and there was a hint of self-pity in his voice. "We've been married for thirty two years, people our age don't leave each other. You can't just up and leave me now. Why in God's name do you want to do this, anyway? I just don't understand."

No, she thought sadly, I don't suppose you do. Was there really any point in trying to explain to a man who didn't see his own problems? "Harry," she said patiently, "it's time to be honest. With yourself, I mean. Why was it so important to sell the house, and just now?"

He looked at her in puzzlement. "It was too big. It made you work too hard. You know that, Iris, so why are you asking me?"

She sighed. There would be little use in continuing this line of conversation, he just wasn't going to face up to her. "Well," she said at last, "I'm tired of worrying about your debts. I've done it most of our married life, and I want to just be quiet and contented. That's all."

"Look," he said desperately. "We could still buy a smaller house together, and I promise you there would be no more debts. I mean it this time, Iris."

"It's too late, Harry, I've heard it all before. When this house is sold, we each get half of the proceeds. We'll work out how to divide the furniture between us. I've quite made up my mind, so you must start making your own living arrangements. Do you understand?"

"No," he shouted, banging his fist on the arm of the chair. "No, I don't understand. It's that damned girl again, isn't it? You wouldn't go off and live alone, I know. I suppose your rich relations are paying for the house, too. Why should you care if it hurts me? I don't have the time to go pottering around estate agents looking for houses. How am I going to manage? Have you thought of that?"

He paused for breath in his outburst, and Iris said quietly, "No. And did you ever think of me when you got into debt after debt? You'll have to sort this one out yourself. I've had enough," and she stood up and went out to the kitchen, closing the door on her fuming husband.

The house Iris and Patricia eventually chose was a mews cottage not far from the castle. Patricia loved it at once. Her parents insisted that they paid half of the cost from Patricia's own money. Iris felt reluctant to accept this, knowing that someone would always be needed to care for the girl, so her money should be saved. Then, realising that she could bequeath the house to Patricia she accepted the offer. After some months of disruption and reorganisation life settled back into a simple routine again for them both, just as it was for Richard and Molly and Jane and Terry. And very soon would for Kitty and John.

CHAPTER SEVENTEEN

Jamie had been watching each morning for the postman. He had entered a competition, and with the optimism of all small boys, was quite sure he would win. He was in the kitchen eating breakfast when he heard the sound of letters dropping onto the doormat. Quickly putting down his spoon he slid from his chair and ran into the hall. Two thick white envelopes, just like birthday cards, lay on the mat. But surely it wasn't anyone's birthday. He picked them up his curiosity chasing away his disappointment. One was for Terry but the other said, "For Jane, Jamie and Debbie Lawson." He hurried back into the kitchen to show his mother. "Look," he said, "this one is for all of us. Can I open it, it's got my name on the front, too?"

Jane smiled at him. "Sure, go on then." She knew exactly what it was. He opened the envelope carefully and drew out a card with a picture of silver bells, and a silver ribbon. That was girls stuff. He opened the card and read aloud, "Raymond Brownlow will be delighted if Jane, Jamie and Debbie Lawson would share in his happiness at the wedding of his daughter Catarina Elena to John Treherne at the church of St. John, Ledminster, and afterwards at the Lockyer House Hotel. RSVP."

Debbie stopped eating. "Why has he asked me? Doesn't he know I'm a bridesmaid. Auntie Catarina knows." Debbie steadfastly refused to call her new Auntie Kitty as the others did. "I expect her Dad forgot."

"Of course she knows, Debs, you're going to Laura's for a fitting on Saturday, aren't you? But you should have a formal invitation too. That's good manners."

"What does RSVP men, Mum?"

"Debbie, don't talk with your mouth full. It means we must write back and say Yes or No, so that Mr. Brown-low knows how many people are going to the wedding. It's French. Now come on, both of you, or you'll be late for school" Jane propped Terry's invitation on the mantelpiece. He was away for a couple of days.

At the other end of Stephen's Lane Molly Hardaker picked up two invitations from the doormat, too. She took them through to the dining room where Richard was just finishing his breakfast, and laid the thick white envelope beside his plate. "Do you want more coffee," she asked as she returned to her own chair.

"Please. Ah, John's wedding invitation." He looked across at her. "So," he said, indicating the envelope beside her coffee cup, "will you come with me?" She had told him earlier when the wedding plans had been discussed that it was a family affair, and she didn't really know the couple that well. Although they had visited Richard several times of course, she had always excused herself and left them to talk together. She was simply Richard's housekeeper companion and hadn't expected an invitation, although Richard had told her one was in the offing. Now he watched her as she opened the envelope and read the card inside. "Oh, come on Molly, you're as much a part of my family as Terry Kennedy, and I don't suppose he's having any misgivings. Come with me, not as my minder but as my friend and guest."

She hid a little smile. It was the way Richard always said "Terry Kennedy. Was he a little envious, for certainly Terry had charm and looks and flair. Or maybe it was because he seemed to have Jane, too. Had Richard once thought of marrying Jane, she wondered. Looking at her employer, she was aware that Richard's face had changed so much since leaving the hospital, and she could now see for herself how handsome he had been, before the pain and despair had etched their lines on him. He had lost the sickly pallor and acquired a suntan during the summer too, which made him look so much better, even younger, perhaps. "Well," she said at length, "if you put it like that, yes I'd like to come with you. As your friend" she added, with a smile. "What a beautiful name that girl has."

"Good, that's settled then. Are you going out this morning? I've run out of stamps."

Kitty was loving every minute of wedding preparations. Laura had agreed to make the dresses, Fran and her daughter, along with Jane's Debbie had agree to be bridesmaids. Not that it had been a difficult decision for any of them. During the summer months she had tracked down John's aunt Heather. She'd asked John if there were relatives to invite and at first he'd said no, none. Gradually she learned that his mother's sister had visited them regularly when his mother was alive, but as she disliked his father, they hadn't seen her in years. Now Kitty had made contact, and Heather was truly delighted to be back in touch. There were two male cousins, Colin was married with a small child and Edward was an officer in the Royal Navy. Heather was now a widow. "Let's invite them all," Kitty said enthusiastically. "They'll balance up all my Spanish relations." John smiled at this; all the Spanish relations sounded like a whole roomful, when in effect it was only half a dozen. She put her arms around him. "I love you, John," she said. "I shall be the best wife ever."

Ray watched his daughter, so happy in all the arrangements for this marriage, with a mixture of love, pride and loneliness. On the nights she stayed at the cottage with John the house seemed so big, and empty, and it didn't seem worth the effort to cook a whole meal. Perhaps when they are settled, he thought, it really would be the right time to make that trip he and Aliss had planned all those years ago. He could let the house for a year, perhaps. Planning to go with Aliss had been fun, maybe just a dream for the future. But his future with Aliss had been cut so dreadfully short. Could he actually do it alone. He didn't know. Best to just wait and see how things worked out for him after the wedding.

The first Saturday in September that year was the glorious summer day that all wedding planners pray for. Terry had taken Debbie to the Brownlow house early that morning, and now he, Jane and Jamie were on their way to John's cottage. John had asked Richard first if he would act as best man, but wasn't at all surprised when his brother didn't agree. John knew he still felt awkward with people standing beside him while he was forced to sit. It had been Richard, though, who'd said, "Why not ask Terry?" So a possibly tricky situation had been avoided, and Terry had been delighted to accept. Now he was on his way to fulfil that duty. Jane watched him as he negotiated the Saturday morning traffic. He was well chosen for his role of "best man". He looked superb in his dark suit and pale shirt, his black, collar-length hair gleaming in the sunlight that poured through the open car window. As she watched he turned his head, caught her eye and smiled, and she felt all her muscles tighten.

She just hoped Jamie had been telling her the truth all those months ago.

They found John in the kitchen, making coffee. His wet hair told them that he'd showered and shaved, but he was still in his dressing gown. He'd changed so much since meeting Kitty, Jane thought. He was still quiet but his face had lost that withdrawn look and he spoke with much more ease and confidence. He smiled a lot more, and could join in conversations with people he didn't know well, sometimes even start them. She was so happy for him, he deserved something for himself at last, after spending so much of his time caring for Richard, and for her and the children too. "Are your cases packed, John?" she asked.

"Yes, Kitty did most of it yesterday morning." He gave a little laugh and added, "Then she disappeared, said she had things to do. She is the most amazing person you know, Jane, and so full of energy. Will I manage to keep up with her, I wonder?"

"She is." I'm so glad for him, Jane thought, the old John would never have uttered such a sentiment, even if he had thought it. They drank their coffee and talked easily together, while Jamie raided the biscuit tin, until Terry took charge. "Come on, John, time you were getting dressed. Unless, of course, that's your wedding outfit you're wearing." They all laughed as John stood up and went to his bedroom. Jane picked up the cups and took them to the sink. We'll leave it all neat and clean for their return, she told herself. She envied them, just a little.

In the Brownlow house, Ray, David and Alan had retreated to the kitchen, where they drank tea and offered it to anyone who came through the door. In the sitting room Great aunt Elena sat and watched as people came and went, her bright eyes taking in every detail. She wore a long black silk dress with a black lace mantilla, and looked every inch the Spanish matriarch, enjoying every moment. Debbie and Natalie were having their long hair taken up, with flowers and small pearls twisted in to look as though they were wearing coronets. Now aunt Anna appeared and as the hairdresser finished her work with them, took the little girls away to dress. Elena's grandsons returned to sit with her and she wrinkled her nose and spoke to them in Spanish. They laughed, "Only one small beer, that's all." They laughed.

The men came to join them from the kitchen. "We ought to be making a move." Alan suggested tentatively. They had spent some time and argument the night before, working out who would take which guests to the church. Alan went to help great aunt Elena to her feet and escort her slowly to his car, with her grandson Juan supporting her on the other side. Anna and Marita, her daughter in law, together with little Carlos, climbed in behind them. Gradually the other guests sorted themselves out and left, until only Ray and David were left together. David would wait for Laura, who was dressing the bride. Francesca, Debbie and Natalie swept into the room, and Ray caught his breath at the sight of his beautiful older daughter. Laura came and joined David, ready to leave for the church, and then Kitty came slowly down the stairs to stand before them, quietly radiant and smiling at them all in turn.

"Oh, Cats," said Ray, almost reverently. "Cats, you look….." but he couldn't finish his sentence, his chest felt too tight with emotion.

She smiled and then the moment was broken by the ringing of the doorbell. The car had arrived for the bridesmaids. Laura and David slipped away to their own car, and Francesca shepherded the little girls gently and carefully into their seat, before joining them. Another car, bedecked with white ribbons, drew up at the gate.

"Time to go, Cats," Ray said softly, and held his arm out to his daughter who, at that moment, looked so like his Aliss that he was finding it difficult to breathe again.

She stood on tiptoe to kiss him. "Thanks for everything, Dad," she said softly. Then she took his arm and they left the house together. "Better not keep John waiting or he might run away," she laughed.

"Not him" her father smiled down at her. "He's much too sensible to run away from you." The chauffeur held the door open, and Ray handed her into the car, then climbed in beside her, and in a few moments they were on their way.

When Kitty and John had drawn up the wedding guest list, Kitty had been adamant that it would be small. "Everyone we invite will be special to us," she said, "and not just there to make a big number." And she had kept her word. Jane and Jamie sat in the front pew, with Molly beside them, and Richard's wheelchair just beyond Molly. John had almost winced, when the family had all met up yesterday - he'd forgotten how much aunt Heather resembled his mother. Now her elder son Edward sat beside her, looking rather gorgeous Jane thought, in his naval uniform. His brother Colin and wife Mary, with their toddler daughter Daisy shared the next pew with John's headmaster, Brian and his wife. And they, John had said firmly, are the only people I care about. Across the aisle David and Laura, with Alan and little Nicky sat together - Ray would join them in a little while. Great aunt Elena supported, well almost carried to her seat by her two grandsons, sat beaming at every-one, with Anna beside her. Jane watched in amusement as a small boy, probably Juan's child she thought, slid from his grandmother's grasp and set off down the aisle with his mother in pursuit. It was a small wedding group, that was true, but everyone there looked happy and friendly, and ready to enjoy themselves. John stood relaxed and at ease at the chancel steps, talking softly to Terry. Then the sound of the organ changed from the soft background music to the familiar wedding march and all eyes turned to the back of the church. A collective sigh of delight rippled through the air as the bride, tiny and beautiful, appeared on the arm of a very proud father. They were followed by two very solemn little brides-maids, even the incorrigible Debbie had been moved by the occasion and stayed quiet. Behind them came Francesca, taller than her sister, but as beautiful, in a more mature way. Jane wanted to cry, it was all so lovely.

Having fulfilled his duties, Ray sat down beside Nicky as the wedding service continued. Cats looked so like Aliss it was almost too much for him, and he felt a hot pricking sensation behind his eyes. He closed them tightly to prevent any unmanly tears. Oh, Aliss, he thought, if only you had been here you would be so proud of her today. Proud of both our girls. He'd brought Cats up alone, been so close to her since she was eleven, and now, here he was handing her over to someone else. It was almost too much to bear without his beloved Aliss. John's a good man, Aliss, he'll take care of her.

Alan watched his father in law's face with a deep quiet pity. He knew he couldn't interrupt, the old man would be embarrassed. So he bent and whispered to Nicky, who nodded and turned to his grandfather. Slowly Ray became aware of Nicky, gently shaking his arm and he opened his eyes at once. "Granddad, don't cry. You've got to go and write your name in a book," Nicky whispered. "Come on, I'll come with you" and he slipped his small hand into Ray's as they stood up together.

Outside the church, standing in the warm sunlight waiting for the photographer to arrange the pictures of John and Kitty, Jane watched as the tiny Spanish boy she now knew as Carlo, having escaped from someone's retaining hand, set off down the path for the gate, with his father in pursuit this time. She smiled as the young man reached the boy and swung him up into the air, both of them laughing. Kitty's Spanish relations certainly were a good looking family, she thought. Suddenly aware of Terry beside her, she turned quickly to him, wondering as always if this was what he had always hoped for himself. He was smiling at the child, then caught her eye and smiled at her, too. "He's a great one for running away, isn't he?"

She was searching his face as she answered him, but then the photographer called for the whole group to assemble, and the moment had gone. What had he been thinking, wishing, wondering? With Terry, there was no way of telling.

As Kitty and John had kept the wedding party small, the room at the hotel was not crowded and noisy. Kitty and John, Ray, Terry and Francesca took their places at the top table, and everyone else found seats for themselves. But apart from flowers, the cake and wine glasses the top table was bare. Jane found this quite odd – were they not going to eat at all? The hotel staff filled glasses for everyone, and the manager, watching over the buffet table, called for quiet. Ray stood up, glass in hand, and all eyes turned to him. "Ladies, gentlemen and children," he began. "I've been told that the speeches must be short, and that suits me fine. But I want to thank you all for joining us in this celebration, and that I'm really glad to say that Cats, sorry, Kitty, has chosen such a good man. So let's drink a toast to Kitty and John." Everyone raised their glasses and murmured "Kitty and John" as Ray sat down, obviously relieved that his speech was over.

Then it was Terry's turn. He searched the guests for Jane and finding her, smiled. "It's hard for someone like me to keep talking to a minimum," he said with mock despair, "but I will. I'm under orders from my future stepdaughter to get this toast right, so please raise your glasses to Catarina and John's future happiness," and as spoke these words a beaming Debbie called "that's right, Terry" while the other guests repeated the toast. He looked into Jane's eyes and smiled. She raised her glass to him, too. He could live without any more children, but he couldn't live without Jane.

John now stood up. Jane watched the man who, until a year ago had been a quiet, unassuming loner, as he turned to look firstly at great aunt Elena. He bowed his head slightly to her for a moment and then spoke in Spanish, to the old lady's great delight. Then he turned back to his other guests. "Kitty and I thank you for sharing in our day like this," he said, "but we don't want to sit here, looking down and watching you all, so we are all coming to join you now. But can we ask one thing. Before you leave this party, we hope you will speak to at least four people you don't know. Including our gate crashing guest, too. Come on out now Monty, and share the fun."

Monty, looking a little sheepish, stepped out from behind a long window curtain. The manager approached Ray, saying "Shall I...." But was interrupted by Kitty.

"No, Dad, it's Monty," she laughed, and clapped her hands in delight, so that all the children clapped their hands too, and Monty stood looking slightly embarrassed. He was wearing a beautifully soft leather jacket, with dark jeans and his blonde hair shone as he stepped from the window.

The manager looked slightly ruffled, and Ray said, "No, it's OK. Add one more to guest to the bill. I'm sure your kitchen staff can find another selection of food to cover an extra guest." The manager nodded and turned away to give an order to one of his staff. Ray smiled to himself; he wasn't going to let this man charge him extra and not provide extra.

Terry found Jane. "before my rampaging stepdaughter finds us," he said, "will you marry me, Jane?" It had been a day of high emotion, and now this - it was too much for her and she felt hot tears stinging her eyes. Terry took out a handkerchief and wiped her tears away. "Is that a yes or a no?" he teased.

"Oh, yes, Terry. Yes." But then Debbie arrived her skirts flying behind her and a rather large sandwich in her hand. She looked from one to the other.

"Terry, did you mean that? About future stepdaughter. Jamie says it means you want to marry Mum. Do you?" Jamie, feeling grown up in his first real suit, had been quite sure, said he knew ages ago that Terry would marry Mum. She didn't believe him.

Jane smiled and said, "Hush, Debs, and watch where you're putting your sandwich. Yes, Jamie is right, as long as that's OK with you."

But immediately the child ran off in another flurry of skirts to find her brother. She met John halfway across the room. "Mum's going to marry Terry" she told him excitedly. "Me and Jamie will have a new Dad soon."

John hurried across the room to where Terry and Jane stood. "Debbie just told me you were getting married, is it true or one of her brilliant ideas?"

"Well, it is a brilliant idea, but not Debbie's. Yes, it's true, Jane just said yes to me, I think." Terry was laughing happily and Jane punched his arm lightly.

"I'm so happy for you," John said quietly. "You've done so much for me lately. I hope you'll be as happy as we are now."

"Thanks, John," Jane said huskily – there was a glint of tears in her eyes again.

"Now," John said, getting the conversation back to the party, "Come and meet great aunt Elena. She can't circulate, but she loves people."

They followed him across the room, and sat beside the old lady. She understood English fairly well and spoke just a little when really pushed to do so, so Jane did all the talking. After a while Terry excused himself and left them.

"Do you know that man across the room in the chair," the old lady half whispered. "I would like to speak with him about it."

"That's Richard," said Jane, "I've known him since I was nine years old and I know he will want to talk to you. I'll go and speak to him, shall I?" The old lady nodded her assent, and Jane walked across to where Richard was chatting to Ray. "Richard," she said when they acknowledged her, "would you go and talk to great aunt Elena? She wants to know about the chair. I think she's more than just curious, she loves people and it must be sad to have to sit and wait for them to come to you."

"It's more than said, Jane. It's totally depressing. Yes, I'll go over in a moment."

Ray stood up and said "I must go and have a word with the manager. They still have to cut the cake, and time's getting on."

Jane walked slightly behind Richard as they crossed the room to the old lady. She introduced Richard who, to her surprise, addressed great aunt Elena in Spanish. The old lady was delighted and clapped her hands and smiled. Then she began to question him about the chair, and Jane sat quietly, watching all the people in the room. Marita was deep in conversation with Mary, and Jane realised they had been together for ages. She had already seen them exchange notes, probably e-mail addresses. Spanish holidays for Colin and Mary in the future, maybe. Their two children played happily with Debbie and Natalie. Colin was sitting at a table with Monty and Jamie, talking about computers, she guessed. Jamie was now learning to use a computer at school. It wouldn't be long before he asked for one of his own. Brian was demonstrating something with his hands to Edward, while his wife was laughing with Heather and Molly. The handsome Spanish solicitor and his mother stood with Alan and Francesca, watching the children at play. Everyone, she thought, had done as John had asked, and met all the other guests. But where was Terry?

After the cake had been cut and passed around, the party began to wind down for John and Kitty were about to leave. Jane went across to them and kissed them both. "It was the most beautiful wedding ever," she said. "We are all so happy for you. Now go and have a wonderful holiday too."

They both kissed her and Kitty hugged her affectionately. "Thanks, Jane, we will; and many congratulations, too. John told me you and Terry were engaged. It's marvellous news."

Other guests came to say their goodbyes, with Francesca ahead of them all. After the newlyweds had left, she came to stand beside Jane and said, "do you want to come back with us for a meal tonight, Jane? We're staying overnight with Dad and Anna is cooking Spanish for us all. Natalie would love to have Debbie at home with her.

"It's a nice thought Fran, but no, thanks all the same. Terry and I will take our kids back home to Oxford now, they must be exhausted. We have plans to make, too" She was smiling at the thought.

"Oh, yes, of course! John told me just as they were cutting the cake, but I got sidetracked before I found you. I'm so happy for you, Jane. I've been wishing it would happen for weeks."

Terry came back into the room and came to join them. The waitresses had begun to collect and stack plates and guests were slowly leaving, calling goodbyes to the room in general. "Let's go and say thank you to Ray, and then take the kids home," he said. "We've a bit of celebrating to do of our own tonight," and he half-lifted a bottle of champagne from the bag he was holding.

"Aaah, champagne again," said Francesca, and hugged them both in turn. "We hope you'll be as happy as we are. We'll keep in touch regularly now, Jane, who knows what scheme we'll need to think up next."

"We'll do that," Jane answered, but no more clever schemes, she thought. She had helped John and Kitty it was true, but had been far off the mark with Karen and Richard. Now she had the business to run, and Terry and the children to care for. She was content with that. With Terry and Francesca beside her she went to speak to Ray, called the children and they all headed for the door. This evening was going to be a very special family celebration for them all. And if she was ever tempted into any new schemes, she thought, they would be just for the family, too.

Bibliography.

The author is a deaf-blind mother of four children She was born with poor eyesight which prevented her from taking up her position in the local grammar school, and was sent to a partially-sighted school in Exeter. At the age of 16 she moved to the Royal National College for the Blind, Shrewsbury, where she graduated with Advanced R.S.A. Shorthand and Typing certificates. Having worked for a few years in Government service, she married and, in between running a busy home, she wrote short stories, poetry and the present novel. She has finally been persuaded to release the novel for publication. It has taken many years for her family and friends to convince her that she has outstanding writing ability.

Printed in the United Kingdom
by Lightning Source UK Ltd.
122734UK00001B/40-78/A